LADY FARAH CREATES A SCANDAL

THE SEASON OF SECRETS
BOOK 2

BRONWEN EVANS

Dearest Reader;

Thank you for your support of a small press. At Dragonblade Publishing, we strive to bring you the highest quality Historical Romance from some of the best authors in the business. Without your support, there is no 'us', so we sincerely hope you adore these stories and find some new favorite authors along the way.

Happy Reading!

CEO, Dragonblade Publishing

Additional Dragonblade Books by Author Bronwen Evans

The Season of Secrets
Miss Tiffany Has A Secret (Book 1)
Lady Farah Creates a Scandal (Book 2)
Lady Courtney's Second Chance (Book 3)

PROLOGUE

London, Late March 1808

LORD ROCKWELL WARE hadn't seen his older brother look so happy for a long, long time. There must be something to this love disease, but he still didn't want to catch it.

Wolf and Tiffany had returned from their honeymoon in Cornwall last week. Married life obviously agreed with the Marquess of Wolfarth and his new wife. In fact, Lady Tiffany was glowing tonight, even though he understood how nervous she was about hosting her first ball as the Marchioness of Wolfarth.

The night was going well, with most of the *ton* present, many no doubt wanting to judge and find Lady Tiffany wanting. How had a bluestocking, poor spinster captured the attention of the Marquess of Wolfarth one of England's most eligible bachelors? That was the question Rockwell knew without a doubt they'd come to find answers to. The answer was simple—she had captured him with love.

That was why, as the second son, Rockwell, hid in the shadows. He was now the only eligible Ware. Most knew he'd accumulated his own fortune from his travels and investments and was now sought after by mothers with young debutantes.

Rockwell would not go there again. He'd loved once and it had cost his love her life. His wanderlust meant he would never settle down and have a happy family. It wasn't fair to those involved. He could never stay in one place for too long.

Now, with Wolf happily married, surely an heir would follow

shortly and he'd no longer have the title of *spare* hanging over him. How he hated being known as the spare. He'd always taken his own path in life. Perhaps his need to explore and challenge the world was because he wanted to prove his life was more than simply sitting and waiting for a terrible thing to happen. Being the second son gave him more freedom than Wolf and deep down inside, he always feared Wolf's demise might take his freedom away. He'd been more relaxed since his brother's enemy, the crooked stockjobber, Mr. Sprat, was now dead.

Rockwell liked adventure, so he'd taken immense satisfaction in making sure Sprat paid for his crimes. While the newly married couple were in Cornwall, Sprat, the man who had nearly killed Wolf, had been tried and hanged. The saga was over, and Rockwell hoped Wolf could get on with his life and put the terrible past behind him. If his brother's contented, smug smile was anything to go by, he had.

Now that the title of spare was pretty much about to be retired, Rockwell was celebrating by planning a trip to Africa to find the rumored precious diamonds of that continent.

Not that he needed more money. His investments were producing great returns. His latest venture, in Armley Mills in Leeds, had brought in a huge sum. In fact, he'd discussed with the mill owners about investing in a large estate and breeding more Merino sheep. Merino sheep were new to England, and their numbers were low. The mill needed more wool to expand. Stock numbers needed to increase. He'd think about such an investment on his return from Africa. Although he was already a landowner, running an estate was not something he'd likely enjoy. He shook his head. That didn't sound something an explorer should consider.

Speaking of hot countries, the heat was unbearable in the ballroom, and he was considering stepping out to the terrace when he heard a feminine laugh. It was Lady Farah, the Duke of Blackstone's younger sister. Her brother was *Stone* to everyone who knew him, because he had about as much emotion in him as a boulder. But Rockwell knew that underneath Stone's ducal persona there lay a man who was all heart. Or he hoped so.

He searched the crowd and found her with the other ladies of the sisterhood who surrounded Tiffany. But his eyes saw only Lady Farah.

He loved the sound of her laugh. It was warmhearted and filled with joy. He shook his head to clear the memory of seeing Farah standing in his bedchamber a few weeks ago, with his Hessian boot on one long slender leg, her skirts hiked up to her waist. His sister and Farah had been secretly raiding his wardrobe for clothes for a charity sale, and Farah had decided to try on a Hessian. Never had he witnessed such a tantalizing display. Was that why he couldn't get her out of his head?

Rumor was, Blackstone was marrying her off to Lord Franklin. That wouldn't be a happy match. Perhaps he should talk to the man, but there had been no announcement yet. Perhaps Farah had finally gathered enough courage to stand up to her brother.

Franklin was as dreary as a cold winter's day, and shy Farah needed a man who could draw out the real woman. The woman he'd glimpsed when she'd stood in his bedchamber in his boot. Hidden under her shyness was a woman full of bristling passion with a love of life.

He felt sorry for Farah. He'd known her since she was a young girl. She'd been a frequent visitor to their home, given she was best friends with his two younger sisters. If Blackstone pushed ahead with this match, she would marry a man who didn't know how to spell *fun*, let alone enjoy life.

As if Lady Farah sensed him watching her, she turned and glided across the floor toward where he hid from the crowd. He couldn't help the seductive smile that broke over his lips. She was exquisite in a pixie-ghost sort of way.

As usual, she could not look him in the eye. "Good evening, my lord. I hear you're traveling to Ireland tomorrow to retrieve the money Sprat stole from Lady Tiffany."

Sprat had cleverly sent his stolen investment money to an Irish bank so he was less likely to be caught. "That's correct. I need to produce the magistrate report and sign some papers at the bank to have the funds transferred back to Wolf."

Farah nodded thoughtfully. "Do you think it will take long for the funds to be returned?"

Rockwell silently stared at her for a moment. Why was Lady Farah so interested in Tiffany's funds? "It should not take more than a fortnight."

She bit her lip. "I suppose that's not too long." She rubbed her hands together.

"Is there a reason Lady Tiffany may need the funds sooner?"

She shook her head. "No. Not Tiffany," and before he could ask more, she brushed past him and out into the corridor.

How strange. Why would Farah, of any of the ladies, need funds? Her brother was very prosperous and she was soon to be married to a wealthy lord.

Before he could give the strange conversation any further thought, Tiffany arrived at his side. "It's time to come out of the corner and dance with your sister-in-law. Why are men so afraid of marriage?"

"Wolf has shown me there is no need to be afraid of marriage, only of choosing the wrong woman."

"Well answered, Rockwell. Is there a right woman for you, do you think?"

An image of Farah in his Hessian flashed through his head.

She chuckled. "Oh, I think there might be." And as they danced, Tiffany ran her eye over the ladies present. Only Farah had not returned to the ballroom yet. Tiffany turned her attention back to Rockwell. "I'll work out who it is. I'm so happy. I want everyone to find what I have found with Wolf."

FARAH BARELY HAD time to catch her breath after leaving Rockwell's side. She had to be quick if her plan was to be instigated tonight. She slipped through the crowd as usual, pretty much unnoticed, until just her damnable luck a familiar voice cut through the ballroom's chatter like a blade.

"Sister." He'd found her as he always did. When out in society, he watched her like a hawk in case she disgraced the Blackstone name. Her brother didn't know her at all. She was usually scared of her shadow.

But not tonight. She giggled inside because for once, she would get one up on her brother. Sometimes confrontation produced worse results than stealth.

She turned, her stomach immediately tightening at the sight of her handsome, but overbearing brother approaching, his imposing figure drawing every eye in their vicinity. The Duke of Blackstone moved through the crowd like a force of nature—shoulders squared, chin raised, his very presence demanding deference from all around him. Ladies curtsied as he passed, gentlemen bowed, and conversations died mid-sentence before resuming in hushed, reverent tones.

But it wasn't just Stone himself that commanded attention tonight. Two exquisite women flanked him, their hands delicately placed upon his arms as if he were some prized stallion they'd captured. Lady Pemberton, a stunning widow with auburn curls and knowing green eyes, simpered up at him from his left, while Miss Ashworth, this season's diamond with her porcelain complexion and golden ringlets, gazed at him with barely concealed adoration from his right.

"Your Grace," Farah managed, offering a curtsy that felt wooden under the weight of those penetrating dark eyes—eyes that missed nothing and forgave even less.

Stone's gaze swept over her, assessing, cataloguing, no doubt, noting every detail from her slightly mussed hair to the faint flush still lingering on her cheeks from her brief conversation with Rockwell. Heat crept up her neck as she felt herself shrinking under that intense scrutiny, her confidence evaporating like morning mist. How at only eight and twenty had her brother learned to intimidate, when she could barely look people in the eye.

"You look flushed, Farah. I trust you haven't been exerting yourself unduly?" His voice carried that particular tone she knew so well—the one that suggested he already knew the answer and was merely testing whether she would lie to him.

"Not at all, Stone. I was simply—"

"Stone, darling," Lady Pemberton interrupted with a breathy laugh, her fingers tightening possessively on his arm. "You didn't tell me your sister was such a lovely little thing. So delicate, so… fragile." The way she said "fragile" made it sound like a flaw rather than a compliment.

Miss Ashworth tittered in agreement. "Indeed, Your Grace. She's quite the opposite of you, isn't she? So small and retiring. How sweetly innocent she appears."

Farah felt her cheeks burn as the two women continued their assessment of her as if she were a piece of porcelain they were considering purchasing. Meanwhile, Stone basked in their attention, his chest puffing slightly with masculine pride at having secured the evening's two most sought-after beauties.

This was how it always was. Stone commanded the room effortlessly, drew admirers like honey drew flies, while she faded into the background—the duke's shy, unremarkable sister who could barely string two words together in company. Even now, as several other gentlemen hovered nearby hoping for an introduction to his companions, Stone remained the undisputed center of attention.

"Perhaps you should retire early this evening," Stone continued, his dark eyes boring into hers. "You look rather overwhelmed by the festivities."

Overwhelmed by you, more like, she thought rebelliously, though she would never dare voice such insolence aloud. Instead, she found herself nodding meekly, staying in character so she didn't raise his suspicions.

"Oh, but surely the evening is still young!" Lady Pemberton protested, though her gaze never left Stone's profile. "Besides, I was hoping Your Grace might honor me with another dance. You move with such…authority on the dance floor."

As the two women continued to vie for Stone's attention with increasingly bold compliments, Farah felt the familiar suffocating sensation that always accompanied these public displays of her brother's magnetism. She was invisible next to him, insignificant, just another piece of furniture in his perfectly ordered life.

Soon nobody would be able to ignore her, and for once, her fear fled on the wings of exhilaration. She would make her life her own and her brother wouldn't be able to stop her.

The image of herself in Blackstone's study, speaking her mind about Lord Franklin, with her brother overpowering every concern she'd raised, flashed through her memory. For just a moment, she'd felt like a real person with real opinions—not just an extension of her brother's will. But as usual, he didn't listen.

"Actually," she said quietly, surprised by the firmness in her voice, "I believe I'll stay a bit longer. I promised Lady Tiffany I would help her until the last guest departs."

Stone's eyebrows rose a fraction—the only sign of his surprise at her gentle defiance. "Did you indeed?"

The two women looked between them with barely concealed curiosity, sensing undercurrents they couldn't quite grasp. Lady Pemberton's grip on Stone's arm tightened almost imperceptibly.

"Well then," Stone said after a moment that stretched like eternity, "I suppose duty must come first." His tone suggested this was merely a temporary reprieve, not a true victory.

As he turned to escort his admirers toward the card room, Farah caught his parting words: "We shall speak tomorrow, sister. There are matters we must finalize."

He was still pushing her at Lord Franklin. The promise—or was it a threat?—sent a chill down her spine. She would not marry that man. Her brother would have to drag her kicking and screaming down the aisle and even Blackstone would balk at that.

For the first time in her life, instead of merely dreading their inevitable conversation, she found herself thinking: *Let him try to intimidate me. I'm beginning to remember what it feels like to have a spine.* She had a plan and a good one.

Soon, *when* her plan worked, she thought with sudden fierce determination, she'd be free of all this. Free to make her own choices, free to speak her own mind, free to love whom she chose. One day, she wouldn't need his permission to simply exist.

The realization both terrified and exhilarated her. Change was coming—she could feel it in her bones like the approach of a storm. And for the first time in her life, she found herself looking forward to the tempest rather than cowering from it.

Before anyone else could stop her, she escaped the ballroom and headed up the stairs.

NEARING DAWN, ROCKWELL entered the bedchamber he kept at Wolfarth House. He was too tired to return to his bachelor quarters after Tiffany's successful ball. He'd told Wolf's valet, Simpson, not to wait up for him. A man like him was perfectly capable of undressing himself.

He pictured Farah helping him. He'd love to undress her and leave her standing naked except for his Hessians… He shook his head. For God's sake, he had to pull himself together. He wasn't ready to marry. He had a big expedition through Africa next month. He couldn't marry and abruptly go off on a dangerous twelve-month trip. It wouldn't be fair to his wife. A pity, really, as he suspected Blackstone would have Farah married off by the time he returned, if not before.

Rockwell slid naked between the sheets. He was already hardening, thinking of a naked Farah in his arms, then his head hit the pillow and…something else. In the dim light from the fire, he sat up and turned to look. It was a roll of parchment tied with a pink ribbon. As he picked it up, he could smell the fine scent of roses. Slowly, he undid the ribbon and rolled out the sheet, tilting it towards the firelight to read it.

Safe travels to Ireland. I shall miss you while you are away.

But my dreams are free and I shall dream of you…

Yours F.

He put the parchment to his nose, closed his eyes, and sniffed. It smelled of the fragrance Farah had worn tonight.

Fancy little mousy Farah sneaking into his room to leave this saucy note on his pillow. What the hell did it mean? He didn't want to examine too closely why he was so pleased.

It made him not want to leave for Ireland tomorrow. As he stroked his cock, picturing Farah in his room, naked in his bed, he thought it would be the quickest trip to Ireland and back he'd ever made.

CHAPTER ONE

London, May 1808—2 months later

A YOUNG LADY in need of a survivable scandal had to choose her unwilling, or was it unknowing, partner, with the utmost care.

Farah was confident in her choice. She'd known Rockwell since childhood, and he'd always made her feel like more than simply the Duke of Blackstone's sister. He listened to her, and he was a safe choice. Her only choice, really.

But she hadn't accounted for Lord Rockwell Ware's extended absence in Ireland, which was now jeopardizing her plan. He was supposed to have been away for a fortnight, but it was almost six weeks. As of last night, he was home, and scandals waited for no man—least of all, a woman on the verge of being pressured into a marriage she didn't want. Really did not want. *Really, really* did not want.

She would outwit her brother, the Duke of Blackstone, if it was the last thing she did. Her brother was only seven years older than her, but it might as well be a hundred. He was such a fastidious stick in the mud who continued to see her as a baby even though she was a young woman of one and twenty. Since their parents' death when she was ten, he'd become incredibly overprotective. She could hardly blame him. She had also been scared that something would happen to him and she'd be all alone.

But looking back, she was honest enough to admit that she'd

let Blackstone make her into a quiet, timid mouse. Still, it was harder than she'd thought to escape the trap she'd allowed herself to walk into.

Hence her plan. This time, she would not let him win. Her life and future happiness depended on it.

Tonight, her courage could not desert her. Rockwell would be here at Lady Skye's ball. He would help her—knowingly or unknowingly.

How could the thought of Lord Rockwell Ware attending tonight's ball have her quaking in equal parts trepidation and hope? Had he found her note? Did he know she'd sent it? What would he do?

She'd been quite surprised he had not mentioned it, but thankfully, he'd not told her brother. Rockwell understood how overbearing Stone could be. Did that mean he'd help her?

Farah stood quietly next to the rest of the sisterhood discussing their favorite topic—investments—but Farah couldn't think of shares when every nerve in her body was stretched so tight, she felt like she might snap in two.

"Lord Franklin is in attendance. Is there anything I and the sisterhood can do to help? Perhaps if we talked with Stone together…"

Farah sighed. "Really? You think that will work?" Hope. She clung to it like a magic crystal, only to see the light dim in Ashley's eyes. Even Ashley understood the strength and determination of Farah's brother after the debacle with Conte Philippe Lambert. Farah's first try at exerting her independence from her brother's ironclad control had been a disaster.

"I know my own scandal made your brother even more concerned about protecting you," Ashley said. "But we could find you someone else to marry. A man Stone would approve of; one you could build a wonderful life with."

Farah knew that Ashley meant well. "I wonder if he'd ever approve of any man I chose. Look what he did to my Philippe."

She remembered Philippe's smile, his teasing presence, and

his sweet kisses. The French Conte had been patient with her shyness and had taken the time to draw her out. He was so handsome and his family, though having lost much in the revolution, escaped to England with some wealth. They had built up their small estate in Norfolk. Yes, her dowry was advantageous to Philippe, but he could have had his pick of heiresses and he'd picked her. Wanted her.

Then her brother found out. "Blackstone knew how much I loved Philippe. But he chased him away and virtually kept me prisoner at our estate until Philippe gave up and married another. I don't think I'll ever get my brother's approval," Farah said.

Her brother had told her that the fact that Philippe gave up so easily was a sign that he was simply after her money. She hated to admit it, but she wondered if he was right. But still. She would have had a happy life with Philippe because she liked him and he liked her. It could have become more.

She'd never love Lord Franklin. She loathed the humorless, mean-spirited little man. Her life would be filled with misery. Unfortunately, Stone was so worried she would be taken in by some unscrupulous suitor, that he was determined to see her married by season's end. Ashley's scandal had scared her brother into becoming an overprotective jailer.

"Then let's try to ascertain a man Blackstone would approve of," Ashley added, refusing to give up, bless her.

Rockwell's face flashed in Farah's mind. While she understood he was a rake, a wanderer, always off exploring the world, he was kind, handsome, and life would never be dull. There was only one problem with her idea. Rockwell had no intention of marrying anytime soon. In fact, he would be off on another of his expeditions in a month. That was why he was the perfect foil to help her create a small scandal. Franklin would cry off with just a scent of the improper. He was such a snob.

Rockwell would leave the country, anyway. By the time he returned, he'd be forgiven, while she would be living in her cottage in Cornwall. The money she'd saved from the sisterhood investment club would help her purchase such a hideaway.

"I have another option," Farah told her friend. "Now that Rockwell has rescued my funds from the bank in Ireland, I have the money Tiffany earned for me through her investing. I could simply slip away and buy myself a little cottage somewhere no one knows me. I have enough to live off if I'm careful, and Tiffany keeps investing for me."

Ashley looked at her in amusement. "And that's going to stop Stone from finding you and dragging you home and marrying you off to anyone who will have you? If you can't say no to a marriage proposal now, how are you going to stop him from saying where and how you'll live?"

And that was where the scandal came in. If she gave in to impropriety, she knew Stone would likely banish her, given how he treated Ashley. And while she'd lose her brother, she hoped in time she could make him forgive her. Besides, she'd lose him if she married Franklin. They'd move to Cumbria, and she'd likely hardly ever see him.

But she couldn't bring herself to tell Ashley that she would rather create a scandal than deal with her own brother. Ashley had been party to her own disgrace and had said nothing about it to any of them. Farah didn't want to tell anyone, either.

So, instead, she replied, "The chance of finding another man interested in marriage within the next few days is unlikely."

"I don't know. Rockwell might come to the rescue if you ask him nicely."

Farah's gaze flew to the stairs where Rockwell was descending into the ballroom with Lady Joanne on his arm. Joanne was a lovely widow, a few years older than Rockwell. Was she his new mistress? Her nerves pulled tighter.

"He doesn't appear to need a wife," Farah replied before turning away from the sight of them both. How could she use Rockwell in her plan if he were embarking on a new liaison? Her night was getting worse by the minute, because coming across the floor in her direction was Lord Franklin himself. "Oh, no."

Ashley looked up and, spying the man approaching, grabbed Farah by the arm and hurried them in the opposite direction. Farah kept looking over her shoulder and saw Lord Franklin lengthen his stride. "He's still coming, ooh…" Suddenly, Farah hit a solid chest. She looked up into Rockwell's handsome face and her heart stuttered in her chest. *Why couldn't it be you?*

Before she could catch her breath, she heard Ashley say, "Save her, Rockwell. Dance with her."

Rockwell's smile died as he too spied Franklin. He turned into her real-life hero as, without a word, he led her to the floor for the next dance, which just happened to be the waltz.

"Why are you still encouraging the odious little man? You deserve better."

"Someone like you perhaps?" Goodness, did she say that out loud? Thankfully, he didn't look at her in horror but just laughed.

"Is that what the note you left in my bedchamber was all about? I'm sorry to disappoint, but marriage, even to you, is not in my immediate future."

Should she deny the note? This was the moment that would seal her fate. *Courage favors the bold. You can do it…* She pushed closer and his arms automatically tightened around her. "I missed you." She looked up at him through half-closed lashes and saw a moment of fear flash in his eyes. But then the rake took over.

"And did you dream of me?"

Her mouth dried. He remembered the words of her note. "Of course."

She couldn't think of anything else to say as he twirled her about the floor.

"Am I to be your plan to thwart Franklin?"

She almost gasped. She hadn't expected it to be this easy. "Would you help me?"

"Well, I know talking with Stone is useless. I've already tried that. Your brother is determined to see you married. He thinks that something similar to my sister's situation might happen to you, and it will ruin your life. He's worried you'll be taken advantage of after the Conte. But personally, I think your life would be unbearable married to Franklin. Besides, I think Ashley would vehemently disagree that her life is ruined."

"I could kiss you for saying that." And Farah meant it. She'd wanted to be held in his arms and kissed for a long time. She wanted her next kiss to be with him. Maybe she wanted only kisses from him, and that was a scary thought, for she doubted he'd want to kiss only her once she set her plan in motion.

"And I'd let you, if we were somewhere more private."

"I thought Lady Joanne might be the woman stealing your kisses at the moment."

This made his grin widen. "No. She is taken by another." At her confused look, he added, "Lord Burberry was running late, so he asked me to escort her to the ball on his behalf."

Her heart wanted to sing.

His next words made her cringe. "If you stay in the ballroom, you'll not be able to avoid Franklin all night."

"He's pressing for an answer and as soon as I politely decline his offer, he'll go running to Stone and my brother will make me change my mind." The heat of the ballroom pressed in on her.

"I would guess that the young lady who was bold enough to leave a note on my bed is most assuredly strong enough to stand up to her brother."

"You really don't know me, do you? I've never been able to stand up to Blackstone. Most people can't." *But I have a plan that will work if you help*, she wanted to add.

He almost stopped moving. "Surely, he won't force this marriage if it's not what you want?" When she said nothing, he cursed under his breath.

She shook her head. No one would understand. Despite her mother's wishes for her to take over the household, she'd never had the chance, even after her mother's death. Stone had hired a new housekeeper who reported directly to him, instead of allowing her to take charge. When she'd protested in her grief, Stone told her she was too young and fragile to be responsible for the house. She hadn't even been allowed to clear her mother's belongings, and she never forgave Stone for that.

"Your note got my attention. What is it you want me to do?"

She took a deep breath. "I have a plan of sorts. I know you set sail in a month for Africa. Could you pretend to court me so I can gain time to attract someone else, or convince my brother to let me have a say in my future?" She added, "My brother is only pushing me to marry Franklin because he's worried after what happened to Ashley. And I'm sure you know that he thought Philippe a fortune hunter."

"He most likely was."

She answered, "But he was a fortune hunter that liked me and I liked him. I loathe Lord Franklin."

"So, I pretend to be the alternative. But what happens when I sail away?"

"Do you not think I can attract another suitor by then? With you by my side, other men will take notice. No one will notice me with Franklin by my side."

"Very true, but I won't lie to your brother."

Hope shriveled in her chest. "How do you feel about bending the truth a little, then? What if you told Stone that you wished to see if there could be something between us? Then, when you take your leave, you can be honest in saying we're not suited."

"I'm afraid I cannot be so gallant. I have an urgent matter that needs my attention. I'm leaving London again tomorrow. I wish you luck, though."

With that, her hope really died. Her plan revolved around him being in London for the next few weeks. If only Lord Dayton Deveraux was back from India. Claire's brother would be perfect. And there was always Lord Axton Fancot but he seemed to be interested in Courtney and the feelings might be reciprocated. And about time, too. Courtney deserved some happiness after her fiancé died in the Irish Rebellion five years ago.

She squared her shoulders. This was merely a setback. She wouldn't give up.

As the dance ended and he released her from his arms, she immediately missed the feeling of security, safety. And her body froze as a voice at her shoulder said, "The next dance is mine, I believe."

Franklin had come to claim her and her night was totally ruined.

CHAPTER TWO

"**W**HERE ARE YOU going?"

Blast. Farah turned to face her brother, the Duke of Blackstone. "I'm going to Lady Tiffany's house with the other ladies to welcome her home from her honeymoon." She held her breath.

"Didn't you accomplish that at the ball last night? Just because I'm going to my hunting estate for the next few weeks doesn't mean I'll allow you to play carte blanche with your reputation. You know how I feel about you associating with Lady Ashley Ware. You know I don't want you at Lord Wolfarth's home."

How could she explain that she wanted to attend the investment club meeting? If her brother knew how much money she had to her name…Tiffany ran the investment club for the ladies, and it was this group that had challenged her brother to an anonymous investment challenge. In twelve months, whoever made the largest return would be crowned the investment champion and keep all the money made. Her brother would be stunned to learn he'd been beaten by women.

"You can't expect me to avoid it now that Tiffany has married Ashley's brother, Lord Wolfarth. It's totally respectable. Besides, she's a good friend." *And she is helping me invest my pin money so I can escape you,* she wanted to add.

"Will that scandalous hussy be there?"

"I expect so. She does live there." Her brother was talking about Lady Ashley Ware, Tiffany's sister-in-law.

"Then I forbid it."

"But all the other ladies will be there."

"I don't care. You are my sister, and I am responsible for you and your reputation. You are not going. What would Lord Franklin think?"

Her mouth ran dry and her heartbeat rapidly. Why couldn't she get the words out of her mouth to say, "I'm going anyway. Try and stop me." Because he bloody well would. He'd carry her upstairs and lock her in her bedchamber as he'd done many times before. She had learned it was better to submit and then sneak out. He was so arrogant, he'd never suspect that she'd disobey him. Sometimes it paid to remain silent and let him think he'd won.

"I've instructed Mrs. Thompson to ensure you act appropriately while I'm away. She will alert me to any misbehavior. If I must return from my hunting trip, I will not be pleased."

"I am not a child, Stone. One day, you'll have no choice but to see it."

He stood watching her as she turned without further argument and made her way back up the stairs, taking her hat off as she went.

She sat in her room fuming, waiting for her brother to leave. She looked at the clock on the mantle. This game was such a waste of time because she always found a way to do what she wanted. Though he had an arrangement with Mrs. Thompson and Cook, it wasn't infallible. And even though they risked everything in disobeying her brother, they felt sorry for her, and gave her some freedom. As long as they had deniability, they turned a blind eye.

At last she heard the carriage draw up and her brother finally left for his trip. The entire house breathed a sigh of relief.

With that, she put her bonnet back on her head and snuck out the servants' entrance.

She and Cook had come up with a plan to thwart her brother. Farah would fall ill at Lady Tiffany's and say she had to stay for a few days. Nothing too serious that would require a missive sent to Stone, but enough to give her a few days away from spying eyes. What freedom that would be, even if only for a few days.

The meeting at Lord Wolfarth's house was the perfect chance for Farah to reassess her plan. Rockwell hadn't returned to his bachelor apartments. He was staying at his brother's townhouse, in a bedchamber upstairs, or so Tiffany had informed them. She needed to learn where he was going and why.

The ladies collectively sighed with relief as they safely received their stolen funds from the bank in Ireland. Last month, Tiffany's evil stockjobber had not only stolen the money they had invested, but they'd learned that several years ago, he'd killed Tiffany's parents. But Rockwell had caught Sprat and saw him hanged, retrieving their stolen money.

This meant Farah had the money to travel. She could simply run away. If she knew where Rockwell was going, could she follow and rely on his help?

Last night the worst had happened. Lord Franklin had offered for her hand in marriage. Unless she developed a completely new personality in two days, one that had a backbone, Farah just knew her ducal brother would force her into accepting Franklin's proposal.

None of her friends understood why she just didn't tell her brother to go to hell, but that had never worked. Even when she did try to hold her ground, Blackstone inevitably wore her down and got his way. Perhaps dukes were born with that skill—the ability to rule with an iron fist and accept no outcome other than the one they wanted.

What her brother didn't understand was that years of his overbearingness had strengthened her backbone and on this point she would not bend. There would be no marriage to Franklin.

"You're especially quiet, Farah," Ashley said in her ear as she leaned closer. "I heard from Wolf that Franklin offered for you last night." Her friend squeezed her hand. "Don't let Blackstone push you into a marriage you'll regret. Marriage is for life."

"Why did it have to be Franklin?"

Farah took comfort in the fact Ashley had survived, if somewhat tattered, her scandal. She didn't know what terrible faux pas surrounded her friend, but Ashley refused to let society's scorn define her. She moved within society as if unaware that the ladies all looked down their noses at her, and the men licked their lips, as if Ashley were fair game. It helped that the sisterhood, as they referred to themselves, had stood by her, as had, of course, her powerful brother, the Marquess of Wolfarth.

Farah would rather spend the rest of her days hidden away in the countryside than face the disapproval of the elite *ton*, and becoming Lady Franklin was even less appealing. If only she were braver… But she would be brave in this. Too much was at stake.

A scandal would be the only thing to put Lord Franklin off and make him withdraw his offer. But could Farah live her life with talk of impropriety hanging over her? She bit her lip. She knew what a scandal could cost her, but a life with Lord Franklin would cost her more.

"If you'll excuse me, ladies, I just need…"

"Use my bathing chamber," Tiffany called out to her. "Wolf and Rockwell are out."

Farah hated lying to her friends, but asking to visit the necessary was the only way she could sneak upstairs and push forward with her plan without alerting her friends. They would not approve, nor likely understand. They would try to talk her out of taking such drastic action, but there was no other choice. Her brother had seen to that.

She took a deep breath before she pushed open Rockwell's bedchamber door. Her nose crinkled at the waft of sandalwood mixed with dirty clothes. Farah had been in Lord Rockwell Ware's bedchamber before. She remembered him catching her dancing around the room wearing one of his huge Hessians with her skirts rucked up around her waist. She should have been embarrassed, but the heat in his eyes made her feel something totally unfamiliar—desired.

Now here she was, once again sneaking into his room to plant another note. But where to leave it? His room was a mess. There were trunks and dirty clothes everywhere. Men were so unreliable. Rockwell returned six weeks later than expected and now she faced complete failure because he was leaving again.

She had so little time in which to create a scandal.

She walked to the enormous bed in the middle of the room and ran her hand over the rumpled sheets, battling the urge to bend and sniff them. She wasn't out to trap Rockwell into marriage. She just wanted him to help her avoid marriage to a man who made her skin crawl. If her plan worked, Rockwell would sail off to Africa before the scandal erupted, and by the time he learned of his part in her downfall, and returned, it would be too late to do anything noble like fall on his sword and offer her his hand in marriage.

The snag was, deep in her heart, she wondered what it would be like to be married to a man like Rockwell. But by making him an unwilling accomplice in her plan, she'd likely kill any chance of a relationship—friend, lover, or wife.

Still, even losing the respect of a decent man was not too high a price to pay for her freedom. That was how seriously she took her situation.

As she moved around the room, a pile of journals caught her eye. *She really shouldn't…* Her fingers didn't listen. She gingerly lifted the cover of one and with one eye closed, as if that made it acceptable, she read, "Norwegian Coast June 1806—the sea is calm and the color of the water is the purest turquoise. We've been anchored in the bay for four days as we take on supplies. I must admit, I'm getting a tad tired of all fish meals. A nice juicy piece of meat would be worth a bar of gold."

Farah smiled. It looked as if Rockwell kept a diary of his explorations. She kept reading, almost laughing out loud at his tale of a husky who got overly friendly with his sheepskin boots, to the point that she almost missed the heavy thump of Hessians on the wooden floorboards and Wolf's voice in a stern argument with someone who could only be Rockwell.

She swung round, desperate for somewhere to hide. The thick, heavy drapes pulled aside from the large windows of his bedchamber would be perfect. They dragged on the floor and she could step on them to hide her feet. Being a hideously thin, tiny-framed woman was, for once, a blessing.

She barely made it to her hiding place when the chamber door flew open with a crash. She peered out through a small gap in the curtain. "I tell you, it was him." Rockwell's words were muffled as he drew off his waistcoat and threw it on the pile of dirty clothes in the corner.

"I just don't want you to get your hopes up." Wolf's tone had softened.

Rockwell swung to face his brother. "I can't sit here and do nothing. I stayed as long as I could in Ireland to search, but... Lauren is barely holding the family together financially, and like Tiffany, she won't let anyone help. Sometimes pride is a damn nuisance."

"Exactly why would he stay in Ireland? Furoe would have come home to his family if he could. He'd never let them suffer. Would he?"

Farah frowned. They were talking about Viscount Furoe, Lauren's brother, but he died in the Irish Rebellion, didn't he? Gosh, if he was still alive... But Wolf was right. Why hadn't he come home?

The two men stood in silence for a few moments. Rockwell finally said, "I'm praying he has an excellent reason. I won't let myself believe the worst of him."

To her horror and, well, maybe not, perhaps to her joy, he wasn't stopping at his waistcoat. Her pulse skipped a beat as he tore off his cravat and pulled his shirt over his head. Her mouth dried at the sight of light tanned skin and muscle. Then her pulse hammered in her veins as he started to remove his Hessians. He was going to undress. In front of her. *Goodness.*

"What if he's hiding from his responsibilities? What if he can't face his family's financial situation?"

Rockwell kicked one Hessian off his foot and sat on the end of his bed. "Then he is not the friend I knew. I'm leaving on the *Doreen* tonight. I just have to attend to a few details regarding my upcoming trip to Africa before I leave."

The *Doreen* was one of Rockwell's ships that he used to sail to exotic places.

The second boot hit the floor.

"When will you be back?"

Rockwell swept a hand over his face, and his shoulders slumped. "I don't know how long my search may take." He looked at his brother. "I'll come back once I've found Furoe, or at least confirmed it was not him I saw."

"That could take a long time."

She watched Rockwell shrug. "I have time. Africa will always be there. My friend comes first."

Wolf turned to leave. "Good luck. I hope you find answers, but a part of me is concerned about his reasons for staying in Ireland. I wish you God's speed."

"Say nothing to anyone. Just in case I'm incorrect or I can't locate him. I don't want anyone to get their hopes up. And that includes Tiffany. Especially Tiffany. She might tell Lauren."

Wolf laughed. "Wait until you're married. There is no such thing as a secret when they know you so well." With that, he left and closed the chamber door behind him.

Rockwell sighed and shook his head.

She really should close her eyes. This was such an invasion of his privacy, but the little timid bird fluttering deep inside her wanted out of its cage, as it always did in Rockwell's presence. She held her breath as he flicked open the fall of his breeches and slowly pushed them over his hips. The light pouring in through the window meant his linen draws hid nothing. However, excitement coursed through her as he pulled on the tie and her hand covered her mouth as she watched them fall to the floor and Rockwell stepped out of them.

He was side on to her view and she marveled at the grace of his hipbone, the pale flesh where the sun had not kissed and she could see the strength in his muscled thighs. She was so bad, but her naughty imaginings were answered when he turned to face the window. She could see all of him and… *Do not faint!*

Drawn to the dark curls at his crotch, he appeared as anatomically correct as the Greek statues she'd viewed. As her eyes moved upward, it was the sculptured chest that almost saw her hand snake out from behind the curtain for a touch.

"My, my, what's this?" For a moment she thought he'd found her, but he was looking at something on the dresser. In a blinding flash, she felt in her pocket, but the note wasn't there. She'd left it by his journals and one journal was open. He'd know someone had read them. Once he'd read the note, he'd realize she'd been nosing through his belongings.

She watched as if in a bad dream as she saw him pull at the pink ribbon. For a minute, she couldn't remember what she'd even written. Then he read it out loud…

I must confess that my heart is a flutter with the prospect of a certain young gentleman. He is handsome and charming, with eyes that sparkle like the stars on a clear night. And yet, I fear he may not notice me, for I am but a mere inexperienced young lady and he is a man of considerable reputation.

Do you have any advice?

Yours F.

It really was cringeworthy to hear it spoken out loud, but to her surprise, he didn't laugh. He folded the note and pressed a kiss to the scented paper. "Oh, my little pixie-mouse, I have plenty of advice, but you'll never hear it. You're off limits to a man like me, no matter how tempted I am."

With that, he slipped the note into the open journal and slammed it shut, then walked into his dressing room.

What to do. What to do. If she stayed here much longer, Tiffany would send someone to find her. And if she were caught in this room, with Rockwell in a state of undress, well, her problem would be solved, but not in the way she wanted. She didn't wish to trap him into marriage. That was no way to start a relationship. Besides, Rockwell was not the marrying kind. He was the intrepid explorer. She longed for a husband who would be happy to stay home with her and the children. If not a grand love like Tiffany found, then at least friendship.

She poked her head through the gap in the curtains and was just about to step out of her hiding place and make a mad dash to the door when Wolf's valet entered, carrying a pressed shirt.

He spoke into the dressing room. "My lord, I have found a clean shirt for you. I shall gather up the rest of your washing."

"Don't bother to rush, as I'll be gone for a considerable time. I have enough clean clothes for my journey." Rockwell reentered the bedchamber in a pair of buckskins, but his chest was bare. What a sight he made. She swallowed hard. "Are my trunks repacked?" To her disappointment, he pulled on the shirt.

"Just a few items to arrive from your lodgings." He pointed to the open trunk. "I'll instruct them to be packed in the final trunk as soon as they arrive."

"Good. I need to catch the tide tonight," he said as he sat on the bed and pulled on his top boots.

"Would you like me to help you with your cravat, my lord?"

"That won't be necessary. I'm not dressing for the opera, merely a long boat trip. While I'm out, can you ensure the trunks are loaded in the carriage and sent to the *Doreen* at Wapping Dock? I'll go straight to the dock from my meeting."

"As you wish, my lord."

Rockwell grabbed his greatcoat and made for the door.

Farah let out the breath she'd been holding. She tried to hold back tears. Her plan was over. Rockwell was leaving, and now she would have to try to deal with her brother alone. Like a rat caught in a trap, she had nowhere to turn. The sun at her back made everything worse because on this beautiful sunny afternoon, her life moved into darkness. Marriage to Lord Franklin loomed, and it was almost too much to bear.

She wiped the tears from her face and thought perhaps it was time to turn to the sisterhood for help. Perhaps Tiffany could get Wolf to talk to her brother. Now, how to get out of this room without being seen?

She peered round the curtain—the room was empty. She moved quickly and was halfway across the chamber when she heard Simpson returning. The valet had someone else with him. Oh dear, what would everyone think if she were caught here? Panic at the thought of trapping Rockwell in a marriage he didn't want made her dive into the open trunk, pulling some clothes over the top of her.

"Put the rest of his shirts in there and then carry the trunks to the carriage. Quickly now, his lordship will require the trunks loaded before he arrives at the dock and it's a good forty-five minutes to get there."

Before she understood what was happening, clothes were placed on top of her and the lid slammed shut. Thankfully, there were small holes near where the trunk straps adhered to the leather, so she could breathe.

Well, it's one way to safely get out of the house. She'd alert the men as they loaded the trunk on the carriage out of sight, near the stables at the back of the house. Then she could sneak back in through the kitchen.

"Gor' blimey, how come this one's so much heavier than the others," she heard the servant say as they began to carry her down the stairs.

Suddenly, on a loud curse, she felt the trunk hit the stairs and tumble downward over and over. Her head hit the edge of stair and even through the thick leather, it hurt like hell. The trunk continued to roll down the sweeping staircase and each time it hit the corner of a stair it smashed her head. Her cries were muffled by a mouthful of clothes. By the time the trunk landed with a crash on the tiled entrance hall, Farah was in no condition to let the men know she was inside. She'd blacked out.

CHAPTER THREE

ROCKWELL ARRIVED EARLY at the dock. His meeting with Captain Clarkson who would be sailing the ship to Africa went as expected—the captain bristled at the indefinite delay until Rockwell explained that he had to go to Ireland first on his other smaller ship, the *Doreen*. However, with Rockwell's money funding the expedition, the captain had little choice but to wait. Let them idle away maintaining the ship. How hard was that?

Rockwell had made it to Wapping Dock in time for the *Doreen* to leave for Dublin at high tide. Night had just fallen and his body hummed with impatience as he stood on the deck watching the many ships journey down the Thames toward open sea.

The air was thick with tension, his mind preoccupied with thoughts of his upcoming hunt.

However, Farah's face haunted him—the hurt in her eyes when he'd refused to help her last night. He wished he could *have* helped her. Wished he could risk even offering for her. She'd make any man a wonderful wife, but he knew a marriage to him would be a disaster for her.

Pain lanced through him at the thought of marriage. He'd proposed once, to Charlotte, a woman he'd met in the Americas. Joy had burst through him when she'd said yes to his proposal. They were on their way home to England to announce his engagement to his family and friends, when she had become ill on board the ship and died in his arms.

He'd had to bury Charlotte at sea.

He'd told no one about his fiancée, not even his brother. That was when he realized he couldn't have everything he wanted. Exploration was best left to men. He'd not risk someone he loved ever again.

Travel and exploring were his first love, and he'd leave the idea of family to his siblings to provide. Tiffany and Wolf had something he'd never have. Couldn't have, when his sailing the world came first. He wasn't that selfish. Not again. Charlotte hadn't really wanted to leave her home, but she did for him. And she paid the ultimate price. He wouldn't ask that of a woman again, wouldn't condemn her to a life of loneliness while he chased every horizon.

He leaned on the railing, as memories of Lord Lucien Cavanaugh, Viscount Furoe, his best friend outside of his brother, pressed in on him. He'd tried to talk him out of taking a commission to fight in the Irish Rebellion, but Lucien, at the impetuous age of three and twenty, had just fought with his father and wanted to escape from under his thumb. Plus, Lucien really thought he could help quell the uprising.

Rockwell shook his head as he gazed at the stars. Only twenty English soldiers died in the short-lived skirmish, but Lucien had been one of them. An only son. It had destroyed his father who blamed himself. Lucien's father lost himself in drinking and gambling and slowly fell into debt.

He remembered the night he thought he'd seen Lucien as if it was only yesterday.

In the dimly lit confines of the smoke-filled tavern in Dublin, Rockwell had nursed his pint of ale, his thoughts lost in the haze of memories. The chatter of patrons and the clinking of glasses faded into the background as his mind wandered, haunted by the specter of his deceased friend, Lucien. He'd died in these very streets.

Rockwell let the guilt sink in. If only he hadn't fought with Lucien about him pulling out of their planned trip to South America. Lucien was in love and had decided to get married to Lady Courtney. He was sure Lucien volunteered for Irish post to prove to Rockwell he wasn't under Courtney's thumb.

Stupidly, Rockwell's gaze had swept across the crowded room, searching for any sign of familiarity amidst the throng of strangers. And then, like a whisper of smoke in the wind, he'd thought he saw him—Lucien, sitting at a shadowy corner table, his features obscured by the swirling mist of tobacco.

Heart pounding in his chest, Rockwell rose from his seat, his movements slow from the alcohol he'd been drinking in his friend's memory. The figure remained still, shrouded in darkness, but something about the way he sat, the tilt of his head, stirred a flicker of recognition deep within Rockwell's soul.

"L-Lucien?" Rockwell had stuttered, his voice barely audible above the din of the tavern.

The figure stirred, turning slightly to reveal a glimpse of pale skin and dark hair, but before Rockwell could fully discern his friend's face, Lucien rose abruptly, disappearing into the smoky haze like a phantom.

Without a second thought, Rockwell tried dashing after him, pushing his way through the crowded tavern and out into the cool night air of Dublin. The cobblestone streets had been slick with rain, the glow of lanterns casting eerie shadows against the ancient buildings.

"Lucien! Wait!" Rockwell had called out into the darkness, his breath coming in ragged gasps as he'd chased the fleeting figure through the labyrinthine streets.

But Lucien was like a wisp of fog, slipping through Rockwell's fingers with each twist and turn of the winding alleys.

Had it truly been Lucien he had seen, or merely a trick of the light?

As the night swallowed the man whole, Rockwell knew one thing for certain—he would not rest until he'd uncovered the truth, until he'd laid to rest the ghost of his dear friend once and for all.

When he'd mentioned it to Wolf, his brother had informed him it must have been his mind playing tricks with him. He *had* drunk a lot that night. But Rockwell owed it to his friend to conduct a thorough search. He turned to go to his cabin. He may as well get some sleep because he would not rest until he'd scoured Ireland and put to rest this obsessive feeling Lucien was still alive.

If the weather held and the breeze stayed strong, they might make Dublin in three days. But if the weather turned, they may have to shelter in Holyhead, Wales until it was safe to cross the Irish Sea.

He pushed open the door to his cabin and washed his face with cold water. He prayed the weather held because he was impatient to begin his hunt. He'd stayed up most of the night ensuring they had sailed well into the English Channel before he left the helm.

One question gnawed at him—why hadn't Lucien come home? He prayed his hunt would first find his friend and then reveal some reason he might be able to forgive Lucien for letting them think he was dead.

He dried his face and took off his boots. Laying on the bunk with his eyes slowing closing, he heard a moaning sound. He thought it was coming from above on the deck, but it grew in volume. Christ almighty, it emanated from one of his trunks across the room. He hoped one of Ashley's cats hadn't stowed away. He wouldn't be held responsible for keeping it from falling overboard. Though he supposed he could confine it to his cabin, if he could tolerate the smell...as he would be gone for at least a month if the search didn't go well.

With a sigh, he moved to undo the ties on his trunk. Throwing back the lid, he peered inside and he could see something wiggling beneath a pile of his linen shirts. He was about to pull them back when he saw a scarlet stain on one. He cautiously lifted them and promptly cursed. Farah, seemingly unconscious, curled up in his trunk, her delicate features red with heat and her forehead marred by a cut.

"What in blazes..." The sight of her small form knocked the breath from his lungs. He knelt beside her, his fingers trembling as he gently brushed a lock of hair from her pale face.

Questions stormed through his mind. How had she ended up here, in his trunk of all places? And more importantly, there was blood… Was she badly hurt?

Years of treating injuries at sea steadied his hands as he assessed her wounds. Had she stowed away on board to defeat her brother? Or had someone else placed her here, with malicious intent? Either way, he couldn't ignore the protective surge that rose in his chest.

She weighed nothing in his arms as he lifted her from the trunk, cradling her against his chest. Moonlight spilled through the porthole, casting silver shadows across her face as he laid her on his bunk. His throat tightened at how fragile she looked. He pressed a cool cloth to her forehead, willing the bleeding to stop.

Her breathing eased with fresh air. When he dabbed too close to the wound, her hand fluttered up to bat his away.

A smile tugged at his mouth. Not unconscious then.

He couldn't tear his gaze away as he kept vigil, his mind racing with the implications. A gentleman and lady alone together, no chaperone in sight… Scandal wouldn't begin to cover it. Blackstone would have his head. How could he shield them both from the inevitable gossip?

But as he watched Farah, her features softened in sleep, desire warred with duty. Had she planned this? Set a trap to avoid marriage to Franklin after he'd refused to help?

The gentle roll of waves matched the tumult in his chest. He had only one option now—and perhaps marriage to Farah wouldn't be the prison he'd imagined. Her dowry would fund his travels, and she'd be waiting at home with his children. Farah, the timid mouse, as most called her. Easy to manage. Easy to leave behind.

Then the vision of her dancing in his Hessian blazed through his mind, shattering his rationalization. He didn't want timid Farah. He wanted the passionate woman he'd glimpsed behind the mask of propriety. And God help him, he wanted to be the one to free her.

But marriage? He barked out a harsh laugh. As if he had any choice with her lying on his bunk, on his ship bound for Ireland.

He forced himself to step away, heading for the door in search of refreshments for when she woke. The trunk must have been stifling. He'd need to find another bunk for the night.

When she woke, she'd better have a damn good explanation for how she'd ended up on his ship.

FARAH WAS HAVING the most wonderful dream. She was at sea, sailing into a future with… Her eyes flew open and she sat up. A damp cloth fell into her lap. Pain lanced through her skull. She gingerly touched her head and felt the cut on her forehead. She looked around. Where was she?

With a groan, she remembered being locked in Rockwell's trunk. She'd probably been knocked out when they dropped her. Dear God. Was she on his ship? Of course she was. She could feel the ship's movements through the waves. She glanced out the porthole. The sun was well up, and she was still fully dressed. She saw a jug and glass by the bunk and eagerly reached for it to ease her parched throat.

After drinking a full glass of water, and then some, she swung her legs out of the bunk and attempted to stand. Her head didn't swim and her stomach was not rollicking. But it did rumble from hunger. She wanted to eat, but she wasn't sure what to do. She relieved herself in the pot provided and then emptied it out the porthole. She had a wash in the basin of cold water and felt better.

Then she carefully cracked open the cabin door and peered out. She could hear some men up on deck and the desire for fresh air overcame her. But when she stepped out of the cabin, a waft of cooking smells sent her mouth salivating and she headed to where the smells were coming from.

"Good morning, the patient is awake then?" the cook said.

"Yes. A tad worse for wear." At his raised eyebrow, she added, "It's a long story. My name is Farah. May I have something to eat? I missed dinner last night."

"Farah! You can call me Rob. How's a nice plate of eggs and ham and a cup of tea?" Her mouth watered even more. "You go to the stateroom and I'll get young Nick to bring it down."

When she looked around, he said, "The stateroom's just further down the corridor at the stern." Still confused he pointed right.

"I might get some air first."

"I don't advise that. Not good to be on deck unescorted. Lord Ware wouldn't approve. Accidents happen. There is a balcony off the stateroom instead."

Smiling, she did as directed and headed further down the corridor, adjusting her balance to the ship's roll. The door to the huge stateroom was open and as she entered, she spied the balcony at the rear. The door out to that was open too. It beckoned and as soon as she stepped into fresh air, her head cleared further. She could see land to the right and left. They must be in the channel between England and France. She took deep breaths and felt more herself.

The idea of having to face Rockwell was what upset her stomach, not the rolling waves. She heard cutlery being laid on the table so she returned inside.

Farah began studying the spacious stateroom. She let out an exclamation of delight. She was very impressed by the sprawling smart, masculine style.

She spied a small bookcase and made her way across the room to see what men like Rockwell liked to read when at sea. To her surprise, there was an eclectic mix. Books on exploration were mixed with philosophy and poetry. Another, she quickly put back on the shelf when she opened it to see an etching of a couple in an intimate embrace.

The smell of coffee filled the passageway. Young Nick arrived. Fresh scones and jam were on the table, and her eggs and ham smelled delicious. If someone could bring her a cup of tea, she'd be in heaven. Soon she was seated in front of a feast. Food was piled on the table along with her teapot. A plate filled with eggs and ham was placed in front of her and she couldn't wait. She dug right in. The meal tasted better than anything she'd ever eaten.

She poured herself another cup of tea. She was finally beginning to feel human again with a bit of food in her stomach after a long sleep, although her head still ached.

She took another sip of her tea and was contemplating selecting a volume from the bookcase when Rockwell strolled in. He stopped when he spied her.

He looked all windswept, like a pirate. His linen shirt hung open at the neck and she could see a large expanse of chest. As he entered the stateroom for breakfast, Farah's breath caught in her throat at the sight of him. Rockwell cut a striking figure, his dark hair swept back from his forehead, the morning light catching the subtle hints of silver at his temples. His angular jaw was set with determination yet softened by the faint trace of a smile as he greeted her with a nod, his broad shoulders hinting at strength tempered by years of experience. But it was the intensity of his gaze, the way his eyes seemed to pierce through her defenses and into the depths of her soul, that stirred something deep within Farah's heart.

There was a quiet confidence about him, a sense of purpose that spoke of a man accustomed to command and respect. Yet beneath the facade of authority lay a vulnerability, a gentleness that tugged at Farah's heartstrings and left her longing to unravel the mysteries that lay hidden beneath his stoic exterior.

As Rockwell took his seat opposite her, pouring himself a cup of steaming tea with practiced ease, Farah couldn't help but feel a tad of apprehension. He was far too calm.

"You, young lady, have some explaining to do."

Don't treat me like a child. Blackstone does that. Instead of verbalizing that, she clasped her hands together under the table. "I know this looks—bad—but I didn't do this on purpose. I swear."

He put down the delicate teacup that made his hands look enormous and with eyes glinting said, "So how on earth did you end up in my trunk?"

She bit her lip and knew she was in so much trouble. "Well, I happened to be in your bedchamber—"

"Happened to be? How does a lady, a young unmarried debutante end up in my bedchamber without an invitation?"

"I went to leave you another note. You read it and put it back in your journal."

His brow furrowed. "You were in my room. When Wolf and I arrived?"

She nodded her head and swallowed.

"So you saw… Christ." He rose from his chair throwing the napkin in his hand on the table. "Jesus Christ." He swung round to face her, his cheeks had a reddish blush. "Where?"

She looked at the floor. "Behind the curtains."

He paced the room. "And the trunk?"

"I waited for you to go in your dressing room and was crossing the room when your silly valet came back with some servants. I dived into the trunk and hid under the clothes, thinking I'd escape after they left, but they put more clothes on top of me and strapped it closed, then went to move it." She looked up at him. "Only it—I—made it too heavy and they dropped the trunk down the stairs. The last thing I remember is tumbling over and over and then waking up on the bunk."

He looked at her as if she had lost her mind. "So you didn't do this on purpose?"

"On purpose? Why would I—" Then her hand slapped over her mouth. She shook her head, her eyes going wide.

He slowly sat down across from her again. "You know your brother is probably looking frantically for you. He'll be out of his mind."

"I don't think so. He went north to Lord Hampton's fox

hunting party in Yorkshire this morning. He's not due back for four weeks."

"But surely the staff will send a missive when you don't come home."

She shook her head again, wanting him to stop looking at her as if she were the enemy. "Tiffany sent word to the house this morning that I'd become unwell with a cold and Mrs. Thompson who is paranoid about illness, readily agreed for me to stay with Lady Tiffany and Wolf. I even organized for a trunk to be sent there." She didn't tell Rockwell she'd done that in case she needed to flee from Lord Franklin. "So maybe no one is concerned. Can't we send Wolf a note when you pull into the nearest port. Then I'll simply take the stagecoach back to London."

"No. We can't send them a note. We're not stopping until Dublin. By then, someone might notice you're missing."

She was starting to get cross. "But I can't sail with you to Ireland."

"Well, you should have thought about that before invading my room and hopping into my trunk." He sighed and ran a hand over his face. "What a mess. You do realize that it doesn't matter if I take you to Ireland, Portsmouth, or Timbuktu. You are utterly ruined. You wanted a scandal to scare off Franklin? Well, you've got it."

"Could you drop me at Portsmouth? Maybe I can get back to London before anyone realizes I've been gone?"

"I'm not letting you go back to London unescorted and I don't have time to accompany you. I must get to Ireland as soon as possible. I have a lead on where Lord Furoe might be. If I delay, he might—disappear again."

"So, I'll come with you to Ireland. I could tell my brother I was helping you."

"The scandal will chase off Lord Franklin, I'm sure."

Her eyes brightened. "That's good, isn't it?" At his look of disbelief, she added, "But Blackstone's going to disown me."

"He'll do more than disown you. He'll very likely challenge me."

"Don't be ridiculous. Once you explain that it was all my fault…" She stopped speaking when she saw the look on his face and noted his hands had formed fists. "It is my fault."

He sat back in his chair and she noted the tiredness around his eyes. "Oh, I'm highly aware of that, but it makes no difference. Your brother will have you marching down the aisle with me faster than you can blink."

She put her hand to her head, suddenly feeling quite faint. "No. I won't allow it."

"Oh, so suddenly you can stand up to your brother without having to hide in a trunk and cause a scandal. What are you going to do to stop your brother demanding I marry you, cause another scandal?"

Yes, she wanted to scream. *I'll run away before I let you sacrifice yourself for me.* "Can we get a message to Wolf? Perhaps he could cover for me until I return. They could say I'm indisposed. Then my brother and the rest of society stays unaware until we get back to England."

"And Franklin? Won't he demand to see you if you are unwell?"

She hadn't thought about that. "It will have to be something contagious so he'll stay away but nothing too serious to have to alert my brother."

"Any illness should be reported to your brother. Franklin will probably send a note—unless it's ladies' problems."

Heat invaded Farah's face. "That could work. I'll write a note to send with your missive to Wolf. It will be for Franklin. That ought to ease his mind." She sipped her tea. This was getting complicated.

Rockwell nodded. "And what am I to do with you while I'm in Ireland."

She closed her eyes. *Think.* Then she smiled. "I could pretend to be Ashley. Your sister and I are both fair-haired. Who would know differently? What would be unusual about a brother and sister traveling together?"

CHAPTER FOUR

F ARAH REALLY BELIEVED that they would get away with this charade unscathed. But then she was the little mouse who lived a life in a safe circle of close friends. But now she'd stepped outside of her circle and it was taking her a while to catch up. He suspected her friendship with Ashley made her think any scandal could be overcome. He couldn't think of anyone in Ireland who'd met Ashley, so it just might work.

Perhaps he should play along. If they came back with Lucien, then perhaps the *ton* wouldn't realize it wasn't Ashley with him, but Farah. The excitement and shock at Lucien's return might make the confusion work.

"That is a good idea, posing as my sister while we are in Ireland." It would be less complicated. However, would his body listen to that advice? The saucy notes she'd left him, and her proximity made it very difficult for him to think of her with brotherly concern. He remembered the feel of her body when he'd carried her and the urge to reach across the table and scare away the naïve trust in her eyes, saw him pick up his teacup once more.

"I'll signal another ship near Portsmouth and ask them to take a missive to Wolf. We'll ask if he can stop your brother returning early to London and spin a story that will keep your scandal from surfacing. Of course, we're assuming I find Lucien and quickly. If not, you may have no choice but to wed me."

She looked at him as if that outcome would be the end of her world. And didn't that just sting.

THE WEATHER THANKFULLY held, and after a brief stop to hand a note to another ship, they reached Dublin harbor within three days. As the sun dipped below the horizon, casting a warm orange glow over the calm waters of the Irish Sea, Farah stood on the deck, watching the coastline get ever closer.

Soon she could make out the quayside. A crowd had gathered, their faces aglow with anticipation and curiosity. Fishermen, merchants, and dockworkers alike paused in their tasks to glimpse the approaching ship, their voices mingling with the distant cries of seagulls overhead.

The sound of creaking wood and taut ropes filled the air as the ship drew nearer, its hull slicing through the water with graceful precision. The rhythmic thud of footsteps echoed along the wooden planks of the deck, accompanied by the occasional shout of orders from the crew.

As the ship eased into its berth, a chorus of cheers erupted from the onlookers, their excitement palpable. Men hastily secured the mooring lines while others scurried to unload cargo from the hold, their movements a synchronized dance of efficiency.

From the ship's deck, the scent of salt air mingled with the tantalizing aroma of spices and exotic goods, hinting at the treasures brought from distant lands. She watched as the ship next to theirs was offloading barrels of rum and crates of silk carefully hoisted onto the docks, their contents destined to fill the coffers of eager merchants.

Farah twirled on the spot with her arms in the air while men ran round her finishing the docking and readying to unload. She was free. Free of her brother's overview and free of society's demands. But only for a short while. Only until they sailed back to England.

She couldn't wait to disembark. The first stop would be to

procure clothes. She needed other items too. Plus, she really needed a bath. A long hot soak in a tub.

Rockwell appeared at her side. He was still angry about the situation she'd put him in because he'd hardly spent any time with her. He worked up on deck most of the days and stayed in his cabin at night. She'd spent most of her days and nights in the stateroom, reading.

"I've organized to have our things sent to the Twin Heads Inn. I've taken private apartments so remember you are now Lady Ashley Ware when we are in public."

She swiped the wisp of hair from her eyes. "I know what part I must play. I swear I won't do anything to make our situation worse, or to trap you into a marriage you don't want. I know what your freedom means to you. You've traveled most of your life, visited places I can only dream of and would be too scared to visit. All the ladies know you're not husband material because we would sit at home alone. Do you think I want to tie myself to a man like that?"

He looked down his nose at her. "But I'm a better option than Lord Franklin? Is that it?"

She looked away at the bustling dock. It seemed a bit more frightening now that night was falling. "My plan wasn't supposed to go this far. You weren't supposed to be trapped into marrying me. I just needed you to help me fall from grace enough to send Franklin fleeing. So, can you try to forgive me?" With that, she stalked off toward the gangplank that was being lowered.

At least he was still talking to her. She could understand his anger. He didn't want to marry her. He'd already told her that at the ball the other night. Still, she was sure she could sort the situation out once they returned home. And she needed to get home as soon as possible. She had better work out a way she could help ascertain, one way or the other, whether Lord Furoe was alive and find out why he hadn't returned to England.

The first place she'd check was with the doctors who'd helped the wounded that night. Surely someone would remember finding him. Furoe was a very handsome man. Lucien was at least six foot three, tall, and broad shouldered. He would be hard to forget. He had black hair with the greenest of eyes. Most women never forgot his face.

There was an idea…

She stood tall at the head of the gangplank, waiting for Rockwell to escort her to the waiting carriage he'd organized. Her body trembled as he stepped close behind her. "After you," he said.

⇢⟫⟪⟸

THE COACHING INN was lovely, clean and tidy and seemed to have a certain upper-class clientele. "Good evening, I'm Mrs. O'Donnell. I own this establishment. Welcome, Lady Ashley and Lord Ware. I have your rooms ready and will have some food delivered shortly to your private sitting room after you have freshened up."

She removed her hat and gloves and said, "That's perfect, thank you. While we are eating, could you organize a bath to be placed in my room and one in my brother's room? It's been a long trip."

Mrs. O'Donnell beamed at Rockwell. "Of course. I'll get it organized at once. By the time you've eaten, the baths should be ready."

"Oh, and could you arrange to have my gown cleaned and pressed? I have nothing else to wear. The men dropped my trunk into the sea, so it seems I'll be needing a whole new wardrobe."

"I'll send word to Mrs. Clearbrook, an excellent seamstress. She can help with your clothes."

Mrs. O'Donnell closed the door of the private dining room and left them alone. Farah wandered around and saw that both bedchambers led off this private living room of sorts. She watched as Mrs. O'Donnell's son put Rockwell's things in one room, leaving the other for her. She'd be quite safe at night. Someone would have to get through the private living area to reach her bedchamber. And she knew that Rockwell would ensure the door into their private quarters was locked.

Rockwell held a chair out for her, and she sat. Still standing, he poured her a sherry before taking his seat.

"I'll organize with the local dressmaker to set up an account for you. I assume you'll need more than a few outfits. Once it's become known we're here, we might be invited to social events."

"How lovely."

"I just pray there is no one in attendance who knows Ashley." He grimaced. "I don't want you wandering Dublin without me by your side. The English are still not very popular here, and a high-born lady could be a target for kidnapping and the likes."

Farah didn't want to think what "the likes" might be. "Then you'll have to escort me to the dressmakers in the morning." He looked even more stern. She ignored his stare. "Then I thought we should talk to the local doctors. Lord Furoe is not a man easy to forget. Surely someone must remember if they treated him or buried him."

Rockwell stopped eating, a piece of bread dipped in stew halfway to his mouth. "I have already talked with as many doctors as I could find. No one remembered him. In fact, I talked to the local saddlers, blacksmiths and taverns…and got nothing. However, I have a lead. I'm going to visit a grain merchant. He deals with all the local farmers. I thought maybe someone had taken him out of Dublin.

"And have you talked to the women?" At his quizzical look, she added, "I suspect women would not forget a man like Lord Furoe."

"How so?"

"Don't be obtuse. He's as handsome as sin. Surely, the ladies of society who mixed with the officers would remember him. If he were still alive, and roamed the Dublin streets, it would be a woman who remembered seeing him."

Rockwell laughed. "I would never have thought of that. But you're right. I've been looking in all the wrong places. We need to check the brothels. Perhaps those near where the grain merchant is situated."

Farah dropped her fork. "No. Wrong again. Lord Furoe was madly in love with Lady Courtney. He would never do—use—prostitutes." Lucien wouldn't disrespect Courtney ever. She'd envied what the couple had shared. They were so in love and so happy. Then she'd watched Courtney fall apart when Lucian had been killed, and for a moment, she'd thought how lucky she was never to have to go through that kind of pain.

"He might not have before he was supposedly dead, but if he hasn't returned to the woman you say he loved, then perhaps you're wrong, and Courtney wasn't as important to him as you believe."

She wouldn't believe that—*couldn't* believe that. Her friends were her guiding light when looking at who and when she would marry. "There must be another reason he hasn't come home, because I refuse to believe that of Lucien. Did you not see them together? Or is it you can't imagine the depth of their love? Have you ever been in love?"

He looked uncomfortable with her question. "No. I have never been in love."

"Then perhaps he really is dead, because I cannot imagine him staying away from his fiancée."

Rockwell's mouth turned down. "I too have thought of nothing but that question on the journey to Ireland. Why has he not returned home? Is he really dead? Did I imagine seeing him when I was here last? But I have this feeling that he is alive. It won't leave me."

She could see how important this was to him. She reached out and covered his hand with hers. "If he's alive, we'll find him."

Rockwell looked to where her hand covered his, and he dragged his hand away and took another drink. He didn't want to feel things for Farah. She was not the type of woman who wouldn't care that he left her behind time and time again. He could only hurt her. There was something in him that drove him. He had to know everything. He had to know about the world he lived in. Why did bees make honey? Why did the winds blow from the east? He wanted to see everything and experience all the world offered.

He would end up resenting a wife who made him stay in England.

A woman like Farah was looking for love and he couldn't let her fall in love with him because he'd break her heart. He would never get over this wanderlust. And he'd already caused one woman's death.

"Tomorrow, while I leave you at the dressmakers, I'll visit the women of disrepute and see what I can learn. Perhaps he was faithful to begin with, but it's been five long years. I don't believe a man could go without—"

"Sex. He couldn't go without sex." She looked disappointed. Rockwell admired the naivety. She was purity herself. She wasn't for a man like him, who took pleasure wherever he could, but never gave his heart.

"Men have needs, Farah. One day you'll learn that sex— passion, desire, is perfectly acceptable without love."

She shook her head. "Not for me," she said softly.

"That's because you don't know what you're missing." And the idea of teaching her about desire and passion swept through him. He forcibly pushed the idea away. He sat staring at her silently. "I hope you meet this man of your dreams, a paragon of virtue, and get your happy ever after."

She looked away and sighed. "I never said I wanted perfection. That is unattainable. I know that most people don't marry for love. Men seem to avoid love for some reason. I want to be happy, that's all. I don't think that's too much to ask. Do you?"

He considered her as he would a painting. Why hadn't some man, other than Lord Franklin, stepped forward for considera- tion? Well, one had. Conte Philippe Lambert. He didn't really know the man, but obviously Blackstone hadn't approved. Was this the man she still pined over? Was he the reason why the idea of marrying Lord Franklin was not to be born? If he recalled, Lambert had married another.

"Friendship and respect are a sound basis for any marriage. I think you are wise to want to wait for a man who can at least offer you that."

"Perhaps I'd be better off remaining a spinster."

He rose and moved round to take the chair next to her. "No. Desire and a shared passion are what make a marriage more— even without love."

His fingers closed gently around her wrist and he turned her palm up and stroked his thumb over her skin. "You have no understanding of what you'll be missing if you decide to remain a spinster. Passion between men and women can be quite remarkable."

"Isn't passion better when there is love?"

He shrugged. *Lie.* "I wouldn't know. I find pleasure with women and I am not in love with them. I wonder if you've ever been kissed?" At her smile, he added, "Kissed properly."

Her smile dimmed, and her cute nose screwed up. "I assure you I have been kissed and properly." She pulled her hand from his and folded her arms over her chest.

With a finger, he tilted her chin and looked into her eyes. They were swimming with a mixture of bravado and question. "Shall we see..." He pressed his mouth to hers, letting his lips dance over hers, and Rockwell felt Farah relax. Her eyes drifted closed as he deepened the kiss. He stroked her cheek with one finger. It was a misdirection as his tongue gained entrance and she stiffened for one moment before once more surrendering and letting her tongue tangle with his.

But soon it was Rockwell who was falling under her spell. The taste of her was like ambrosia, and his tongue possessively stroked hers. His hand cupped the back of her head as her shy participation created a yearning inside him that he'd never experienced before. He should stop before he lost control, but the idea that Lambert had kissed her before him made Rockwell want to eviscerate the man's memory from her mind.

It was the sound of Farah's moan that saw him break off the kiss and rock back in his chair, stunned from the need to take her that coursed through his veins. All he could hear was her rapid panting. He watched in masculine satisfaction as her fingers feathered over her lips, as if in awe.

"Goodness. That was—goodness," she murmured shakily, forcing a lightness to her tone.

Happy that he'd made his point, he stood. "Marriage based on friendship but with desire and passion is not to be sniffed at. Love is a bonus, but not a necessity." He needed her to understand this because when they returned to London, they would likely have to marry. Perhaps she would not see a marriage to him as she did a marriage to Franklin—the end of her world. "If you'll excuse me, I shall retire for my bath. Don't stay up too late. We have a busy few days ahead."

Then he walked into his bedchamber, right next to hers, and images of Farah naked in a bath in the room next to his flooded his vision. He groaned out loud. Having her so close would be torture. But he owed her the chance to see if they could return from this voyage unscathed.

CHAPTER FIVE

FARAH REACHED FOR her glass with a shaky hand and took a long gulp of the wine within. She sat there for a moment, swaying, dizzy, trying to regain her composure. Shaken to her very core, she couldn't believe the power in Rockwell's kiss. Even Philippe's kisses hadn't affected her so, but then again, Philippe's kisses had been chaste compared to Rockwell's. His tongue had entered her mouth and—she'd liked it.

Her skin still tingled all over. She shifted in her chair. Her whole body was warm, but there was a yearning in her feminine center which still throbbed. She looked at her plate of half-eaten food but pushed it away. This was terrible. Now she would think of Rockwell in a new light. Seeing him naked was bad enough, but now that he'd kissed her....

She chided herself for allowing such a liberty. She was supposed to be his sister and already they had acted inappropriately. It must be because she was tired and worried about her—their—situation. She threw her napkin on the table, chiding herself. It was time for a bath and then for bed. Tomorrow was another day, and she planned to find Lord Furoe as fast as she could and get herself home with no scandal. She would not put Rockwell in a position where he had to marry her. She'd have to find another way to deal with Lord Franklin.

She couldn't end up in a marriage of convenience with Rockwell. She might lose her heart to him and she was pretty sure love was something he didn't want in a marriage. She'd be just as miserable with him as she would be with Lord Franklin—maybe more. She was right in her thinking. For her, it was love or nothing in a marriage. She wanted what Wolf and Tiffany shared, or she'd rather become a spinster.

A few minutes later, as she lay soaking in the hot water, her gown taken for cleaning, all she could think about was that Rockwell was in the chamber next door—naked too. She closed her eyes and relived the kiss. His finger on her cheek was like fire on her skin—almost branding her. She'd wanted him to touch her everywhere.

Rockwell was like laudanum. It gave such pleasant dreams, you had to fight to keep from using it every day. She, of course, didn't have any with her, as she hadn't expected to be shanghaied on a ship bound for Ireland. When her courses came, she often needed it for the pain. Now she would avoid it in case she dreamed of him. From now on, Farah vowed earnestly, she would make a concerted effort to always play her role as his sister and remind him of such.

She had no choice. For the first time in her life, she was conflicted. She could envision letting a man like Rockwell take her to bed, but he would only do so as her husband, and that she couldn't afford to contemplate. A wanderer who didn't believe in love would likely have a woman in every port while she was left behind.

That could work if she didn't feel her heart might be in danger. The wisest thing would be to keep away from him, but it was impossible to do when stuck in Ireland with him.

Just then, she felt something touching her arm as it hung over the tub. She looked over the side of the tub and spied a very large brown spider with legs as long as her fingers crawling up her arm.

The scream she issued was followed by a violent shaking of her arm to try to remove it, but it wouldn't budge. She was screaming her head off while jumping out of the tub and swatting the spider away with her other hand.

The spider dropped to the floor and scurried away towards

the bed. She quickly threw her towel over it, not wanting to sleep in a bed she knew an enormous spider had crawled under. Her breathing got back to normal just as the door burst open to find a dripping wet, and naked Rockwell, his face pale with a pistol in hand standing in the doorway.

He looked about the room and then at her, also naked in the middle of the room.

She pointed to the towel. "A spider," she croaked out. "A very large spider," she said, and shuddered.

But Rockwell stood like a stone statue, his mouth hanging open. As she let her eyes sweep up his magnificent body, the cold night air was forgotten as she found the heat and desire flaring in his eyes. Only then did she remember she was naked, too.

She looked around and grabbed for the quilt on the end of her bed but gave it a good shake before wrapping herself in it. "Can you get rid of the spider, please? It's under the towel. I won't be able to sleep unless I know it's gone."

"Sleep… I'll never sleep now that I've seen…" Rockwell growled. "Why didn't you simply kill it?"

She shook her head as she tried not to look at him—still naked. "Just pop it out the window. It's not hurting anyone. Perhaps you should—cover yourself first, now that I have the spider contained."

Rockwell flashed her a look she couldn't understand before crossing naked to the towel and picking it up. He walked to the window and shook it out. As he turned back to face her, he held the towel in front of him, blocking the view she was coming to crave.

He stood there, looking at her wrapped in the quilt and a pained look crossed his face. "I'd hand you the towel but I suspect the sight of my…" he swallowed hard, "my reaction to your nakedness might be inappropriate. I'll fetch you another towel from my room." With that he stalked out, leaving her staring at his bare buttocks clenching as he walked. Her body heated and her mouth fell open.

He was gone for quite some time and she stood, still wet, in the middle of her room in the now completely soaked quilt. Finally, he returned, but this time, to her disappointment, he had a deep blue dressing gown tied tightly around him.

"Your towel, madam."

She reached out to take it from him.

"Don't look at me like that," he said.

"Like what?"

"With disappointment that I'm no longer naked. I'm having enough troubling trying to remember you're supposed to be my sister."

She moved closer, knowing it was a bad idea, but no man had ever looked at her the way Rockwell was doing, nor had her body reacted to any man like this before. It was as if it had a mind of its own. "But I'm not your sister."

Rockwell briefly closed his eyes. "What are you doing? This is not a game. Do you *want* to end up married to me?"

She shook her head but held her ground. "I don't intend to marry unless it's for love. You mentioned I'd be missing out if I remained a spinster. Well, I can be a spinster, but that doesn't mean I can't experience desire and passion." So she dropped the quilt to the floor.

Once again, heat flared in his eyes. He took a step towards her until her breasts almost rubbed against the satin of his robe. "But what if you met a man you could love and—"

"If he loved me, he wouldn't care about my past. If he does, he's not the man for me." She tentatively reached out and cupped his cheek. "No one needs to know what we do in Ireland. Besides, you're saying I'm already ruined for being with you here in Ireland. So perhaps I want to be ruined for real."

He reached up and gripped her wrist, gentling peeling it from his face. "But I would know. If you want this to go any further, realize you're agreeing to marry me. And I warn you, I'm not husband material. But I can promise you passion. Just not my heart."

She stepped back, stooped to gather the quilt around her once more. "Then we are at an impasse. I'm happy to explore passion with you, but I won't marry you unless I own your heart. I guess it will be a frustrating trip."

With that, she pushed him out of her room and slammed the door.

Men were so confusing. Rockwell wanted her. She saw it in his eyes and the way his robe was moving when she revealed her body to him. Yet honor got in the way.

She sighed as she donned her slip to sleep in and crawled into her cold bed—alone. Really, she admired his honor. That was what made him a good man, and why she utterly believed him when he said he wouldn't make a good husband.

He would never lie to her.

The fear that grew deep in the pit of her stomach was that if they didn't get home soon, the ruse would be revealed, and Rockwell and her brother would make her marry him. Franklin wasn't stupid and would not believe the story. She was ill for too long. He'd want to see her. Or worse, contact Blackstone and ask what was wrong with her.

Wouldn't it be ironic if Rockwell behaved like a gentleman on this journey and ended up having to marry her, anyway?

She turned over for about the hundredth time and punched her pillow.

What she was even more scared of was that maybe she didn't care they would have to marry. Having a man like Rockwell for a husband could be very desirous—while he was at home in England, anyway. The nights would be long when he went adventuring.

An image of Rockwell with mistresses or ladies in countries he sailed to, made her cringe and wish she'd never thought marriage to Rockwell would be anything but a disappointment.

As she drifted into sleep, she promised herself that they would do everything they could to find Lord Furoe. And soon.

FARAH SLEPT LATE and by the time she had risen and dressed, Rockwell had left the tavern, which meant she was stuck here until he returned. She'd promised. She sat in their private salon drinking another cup of tea and thinking about Lucien. She prayed they found him because both Lauren, his sister, and Courtney, his fiancée, would be so happy…

Perhaps a book might keep her busy, but just as she stood to peruse the shelves, the door opened and Rockwell strode in and threw his gloves on the table. "Well, the meeting with the grain merchant only led to more confusion. I showed him the small painting I have of Lucien and he thought it looked like a man who lived in a small village north of Dublin, Malahide. But he wasn't sure, as the man had a thick beard."

"So not all bad news."

Rockwell sunk into the chair and rubbed his head. "But he was sure the man had a little girl with him—a daughter, he thinks."

"Oh, that can't be him then." She sat watching his inner turmoil. "But you want to check?"

"This man is the first person to show any sign of recognition. I can't ignore that."

Farah eyed him and finally plucked up the courage to ask, "Why is finding Lord Furoe so important to you?"

"Because they never found his body. His grave lies empty. His father and his sisters had no one to mourn. When I thought I'd seen him… Perhaps he's not dead." He looked at her, his eyes full of anguish. "He was my best friend. He and I were supposed to go off on an adventure, but he signed up to help in the Irish Rebellion. Did you know his mother was Irish and he spoke Gaelic well? He thought he could stop them before anyone was hurt." Rockwell gave a harsh laugh. "That didn't turn out as he planned."

"So, you were friends? But he was engaged to Courtney, so I doubt he'd go traveling with you." She wanted to learn what made Rockwell need to keep adventuring.

It was as if she were no longer in the room. "The last words we spoke to each other were harsh. I was angry he wouldn't come with me as planned because he'd fallen in love with Courtney. I told him to go off and get himself killed then… and when he was…" He looked up at her with anguish deep in his eyes. "It's as if I cursed him. He got angry with me and my selfishness, and I think he took the commission to spite me. It's my fault he came here to fight. It's my fault he died. Now all I have of him is the locket his sister gave me, something of his to remind me of him."

She moved and crouched at his feet, taking his hand. "It most definitely is not your fault. You were young and headstrong, as was he. He should have thought about Courtney and his family before haring off."

He smiled down at her. "I suppose we were. We both thought we were invincible."

She rose, letting go of his hand, and tried to ignore the tingle of sparks racing up her arm at the contact. "At least I now understand why finding him is an obsession with you."

"He'd do it for me. If he thought I were dead and then he saw me, he'd keep looking."

"Well, we have only just started our search. Let's crack on and see if we can find out more information. I'd like to come with you to this little village the grain merchant mentioned. Can we get there and back in one day?"

"Probably not there and back. I was thinking of leaving you in Dublin as there is an inn in the village, but it's very basic."

"I'm sure I can survive basic. Besides, I've never been to Ireland, and I'd love to see some of it. And if it is Lucien, then I want to be there when we find him."

Rockwell nodded. "It's probably best that I don't let you out of my sight, anyway. We'll go in a few days." He nodded his head to the window. "A storm's passing through. We'll wait for the roads to dry out."

She could tell that he wasn't happy to wait for the weather to clear any more than she was, and that he was only waiting because of her. Guilt fell heavily on her shoulders. "You could go without me. I swear to stay in the tavern."

He sat in silence for a moment. He stood. "No. We go together. Anyway, I've come to escort you to the dressmakers. Questions will be asked if you're seen with no luggage or change of clothes." He watched as she donned her bonnet and cape, since it was drizzling. "Once you've selected your materials, I'm sure the dressmaker won't mind coming here for fittings. We need to get as much as possible done over the next few days before we head out of Dublin."

ROCKWELL HAILED A hackney, and she hurried into the protection of the carriage. "You don't need to stay with me," she said. "You could do more investigations and collect me in a few hours."

He wanted to do just that. But he worried about leaving her alone in a city where she knew no one and didn't have anyone to call on for help. She was his responsibility. It would do no good to find Lucien but lose her. So, he simply nodded. He'd have to leave her at some stage to visit with the ladies of the night, so to speak. But he'd do that while she was tucked up in her bed with the door locked.

Perhaps he should call on his friends, Simon and Bridget Boyle. He'd met Simon in the Caribbean on one of his trips. Simon's father, Baron Boyle, owned a plantation and Simon had been to check on his father's holding. They'd stayed in touch and Rockwell had stayed with the couple when he'd come to get Tiffany's money back.

He'd feel relieved leaving Farah with them. The couple had

never met Ashley, so that should work, but Farah might get tripped up. He couldn't remember how much he'd shared with Simon about his sisters. They would look after her, but it was a lot to ask of new acquaintances, and would she agree? Perhaps they could pay the Boyles a call on the way back to the tavern from Malahide.

The rain was heavier, and luckily the hackney could stop directly outside the dressmakers. He helped Farah down, and they both rushed for the door. He flung it open and stood back for her to pass. As soon as he entered, he heard a cry of delight.

"Lord Ware? How wonderful to see you! I didn't realize you were back in Dublin." The woman paused. "And with company."

"Good day, Mrs. Ahearn. I've only just arrived with my sister, Lady Ashley Ware. One of my ship's crew dropped one of Ashley's trunks in the water as we disembarked and she's in need of replacements."

Blast. He would have to run into the widow he'd enjoyed a tryst with while in Dublin recently. She'd gotten clingy back then. Her frown had turned into a seductive smile when he mentioned his sister, while Farah's eyebrow had risen in a knowing smirk.

"Your sister, you say. How lovely." And Mrs. Ahearn turned to Farah. "You must let me help you, my dear. Orla Clearbrook and I can take care of this." Mrs. Ahearn nodded in the dressmaker's direction. "Orla is very experienced. You'll be in expert hands, Lady Ashley. Your brother must have more important things to do than chaperon your shopping expedition." She waved her hand at Rockwell. "Off you go, Rockwell. I'll see your sister safely back to…?"

"Twin Heads Inn," Farah piped up with a smile that said, *I'm going to have fun.*

"There you go. I know where that is, don't I?" Mrs. Ahearn—Fiona—winked at him. He gritted his teeth as Farah tried to hide a giggle with a cough.

He could use the time to visit the unsavory areas that Farah suggested. There were a couple of gentlemen's clubs nearby he could visit. "That would be very kind, if it's all right with Ashley." It took Farah a moment to realize he was addressing her.

"Oh, yes. That would be lovely. Mrs. Ahearn—"

"Call me Fiona, my dear."

"Fiona might like to join us for dinner too," Farah added as she noted his embarrassment.

"Of course." He flashed Fiona a smile through gritted teeth. "I shall leave you ladies. Enjoy your day."

"I'm sure I will," Farah added as he took his leave out into the horrid weather.

He didn't need to hail a hackney. The first of the gentlemen's clubs he wished to visit, a more upmarket establishment, was around the corner. This was the more fashionable area in Dublin. That was how he knew the dressmaker was here. He'd passed it many times on his way to the club.

Kevin the doorman greeted him like a returning friend. "Lord Ware. How nice to see you so soon again. I thought you'd returned to England."

He took off his hat and shook the water off it, handing it to Kevin. "I'm back in Dublin to find a friend." He fished out of his pocket the painting he had of Lucien. It was over five years out of date and no doubt, if his friend were alive, he would have matured somewhat. Certainly the man he'd spied in the tavern had been bigger and wider. "Have you ever seen this man in here?"

Kevin took the small portrait and studied it. Finally, he shook his head. "No. I don't think so, m'lord. Are you sure he's a member?"

This high-class club was a member-only place. Rockwell couldn't imagine Furoe, if he were alive, not being a member here. "Do you think I could talk to the ladies and see if any of them recognize my friend?"

"Lord Ware, you're back so soon?" Down the stairs glided one of the most stunning women he'd had the pleasure of meeting. Mrs. O'Rourke owned the club, but that was all. She did not provide services to her male members unless she wanted pleasure for herself.

He bowed over her hand and kissed her knuckles. "As beautiful as ever, Maeve. You always take my breath away."

"And you, my lord, are still a smooth talker." But her smile showed she was pleased with his observation. "Are you after male company in the card room this early or other entertainments?"

"Neither." He handed her the image.

"And who's this handsome gentleman?"

"He's my friend. He went missing a few years ago and is believed to be dead, but I thought I saw him in Dublin when I was last here."

She nodded her head. "He reminds me of a young man that was brought in here after the uprising a few years ago. He had a terrible head injury." She peered closer at the picture. "It could be him."

Rockwell could barely contain his excitement. "What happened to him?"

She turned to Kevin. "Didn't Ava nurse him?"

Kevin nodded. "Aye, I think she did. I remember she nursed him for over a month."

"Is Ava here? Can I talk to her?"

The smile on Maeve's face dimmed. "Ava left us almost five years ago to go home to her family. This life wasn't for her." She tapped a finger to her lips before adding, "But I think this man went with her."

"Went where?" Rockwell asked hopefully.

"Malahide," Kevin answered. "Young Ava came from north of Dublin. Not far, about ten miles up the coast."

Malahide! The same place the grain merchant mentioned. Rockwell could kiss him. "Thank you, Kevin. That's most helpful."

She clapped her hands. "Now that we have settled your inquiry"—she linked her arm through his—"can I tempt you—to partake in some of the house's offerings."

The way she ran her fingers over his arm made it clear she was inviting him to her bed. It was an offer he would love to take, but to his annoyance, an image of Farah standing in his bedroom, skirt hiked up to her waist and his large Hessian on her foot filled his mind. Why did that image haunt him so?

To his horror, he also realized he didn't want to have sex with this woman. The woman he wanted beneath him, above him, every way a woman could be taken, was Farah. Damn it all to hell.

CHAPTER SIX

"N ORMALLY, I'D LOVE to accept, Maeve, but I've left my sister, Ashley, at the dressmaker's around the corner and I must get back. I promised her a trip and she was most keen to also try and locate our friend. The man I'm looking for is her best friend's fiancé. May I hold your wonderful offer until another day?"

She hid her disappointment well and exclaimed, "My club is always open to you. Come and visit me when you don't have your sister in tow."

He kissed her cheek. "I most definitely will do that. Thank you." He skipped down the stairs and didn't even care that it was now torrential rain. He had a lead that matched with what the grain merchant had told him. He needed to get to Malahide as soon as possible. The sooner he found Lucien, the sooner he could get back to London and try to avert a possible scandal.

But a part of him wondered if it wouldn't be the end of the world if he had to marry Farah.

IN THE ELEGANT parlor of Orla's dressmaking establishment, Farah sat perched on a cushioned chair, her fair hair cascading in loose waves around her shoulders. Orla, a seasoned dressmaker with a keen eye for fashion, bustled about the room, pulling out bolts of fabric in an array of colors and textures.

Farah was having fun. Mrs. Ahearn—Fiona—was so obvious in her need to learn all about her "brother." Talk about infatuation. Mrs. Ahearn almost hero-worshipped Rockwell. It wasn't every day a young lady got to spend time with a man's paramour.

"Your coloring is nothing like your brother's," the woman said as they poured over some fabrics.

"I take after my mother. The rest of my family are dark haired. I like light blues and greens," she suggested to Orla.

"How many gowns will you require?" Orla, the dressmaker, said.

Remembering what Rockwell had said—another lie—she said, "My trunk went overboard, so I have nothing. I really need about three dresses for everyday wear and two that I could use if going out on a social occasion. And I'll need undergarments too. Plus a night robe—a warm one. The nights are cold here."

Right now, all she had was the gown she wore when she'd been locked in the trunk.

"When will you require the gowns?"

She hesitated. They would travel north in a few days. "As soon as possible, I'm afraid. Perhaps you could add a warmer cape, with some muffs if you have them. I didn't realize it would get so cold at this time of year."

"When the storm fronts come through, the temperature drops. It should be warm again in a few days."

There was no way she was letting Rockwell leave her behind. She could just picture him thinking she could stay with Mrs. Ahearn, but that would not happen. She wasn't about to be pawned off on his ex-mistress, even if the woman was entertaining. "Could I have them all within two days? Rockwell will pay whatever is needed to make it happen." He had said he would pay, and Rockwell had plenty of money.

"I can do that. But we need to get on and choose fabrics and then take the measurements," Orla said.

Then she walked over to the other side of the room. "And

Lady Ashley, my dear, I have just the thing for your gowns," Orla declared, her voice brimming with excitement as she presented a selection of fabrics before her client.

Farah leaned forward, her green eyes alight with interest as she examined the offerings. It was quite odd to be playing the role of Rockwell's sister. "What do you suggest, Mrs. Ahearn? I want something that will complement my complexion and flatter my figure."

Mrs. Ahearn nodded thoughtfully, her fingers deftly unfurling the delicate folds of fabric. "For your fair complexion, I recommend soft-pastel shades that will bring out the rosy undertones in your skin. Perhaps a blush pink or a pale lavender?"

Farah's lips curved into a smile of approval. "I do adore pastels. They lend such a delicate charm to any ensemble."

"Indeed, my lady," Mrs. Ahearn agreed, her eyes twinkling with enthusiasm. "And for the fabric, I would suggest a lightweight silk or muslin, something that will drape gracefully and move with your every step."

She looked at Orla for confirmation. Farah nodded in agreement, her mind already envisioning the finished gowns. "That sounds perfect, Mrs. Ahearn. But I would also like to incorporate a touch of richness into some of the designs. Perhaps a deep emerald green or a regal sapphire blue?"

Orla's smile widened at the suggestion. "Ah, a pop of jewel tones to add contrast and sophistication. An excellent choice, my lady."

As they continued to discuss colors and fabrics, Farah and Mrs. Ahearn worked together to curate a stunning selection of gowns that would not only showcase her beauty but also capture the notice of a man. This was the first time she'd created a wardrobe just for her, not worrying what her brother would think. It was so very liberating. So why then did Rockwell's face swarm into view. It infuriated Farah that she wanted Rockwell to notice. But she couldn't compete with a woman of Fiona's beauty and experience.

With each bolt of fabric chosen and every detail meticulously planned, Farah's anticipation grew, knowing that the gowns would soon come to life in Orla's expert hands. Dublin wasn't nearly as backward as she thought. These were very rich French fabrics.

Mrs. Ahearn picked up on her thoughts. "The French and Irish trade freely. The Irish are more aligned with France than England. It's wise to remember that if you are out and about by yourself. The English are not well liked here."

"Have there been other uprisings since the one in 1803?" she asked. Orla's head popped up. "My best friend lost her fiancé in the uprising," she added.

"Is that why Rockwell—Lord Ware is back? He's still looking for this friend?" Fiona asked. "I told him that no Englishman wounded in the uprising, who was captured by the Irish rebels, would still be alive." She sighed. "I admire his loyalty, but it's a waste of his time." She gave a saucy smile. "I can think of other ways to amuse your brother."

"He is quite focused on his task. We only came back to search for our friend."

Fiona sighed. "I knew he was not looking for anything other than amusements when he was last here. Lord Ware is a wanderer. A restless soul. I pity any woman who marries him, for his heart desires only adventure." She winked at Farah. "But a woman can enjoy him while she can."

Farah tried to hide her shock. "My brother does like to travel. But I'm sure the lure of hearth and family will soon catch up with him as he gets older and realizes there is more to life than sailing around the world by himself."

"Perhaps. Although I got the impression that since he lost his fiancée all those years ago, he's quite reluctant to let his heart engage."

Farah almost tripped over the trail of fabric she was holding. "I beg your pardon. What fiancée?"

Fiona's face colored, and she cursed under her breath. "Oh,

no. He said no one in his family knew the story. But he let slip Charlotte's name one night in—that is—I asked him who Charlotte was. He didn't want to tell me, but I persisted and he told me the story."

"What story? Who is Charlotte?"

"She is no one of consequence," a deep voice said from behind her.

Rockwell. "You're back early," she said gaily, trying to hide the fact they'd been talking about him. "I've selected the material, but they need to do my measurements yet. Why don't you come back in half an hour?"

He looked at Fiona, who seemed to have shrunk under his gaze. "That's all right. I'll wait. Then he sat on the chair near the window.

Orla looked at the two women. She clicked her fingers. "Refreshments for Lord Ware. Come, Lady Ashley. Behind the screen you go and we will get your measurements and soon have your garments in hand."

Fiona gathered her things. "And I must dash. Orla, can you deliver my gown by Friday? I'm happy to wait longer if Lady Ashley's order needs to take priority."

"Of course, Mrs. Ahearn."

"Oh, that's too kind," Farah added.

"Then I bid you good day." Mrs. Ahearn hugged Farah. "I wish you luck on your hunt. But remember what I said." Then she whispered in Farah's ear. "Your brother may need a shoulder to cry on when he realizes his friend is dead."

Before Fiona left, Farah called, "Oh, but you will dine with us tonight?"

Fiona looked at Rockwell's face and shook her head. "Another time perhaps."

Farah bit her lip as she looked into Rockwell's stony eyes. He was angry. Really angry. He didn't like that she had learned about his fiancée. What did that mean? Who was she? Where had they met? Did his heart still belong to her?

Most of all, it made her think Rockwell knew how to love. It was likely the problem was that he didn't want to.

Rockwell didn't utter a word while her measurements were taken, and the tension in the room could be cut with a sword. Even when she was ready to leave, he still said nothing. The rain had stopped, but a blustery, cold wind blew as they hailed the hackney.

She settled into the carriage and couldn't bear the silence. "Did you find out anything important?"

He turned to stare at her. "You will never bring up the name Charlotte in my hearing or mention her name to any of my friends and family. Is that clear?"

She swallowed. "If that is your wish, then I promise."

He merely nodded and then he carried on talking as if nothing strange had occurred. "I think we have a valid lead. The gentleman's club revealed they think a man who looked a lot like Lucien left with a young lady named Ava who worked at the brothel. They went to her village, a place called Malahide."

She leaned forward, and a smile broke over her face. "But that's the same village the grain merchant spoke about." She clapped her hands in glee. "We are close. I can feel it. When do we leave?"

She looked so beautiful in her excitement. But he'd been shocked to hear the questions about his fiancée cross her lips. Charlotte was his ghost, his pain, and not one he wished to share. He didn't want anyone to know.

Trust Farah to uncover his darkest secrets. She was worming her way into his life and he couldn't stop her. It was as if she were peeling back all his layers and he didn't like it. He didn't want to let a woman into his life again. He was better off as a loner. A man with a woman in every port. He ran his hand over his face.

He didn't want to take her to Malahide, but he couldn't leave her here. What more would Fiona tell her? "If it doesn't rain overnight, we'll leave soon."

"I guess I'll be fine with what I have on for a few days in a small village. I won't need anything expensive in Malahide. And my new clothes will be waiting when I return—with Lucien."

He sighed. "Has it never occurred to you that if Lucien is living with this woman in Malahide, he may not wish to return with us? He has lived here for over five years, letting no one know that he's even alive. He must have a good reason."

The light in Farah's eyes dimmed. She slumped back against the squab. "There must be a reason. I won't think ill of him. Courtney has been pining for him all this time. Surely she couldn't have been so wrong about the depth of his affections."

Rockwell would have said his friend would never have hurt Lady Courtney. If he said he loved her, he did. But now, he doubted everything he knew about his friend. Why hadn't he returned to England? A part of him thought that he just might punch him if he found Furoe alive. Lucien had let him think he was dead. Dead! For five years.

"If we find him tomorrow, we'll have our answers."

When they arrived at the inn, he helped her out. "You go up to our suite. I'll organize the carriage hire and whatever else we need for tomorrow."

She bit her lip and he wanted to kiss her so much it was like a constant ache deep in his balls. What was it about this pixie woman that stirred him so?

She finally said, "I'm sorry if what Fiona told me was a secret, but I didn't purposely—"

"Yes, you did. You wanted to learn more about me." Then he got back into the hackney.

The wind was buffeting her tiny frame so much, she was almost swept off her feet. "You can't hold that against me. If things go wrong, we may end up married. That's scary. While I know you, I don't really know you. Can you understand? You've always just been my best friend's older brother. Not an actual flesh and blood man." She stamped her foot. "I'm not explaining this properly."

He leaned out the window and cupped her cheek. "I understand. But if we must marry, my life before our marriage is just that—my life." Then he drew in a deep breath as the pain flashed in her eyes. As the carriage drew away, he thought the wind carried to his ears, "True love has no secrets."

That was what he was afraid of. She wanted more than he could ever give. If they couldn't sneak home and avoid a scandal, he was going to hurt her.

And he hated that.

CHAPTER SEVEN

TWO DAYS LATER, they set off for Malahide. As the carriage rattled along the uneven road, Rockwell and Farah exchanged worried glances. The verdant Irish countryside passed by in a blur. Farah wished she could take it all in, but maybe on the way back, once they'd found Lucien, she could relax and enjoy this trip. At the moment, the two of them had their thoughts firmly fixed on their missing friend.

Rockwell, his normally composed demeanor slightly frayed around the edges, broke the tense silence. "What am I going to say to him if I find him?"

Farah, her brow furrowed with concern, leaned forward in her seat. "Be truthful, Rockwell. If he deserves your censure, then do so. It seems unlike him not to send word home or not to go home. If it is him, I fear something dreadful has occurred. Maybe he's being held prisoner."

He reached across the space and squeezed her hand. "I'm almost hoping that's true." He shook his head. "How awful is that?"

"You're just being honest. His disappearance hurt you, too."

He turned to look out the window and she left him to his thoughts. She too had tossed all night, wondering if this romantic image she had of Courtney and Lucien was a charade. If he had run from his obligations and family, she'd make Rockwell swear that when they returned to London, he'd say Lucien was dead. She could not bear to hurt her friend by revealing the truth.

"What time will we make Malahide?"

He gave her his attention. "We should be there just after lunch. It will give us time to do some initial scouting."

She was pleased that she wore gloves to prevent her nails from being bitten to the quick.

"Why did your brother refuse your marriage to the Conte?"

Gosh, where had that question come from? What had Rockwell been thinking about? Perhaps the most likely outcome of this adventure. A scandal-ridden engagement and marriage. Not if she could prevent it.

"You know why. He thought Philippe was after my money and not good enough for me. Blackstone has a grand dislike of the French."

"Didn't you explain to him you loved him?"

She didn't know how to respond to that question. Had she loved Philippe, or was it simply because a handsome man had shown interest in her, and she saw a marriage to him as a way out of her brother's grasp? To always live under her brother's rule, even though his behavior stemmed from love for her, never knowing if he'd approve of anything she did… It was so tiring. Farah saw that she would have to stand up for herself because no one else would. When they returned to London, she'd make Blackstone see her. Make him understand she was an intelligent and capable woman.

Although if he finds out about this trip, any chance of that will vanish.

"Of course, but he didn't care. I think I would have been content with Philippe."

"Content? Is that enough for you? I thought you told me you want a grand love like the one between Tiffany and Wolf."

"I didn't back then. But I'm older and wiser now, and I know what I want. I don't think Philippe and I would have had a grand love affair, but we could have been happy." She paused and took in the look on Rockwell's face. "What is it? What is on your mind?"

He shrugged. "I'm just thinking of Ashley and Ivy. Both Wolf and I would do anything to protect our sisters, but we would also want to ensure they have happiness in their lives. I can't imagine Wolf or me forcing them to do anything they didn't want to."

"Is that what you did for Ashley? You let her make her own choice, regardless of the scandal?" What was the scandal? She was dying to know. Would he tell her?

"Absolutely. I love her and we would both do anything for her. That's why I cannot understand Blackstone's treatment of you."

She turned to look out the window. "You are nothing like my brother. If you were, I would not be in this carriage with you. I would have been sent home and married off with no say in the matter. Is my scandal going to be so different from Ashley's? She's survived hers. Surely I can survive mine."

"Yours is nothing like Ashley's." She watched Rockwell's hands clench into fists. The venom in his voice shocked her into silence. What on earth had happened to Ashley? The mood in the carriage thickened.

Finally, he said, "You think you're this timid, shy woman, but I think you are stronger and more determined than you realize. I'm pretty sure you can survive anything. Ashley proved to me just how strong women are. Women are called the weaker sex and it's absolute rubbish."

She hugged herself inside. He sounded as if he admired her. Or was he simply telling her this so she would fight being forced to marry him? It would set him free too—and his honor would remain intact if she declined him. She eyed him warily but couldn't ascertain his true thoughts on the matter. She guessed she'd learn her fate when they returned to London.

After a few hours, their carriage finally rumbled into the quaint village of Malahide, a pretty village by the sea. She shook herself awake, since she'd dozed the last few miles due to lack of sleep the night before.

She peered out of the carriage to take in cobbled streets that were lined with charming cottages and bustling with locals going about their daily routines. Farah's gaze scanned the surroundings, searching for any sign of their friend.

"Let's start at the inn where we're staying," suggested Farah, her voice tinged with determination. "Perhaps someone here has seen him or knows of his whereabouts."

The inn wasn't up to the standard of their accommodation in Dublin, but it was clean and had two rooms available. It also had a private dining room, which they could use for meals.

After refreshments and other needs were taken care of, they made their way through the village, inquiring at every shop they passed. Despite their efforts, the answers they received were vague and inconclusive. They were told in no uncertain terms that no English gentleman lived here.

Rockwell sighed heavily, frustration evident in his voice. "It's as if Lucien has vanished into thin air. But we can't give up hope just yet."

Farah nodded in agreement, her resolve unwavering. "Perhaps they are suspicious because we are English? We'll continue our search. We owe it to Lucien to leave no stone unturned."

Rockwell pointed back toward the inn. "I'll go and speak to the blacksmith. Surely he must service all those around this village. Do you want to wait at the inn?"

Farah shook her head. "I'll visit the church at the top of the hill. It looks out over the sea, so at least I'll take in a beautiful view. Besides, I'll stop at the vicarage. The vicar must know all his congregation."

"Good idea." He pressed a kiss to her cheek. "I'll meet you up there." He strode off down the hill toward the sounds of the smithery.

Farah took off her bonnet and let the crisp sea air clear the tension headache that had been building all morning. The view as she walked was breathtaking and for one moment, she forgot all her troubles. Soon she game to a rickety iron gate that was the entry to the graveyard. She could see the vicar's cottage further up the hill, but she wanted to read all about the people who had lived and died in this little village.

She wandered through the weathered gravestones in the yard, her footsteps muffled by the damp grass beneath her feet. The sun cast a glow over the ancient burial ground as she trailed her fingers along the cold, moss-covered stone markers.

Her eyes scanned the inscriptions, each one telling a story of lives long gone. Some names were faded with time, barely legible, while others stood out in bold relief, their memories preserved for centuries. Farah paused at one particularly ornate tombstone, tracing the elegant script with a gloved finger.

Lost in thought, she was startled by the sound of light footsteps approaching. Turning, she saw a little girl, only around three or four, her dark hair tousled by the wind, racing toward her with a wildflower clutched in her hand.

"Dia dhuit," the girl said breathlessly as she skidded to a stop in front of Farah and handed her the flower.

Tears welled in her eyes. She recognized that smile, and the look around the eyes, and the child's hair coloring were the same. She smiled warmly at the child's kindness, taking the offered bloom delicately between her fingers. "Thank you, sweety," she said, her voice carrying the lilt of a foreign accent that piqued the girl's curiosity.

The child tilted her head, studying Farah intently. "Who are you?" she asked, in Irish English this time, her blue eyes wide with wonder. "And why do you talk funny?"

Farah chuckled softly at the girl's blunt question, kneeling to meet her gaze. "I am Lady Farah Perrin," she replied. "What's your name?"

The child eyed her as if judging if she should talk to a stranger, but she must have thought Farah was nice because she said, "I'm Ava-Marie."

Farah's excitement grew at hearing the name Ava. It couldn't be a coincidence. She looked around the graveyard. "Are you here alone? I'm a friend of your father's. Is he here?"

The girl's eyes widened in awe at the mention of her father. "Daid?" she repeated, the word rolling off her tongue. "He's visiting with Máthair."

She held out her hand. "Shall we find them?"

With a sudden burst of energy, Ava-Marie took Farah's hand. "Or we could play a game," she said with a mischievous grin. "Would you like to explore the graveyard with me? I know all the best hiding spots!"

Farah laughed, her heart warmed by the innocence and enthusiasm of the child. Taking the girl's hand, she rose to her feet. "But I haven't seen your father in a very long time and I'd love to say hello."

"I suppose. But we could play afterwards. Daid always finds me, though."

Ava-Marie skipped along beside her, chatting, sometimes in English and sometimes in Gaelic. Farah's heart was so full. He was alive. But with that came a dread regarding questions. Was this child the reason he hadn't returned home? Was he ashamed that he'd been unfaithful to Courtney?

They rounded the corner of the church and she saw a man over by the tree, standing over a grave. She could tell he was talking and she could also see it was Lord Lucien Cavanaugh, Viscount Furoe, the heir to the Earl of Danvers.

"Daid is talking to Máthair."

The truth hit her squarely in the chest like a cannonball—Ava-Marie's mother was dead. Just as they drew near, he leaned down and cleared some old flowers off her grave and placed fresh ones on the headstone. She saw him wipe a tear from his face. As he heard them approach, he swung round to face them. She hardly recognized the man in front of her. His beard was full and his face had a deep slash from the top of his right forehead down his cheek.

"I'm sorry. I hope my daughter hasn't been bothering you."

In an instant, Farah knew something was very wrong. There was no recognition in his eyes and he spoke with a heavy Irish accent. But it was Lucien, all right. She drew in a breath before saying, "No. She hasn't been bothering me. I'm here in Malahide looking for someone."

"Oh, you're English. I'm John Collins. This is my daughter, Ava-Marie," he said, swinging the little girl who looked so much like her father it hurt, into his arms. His Irish accent was broad. A commoner's accent.

"Yes, she introduced herself to me." To fill the awkward silence, she asked, "Have you always lived here in Malahide?"

A frown crossed his face. "No. I think I lived in England before coming home, because I got injured in France, I believe. Or so my wife used to tell me. I can't remember anything from before five years ago." He touched his head near his scar. "A head wound took my memories."

Farah bit down on the urge to stamp her foot and yell into the breeze. Someone had told a man who had so obviously lost his memories, lies to keep him here. He'd never fought in the war with France. She was out of her depth and wasn't sure what to do when a voice behind her boomed out, "Christ. Lucien, oh, my God you *are* alive!" The next minute Rockwell came barreling into them, hugging Lucien and his daughter while tears poured down his face.

Lucien began to struggle and Farah could see the panic in his eyes. She pulled hard on Rockwell's coat, pulling him away from Lucien. "He doesn't know who you are, let alone who he is. He's got amnesia."

Rockwell stumbled backward, shock and then relief on his face. Farah guessed what he was thinking. Lucien hadn't deserted his family. He just didn't remember them.

Farah focused her attention back on a shocked Lucien. "Mr. Collins. This is my—friend—Lord Rockwell Ware, and he has been looking for you for a long time. He's simply overjoyed at finding you." She smiled at the man she'd known most of her life, who now looked at her like a stranger. "Is there somewhere we could go to explain why we are here?"

CHAPTER EIGHT

ROCKWELL'S HEART WAS still pounding in his chest. Lucien was alive, and he'd found him. He wished he could hug his friend until the memory of standing over his graveside vanished. He didn't even care that the man before him couldn't remember who he was.

How awful that all he could feel was relief in learning that Lucien had lost his memory and hadn't just turned his back on his friends and family. He stood looking at the man he'd grown up with and considered one of his best friends, but the blankness in his eyes proved beyond a doubt that Lucien didn't have a clue who he was. He ran a hand through his hair and wondered how to proceed. It was going to be a lot for Lucien to take in.

"What on earth are you talking about? Why do you keep calling me Lucien?"

He watched as if in a dream, as Farah put her hand on Lucien's arm to calm him. Rockwell could see fear and confusion enter his friend's eyes. Farah gently spoke. "We know you. We have a story to share with you and it will not be easy to hear." She turned to Rockwell. "Show him the locket."

He scrambled in his pocket, pulling out the locket Lauren had given him when he'd asked for a keepsake of Lucien's, and opening it. He shoved it toward Lucien and let him see. Lucien's hand reached out and took the jewelry from him and he stood staring at the images inside for a moment. There was a picture of Lauren and one of Lucien, himself.

He handed it back, then shifted Ava-Marie onto his other hip, and said, "My cottage is about a mile from the village. We can talk there. I have my cart here, so you don't need to walk."

Rockwell looked at Farah. "We have our own carriage. Why don't we just meet you at your cottage? I'll need directions."

Lucien nodded. "If you keep following the road along the cliff tops past the vicarage, after a mile, you'll come to a small cottage with a swing in the front yard. That's my home."

Farah smiled tentatively. "Thank you. I know this is very confusing for you. But you need to hear what Lord Ware has to say."

Lucien nodded. "Aye, I think I do. Come Ava-Marie, we need to go."

"But we haven't played hide and seek today," she complained.

"Next time," Lucien promised, and they walked off. At the gate, he turned to look at them, or was it Ava's grave, before leaving?

"We're going to hurt him—a lot. All those around him have lied to him. He thinks the woman in that grave is his wife. I wonder if they were ever married or if she merely told him they were."

Rockwell cursed into the wind, and if he could have hit something, he would have. "How could she have done that to him? How could she take advantage of an injured man?"

"We will never know. But you said it in the carriage—women are strong and will do anything to survive. Ava saw an opportunity and took it. She wanted out of the horrible life she'd obviously had in that brothel. So, she brought a man with no memory home from Dublin as her husband and I suspect no one was the wiser. I also think she hoped he'd be happy and that she really wasn't hurting anyone. He probably was happy, for he was crying over her grave. He must have loved her." She sighed. "He'd have remained happy or at least content, and he'd be none the wiser if we hadn't showed up. The one thing I know for certain is the child is his."

"Agreed. The little girl is the spitting image of him. But he deserves to know the truth, doesn't he?"

She turned to him and slipped her hand over his arm and tugged him along to walk back to the village. "Yes. He does. But it doesn't mean he will not be hurt as we turn his life upside down. And perhaps, he won't want to leave here."

"Of course he will. He's the heir to an earldom."

"An earldom that is all but broke."

"I'm glad you're here with me. I don't think I could have handled this very well on my own."

And that was the truth. He didn't care that there would be consequences. Rockwell needed her. He was so cut up inside and now filled with such anger for his friend and family, that he needed Farah's touch to calm him. She would know how to help his friend and for that, he would be forever grateful.

She smiled like an angel. "I'm glad I'm here with you, too. I'm so happy you've found your friend."

THEY EASILY FOUND Lucien's cottage. Nestled amidst the rolling green hills near to the sea, stood the cottage, weathered by time and the elements. It was nothing like Lucien's ancestral country house, but it was obvious that he took pride in it, as the gardens were immaculate and the stone fences well kept.

The cottage was constructed of rough-hewn stone, its walls coated with a layer of whitewash that had faded to a soft, weathered hue over the years. A thatched roof, now patched in places, sloped gently downwards, offering shelter from the frequent rains that swept across the countryside.

Outside, a small garden flourished, its borders delineated by neatly stacked stone walls. To the side of the cottage were rows of potatoes, cabbages, and carrots thriving in the rich, dark soil. A path of worn cobblestones led from the garden gate, passed the swing to the cottage door.

As they approached the cottage, the scent of peat smoke hung heavy in the air, mingling with the earthy aroma of the surrounding fields. Rockwell glanced through the small, paned windows, and noted the warm glow of a fire flickering within, casting long shadows across the worn wooden floorboards.

Lucien flung the door open and waved them in. He'd placed chairs by the fire for them to sit.

Inside, the cottage was cozy and inviting, despite its modest size. A hearth dominated one wall, its stone mantle adorned with an assortment of trinkets and keepsakes—a wooden pipe, a faded daguerreotype, a rosary blessed by the local priest. Above the mantle, a crucifix watched over the room, its presence a silent reminder of the family's faith. Another lie. Lucien wasn't Catholic.

Furniture, though sparse, was sturdy and well-made—a wooden table and chairs, but Lucien sat in a worn but comfortable armchair by the fire, a simple wooden bed tucked into the corner looked feminine with a quilt a rainbow of colors. Was that Ava-Marie's bed? Shelves lined the walls, filled with books and crockery. Each item appeared cherished for its practicality or sentimental value.

Despite the obvious hardships of rural life, the cottage was an inviting place of warmth and hospitality. Only Rockwell understood how Lucien would feel about this cottage once he returned to England.

"Ava-Marie and her cousin Caitria, are in the barn. I thought it would give us privacy to talk, as I'm pretty sure I will not like what I hear."

Rockwell smiled. "I can see the head wound hasn't scrambled your brain. You were always a clever man."

"I must be mad to believe this tale, but something inside me always felt that this wasn't really my home. Besides, why would anyone come and tell me I'm English nobility unless it were true?

Plus, how is it I can talk like this?" Lucien had swapped to a very upper-class English accent. "I take it you know me and know me well?" Lucien's eyes swept over them.

He leaned forward. "We were—are—best friends since we could walk."

With desperation in his voice, Lucien said, "Please tell me. Who am I?"

It was Farah's soft voice that responded. "You're Lucien Cavanaugh, Viscount Furoe, heir to the Earl of Danvers. You have two sisters called Lauren and Madeline, and your father is still alive."

Lucien looked at them as if they'd gone mad and promptly burst out laughing. But his laughter turned into a croaking cry as he said, "Then how did I end up here?"

Rockwell told Lucien bluntly, not holding anything back. "We know some of the story but have had to surmise the rest. You left England to help quell the Irish rebellion in 1803. Your mother was Irish and you could speak Gaelic, so you thought you might stop the bloodshed."

Farah butted in. "You were in the British Army in Ireland fighting in the Irish rebellion. I think you got wounded and taken into a gentlemen's club where Ava nursed you back to health." She swallowed and looked at Rockwell, who nodded his encouragement. "I think Ava must have fallen for you, and when she learned you'd lost your memory, she brought you here as her husband."

The anguish in Lucien's eyes was almost too much for Rockwell to bear. "She tricked me. It was all a lie. We were never married, were we?"

"I don't think so," Farah said. "We would have to check the parish records in Dublin. If you married Ava, it must have been before your injury or you would remember. And I don't think you were in Dublin long enough for a marriage to occur." She didn't want to tell him about Courtney just yet. Lucien had enough to take in.

"That means Ava-Marie is illig…" And Lucien swore and got to his feet to pace the room. "How did you find me? After all this time, why did you come looking?" Lucien retook his seat.

Rockwell leaned back and told him the tale. "I was in Ireland on an errand for my brother, the Marquess of Wolfarth. I thought I saw you in a tavern one night. I tried to follow you but lost you in the street."

"That was you? I thought some drunkard was after my money. I had just sold some potatoes to the grain merchant. I hid from you because you kept calling me Lucien." He sighed. "Now I understand why."

"I came back a few days ago to see if it was you."

"On a hunch? You really were—are—a good friend. Thank you, I guess."

Rockwell didn't know what to say. "I know this is a lot to take in, but your family needs you. Your father—"

Farah interrupted. "You deserve to know the truth. It's over to you what you want to do with it." Farah gave him a stern look, as if to say, *don't overwhelm him all at once.*

"Do my family in England know I'm alive?"

Rockwell's heart almost seized. Was he considering not returning to his old life? He looked around the small cottage. While Lucien's family's finances were not the best, if Lucien took control of the estates, he could turn it all around, especially if he married well. And he was sure Courtney would welcome Lucien back with open arms. "I didn't want to tell anyone I thought you were alive until I was sure."

Lucien nodded. "That makes sense."

Farah leaned forward. "We are here to take you home."

Lucien really looked at her. "And how do you fit into this situation? Are you Lord Ware's wife?"

Rockwell spluttered and coughed. "Please, call me Rockwell."

Once again, Farah saved him. "No. I'm a friend of his sisters. I accidentally got caught up in this adventure."

Lucien seemed to accept this because, of course, he'd forgotten how the *ton* worked. He likely did not know the consequences of Farah being here.

Lucien sat quietly for some time with his chin resting on his peaked hands. Rockwell prayed his friend would come home with them, even if they never returned to their previous friendship. Regardless of his friend's memory loss, Rockwell only wanted the best for Lucien and he wasn't sure this was it.

"If I return with you, Ava-Marie and Caitria come with me. Ava and her father died two years ago from the lung disease, and I would not have survived without her cousin, Caitria. I don't believe Caitria has any idea that this is all a lie. She came from Cork to help when Ava fell ill and had not seen this side of the family for many years."

Rockwell inwardly gave a sigh of relief. Farah spoke once again. "Of course your daughter must come and Caitria, too, if she wishes. Her life will be very different in England, however. You might wish to ask her first if she wants to go home to Cork instead."

Lucien nodded. "Of course."

"How long will it take you to be ready to leave? We have a coach that will fit us all, and my ship is docked in Dublin." He was conscious, as was Farah, that the sooner they left, the better for her ability to stop a scandal arising.

With a great sadness floating in his eyes, Lucien looked around the cottage. What did he see? Happy memories or hurtful lies. He watched Lucien's mouth firm and his jaw tighten. "Let me talk with Caitria and get her decision. If she wishes to come with me, we can leave tomorrow."

"That soon?" Farah asked tentatively. "What will you do with this holding?"

Lucien stood and moved to stand before the fire. "I shall keep it to remember this part of my life. Besides, this is where Ava-Marie was born." His tone softened when he talked about his daughter.

"I can help you arrange for someone to look after the cottage and land once we are back in England."

Lucien looked at Rockwell. "Thank you, my—friend." He smiled.

Farah stood. "We'll take our leave. Ava-Marie will need supper and to get to bed. It's going to be a long journey for her. Besides, it's likely getting cold out in the barn."

As he showed them to the door, Lucien shook Rockwell's hand, but he couldn't help pulling Lucien in for a manly hug. Lucien took Farah's gloved hand and pressed a kiss to her knuckles. "Thank you for your kindness."

Farah too pulled him in for a hug, and he saw tears form in her eyes. "I'm just so thankful you're alive."

CHAPTER NINE

THEY SAT IN silence on the carriage ride back to the village. It wasn't until they reached the inn and were sitting before a wholesome dinner in the private dining room that Farah let go. And once she started crying, she couldn't stop.

She was crying for all that had been lost due to his injury. Lucien was alive, but he wasn't the Lucien they knew and loved. Lauren and Madeline would be so happy that their brother was alive. It almost meant their financial situation could be helped if Lucien married well. And Courtney? She couldn't stop thinking about what this would do to her friend—to all of them.

Rockwell gathered her close. "Don't cry." Although he sounded like he wanted to cry, too.

"He's Lucien, but not Lucien, and he never will be again."

Rockwell uttered as if in denial, "We don't know that. Maybe once he's home and sees family and friends, something will trigger his memories to come back."

She clung to his coat, not caring that her tears were wetting his clothes. "Courtney will be caught between heaven and hell. She'll have him back, but not really. What will it be like to see him every day, the man you love and who once loved you, but he doesn't remember that love or that life?" And she cried harder.

She let Rockwell simply hold her and gently rock her against his muscular frame. She felt safe, so safe. When she got home, would she ever feel safe again? She lifted her head and gazed into eyes that were as filled with loss as hers were. Rockwell must be feeling everything that Courtney would feel. To have his friend alive, but not the same, not the friend he remembered.

Perhaps there was only the here and now. No one knew what would happen in the future, so it was important to live in the present.

On impulse, she kissed him. She wanted to ease the pain they both felt. But Rockwell captured the kiss. Captured and deepened her naïve attempt to offer comfort. However, she'd miscalculated his need.

Farah felt his hunger as his strong hands pulled her even closer. It was as if he wanted pleasure to take away the pain he felt. She didn't even try to resist. With a need to match his own, she wanted to block out the image of Lucien's pain and Courtney's coming disappointment. She melted against his warmth, kissing Rockwell back with ruthless abandon.

She reveled in his growing need, evidenced by the thick length of him pressing into her stomach. Their kiss became wild, delicious, and as she expected with him, sensual. Farah gave a whimper at the sheer power of her need for him—only him.

Her heart was hammering and her breath came in ragged pants when Rockwell slowly drew back to stare at her, his chest heaving. Desire coursed through the air, accompanied by a deep ache between her thighs.

The shock and the pleasure battled within her. Rockwell's eyes told her he wanted to make love to her. They were at a crossroads.

"I want you, Farah," he stated, his voice a low, husky rasp. "And you want me too. This is desire. But giving in to our desires has consequences."

"I know. I'm not sure I'm ready to face those consequences." She never imagined creating this scandal would have such high implications. She was falling for Rockwell. Who wouldn't? He was handsome, kind, wealthy, confident and he really listened to her. But his life was not one she wanted to be a part of. If she lost herself to him...if she fell in love, what would happen when she walked away? Worse, what would happen if he demanded marriage? She couldn't see it being a happy one, with him away all the time.

She would be alone once more but with a broken heart.

"I like your honesty." He cupped her face and gently pressed a kiss to her lips. "Tonight I'll come to your bed. But we will go only as far as you're ready to go. There are ways of sharing pleasure without ruining you."

She stilled, which was difficult given the excitement skittering over her skin. "And if we share this pleasure, you won't force me into a marriage I may not want?" She wasn't stupid. Rockwell had to promise that he wouldn't try to be a hero and save her from scandal.

"At this moment, with you in my arms, I'd promise you anything." When she raised an eyebrow, he added, "I promise."

The half-eaten food was forgotten. She stepped back and held out her hand. "I need comfort of a different kind." He slipped his hand in hers and needed no persuasion to follow her upstairs.

She chose her room. It would be easier in the morning for Rockwell to slip away than her. He kicked the door closed behind them and locked it.

She stood trembling in the middle of the room, wondering where her sudden bout of bravery was disappearing to. Rockwell filled the room with his size.

"Don't turn back into the timid mouse. You wanted this as much as I."

Want was such a tame word—need, was more appropriate. She needed him more than her next breath.

She swallowed as he slid one hand around her nape and stroked the base of her neck in a light, tantalizing massage before gently tugging at her coiled hair. "I want to see it loose."

She helped him unpin it, the pins scattering on the floor. She'd need to find them in the morning. He ran his fingers through her hair until it hung in waves over her shoulders.

Then his hands slid over her body, exploring every curve with enthralling seductiveness, making her breath hitch.

"Turn around." His soft command made her shiver.

When she presented her back to him, he slowly began undoing each catch, pressing his lips to the skin he was baring. The gown fell to her feet, and he unlaced her corset, throwing it aside to lift her chemise over her head. Slowly, he knelt and rolled her stockings down her legs until she stood gloriously naked before him.

The erratic rhythm of her heartbeat grew stronger as he slowly walked around to face her. She stood proud and tall, not letting the timid mouse ruin this moment for her. His expression was almost reverent as his eyes traveled up and down the length of her. "I've been wanting to gaze upon your beauty ever since you stood in my bedchamber with my Hessian halfway up your leg. And you do not disappoint." He reached out and cupped one breast. "You are exquisite."

She didn't feel shy standing under his heated gaze. She felt powerful and womanly and totally in control. She stepped forward and began removing Rockwell's clothes. Impatiently, he helped. Soon she was giggling as they both raced to get him naked as fast as possible.

But she wasn't laughing when finally he stood before her in all his masculine glory. Her breath caught in her throat, and she just had to reach out and touch him. Her enthralled gaze wandered freely this time, over his magnificent shoulders, his chiseled chest, his narrow waist and hips, his long powerful legs.

He took her hand in his and lifted it to his lips. Muscles rippled and played beneath the satiny skin and his arousal thrust out thick and swollen from the juncture of his thighs.

With a chuckle, Rockwell put a finger under her chin, lifting her gaze to his. "Looking at me like that is likely to end this far too soon." She found herself drowning in the need and desire she saw on his face.

Her impatience to touch him grew when he took both her hands in his and urged her back upon the bed. He gently pushed her back and followed her down, stretching out his full length on top of her, making the muscles in her stomach clench in anticipation.

"I'm going to need all the willpower I have not to sink deep within you, but a promise is a promise. No ruining tonight."

The naked flesh above her made her blood warm. Warm, smooth, and hard muscles made her senses come alive. The softness mixed with heat and steel. And his loins… His erection pulsed and strained against her abdomen. She wanted to touch more than she wanted to take her next breath.

Stirring restlessly, she tried to snake her hand down between their bodies, but he captured her hands and raised them above her head. "Let me teach you about pleasure. Then see if you can live your life as a spinster."

On those words, he stroked her, his hand tracing over her skin as if she were soft fur to pet.

Her nipples pebbled into hardened nubs and when his palms brushed over them, a spark lit inside and flowed downward to her womanly core.

Her body fell under the pure sensuality of the feelings. The moonlight pouring through the window added to the heavenly experience. His magical touch swept her away into another world. She finally understood why men and women risked ruination.

His hands tangled in her hair as his mouth found hers, and her sanity fled. His feathery kisses were a tantalizing caress on the underside of her throat before moving upward over her jaw to her cheekbone. But it was when those lips trailed down her neck and latched firmly onto a turgid nipple that a moan escaped her lips, and she squirmed restlessly beneath him. He moved across to the other nipple and she was enraptured… held spellbound by the pull deep within her. Farah dragged in a shuddering breath as melting heat consumed her. She sank her hands into his hair and anchored his mouth to her breast.

"Easy, my pixie." He shook free of her grip and trailed his

mouth lower. She burned where his lips caressed her skin, but it was too much when those lips nuzzled her nest of curls at the vee of her thighs.

She tried to hold her thighs together, but it took only one large hand to push them apart. She closed her eyes and concentrated on breathing. He would show her a new world tonight, and she couldn't wait.

"It's intoxicating knowing I'm the first man to touch you here," he whispered, covering her mound. He cooed her name repeatedly as he slowly parted her thighs wider. She gripped the sheets in her hands and moaned into the still night air as he rested his hand between her parted thighs.

"Don't be scared, my brave pixie."

"I'd never be frightened of you. You'd never hurt me." She prayed that was true. Falling in love with him could hurt her deeply and each time he intimately touched her, her heart cracked open more. Giving herself to him for pleasure was a terrible idea, but she couldn't bring herself to stop.

Before she could gather a breath, his hand ran up the inside of her calf and further up her thigh. She bit back a cry of anticipation. Then his finger caressed her wet, pulsating flesh, gently stroking her secret place.

"Oh, dear, God."

"So responsive. I was right. My timid mouse is full of passion." He kissed her lips as he slowly penetrated her with two fingers. Then he took her mouth once more.

She shifted restlessly as he continued to kiss her, his tongue in her mouth and his fingers deep within her. Eyes closed, she kissed him back encouragingly, her whole body beginning to undulate.

With his gently thrusting caress between her legs, in and out, her hips lifted to meet the exquisite torture. She let herself fly free, demanding an ever-faster rhythm.

He lowered his head and began licking her nipple in delicate circles as his clever, coaxing fingers worked a slow, sensuous magic. Wantonness enveloped her, and she suddenly understood why women could be so easily seduced. But the thought of letting any other man do this to her turned her cold.

She spread her legs wider for him, arching helplessly against the slick, expert touch. He took her breast and suckled her. Only Rockwell could make her feel this way. No other man—ever.

She clung to his shoulders, her nails digging deep as his thumb joined his fingers, pressing against her mound as his fingers entered her again and again. She was wholly under his control. Mindless passion owned her. Every muscle was tight, poised for the splendid release that she could feel was just a stroke away. Her eyes closed, and her head fell back on the pillow, her center totally focused on a bright light beckoning her.

She could feel him watching, but she didn't care. She wanted to fly…

"You are so beautiful," he whispered, his voice husky with desire.

She moaned his name as her head thrashed on the pillow. She would never forget this moment. Never forget *him*.

She bucked and gripped the sheets, gasping in a strangled cry, as explosions of shattering pleasure burst in a series of stars behind her eyes and pulses radiating from her feminine core. Tingles raced through her limbs, rushing along her nerve endings, flooding her body with a sensation that went on and on. She closed her eyes as aftershocks of pleasure hit her.

He lay beside her, stroking down her body. "That, my pixie, is pleasure."

She could hardly get her breath. She swallowed hard, thinking she could happily spend the rest of her life in bed—if it were with him.

"Is it always like that?" she asked in wonder.

"Like what?"

"I think it's like touching heaven."

He smiled against her cheek. "I'm glad you enjoyed it. But making love is better than that."

She felt his erection pulsing against her hip and realized he hadn't—found his release. She turned to face him and ran her finger down over his chest to his groin.

"I'm not really sure what to do," she said, but her small hand wrapped around his cock and he shuddered. He shouldn't want her so, but denying his attraction was difficult given she had his erection in her hand.

He took her hand and wrapped it firmly around him, showing her just how tight she could grip him before moving them both slowly up and down his shaft. She watched, and she saw the heat flame in his eyes. His hand guided hers in urgent insistence. He grew rigid and his hot, silky flesh pulsed as he thrust in time to their hands, his muscled body rippling and straining.

He closed his eyes on a groan and his hand fell away, leaving her completely to see to his pleasure. Her power over him was exhilarating. He was under her command and she loved it.

With another groan, he cupped the back of her neck and pulled her down for a frenzied kiss. She gripped him harder and was rewarded with another groan, then suddenly he gave a low, anguished cry of release, his back arching off the bed as he discharged the hot shooting glory of his seed, raining it on his hard, flat belly.

Her inner core pulsed. Never in her life had she witnessed anything so erotic and beautiful. He was beautiful. His rigid body slowly relaxed, as if all the tension flowed out of him. He lay on the bed, spent, panting, his expression one of wondrous bliss.

Still with eyes closed, he murmured, "You know when we leave here tomorrow, we can never do that again."

Her mouth firmed. He might think that, but she had at least a week of freedom left before returning home. She intended to make the most of it.

He cast a forearm over his brow and swept his lashes open, gazing at her from under his arm.

Now it was her turn to smile. That look didn't speak of never doing this again. It spoke of promises of more wonderful nights in his arms.

With a playful growl, he reached out and pulled her down onto his chest, then pressed a kiss to her lips. "You little minx. Only until we get back to London."

On a satisfied sigh, she curled into his side and promptly fell asleep.

Rockwell lay awake as she slept beside him, gently stroking her silken skin. *What a cad.* He'd taken advantage of her sorrow. *But you needed her.* Besides, she might not have accepted it yet, but there was no escaping this scandal. The only honorable thing to do was to marry her.

He looked down at her beautiful face. Those lips that made him want to kiss her every time she smiled. He had been right. Hidden behind the shy exterior was a passionate woman who needed the right man to reveal her inner strength. He was the right man, and the idea of any other man touching her made his blood boil. She was his.

But as that thought entered his head, the horror-filled idea of his freedom being curtailed coiled around his heart. The thought of being trapped made him gasp for air. His life would no longer be his, and he still had so much of the world to discover.

It was his father who had instilled wanderlust in him. Perhaps his father did so because he understood what the life of a second son might be—empty, meaningless.

His father used to bring him into his study and show him the map of the world. They'd play a game where he'd spin the globe and his father would stop it and wherever it stopped by the marker, they would talk about the country. His father had told him vivid tales of countries he now understood his father never saw. He could remember the awe and longing in his father's voice.

He thought his father was very much like him—a wanderer who could never wander because he was the marquess. Rockwell's uncle had all the adventures instead, and he wondered if his father resented the life he'd had to live.

Would he?

What a mess. He pressed a kiss to Farah's head as he finally closed his eyes. He needed sleep, but he thought it was quite a shame that if he let himself, he could easily love this woman curled into his side. But he had a world to conquer first.

CHAPTER TEN

I**T WAS A** solemn carriage ride back to Dublin. Caitria looked as if she'd been crying, and Lucien looked like he carried the weight of the world on his shoulders. Rockwell had barely spoken to her since breakfast. She'd woken alone in her bed as she knew she would. He'd already broken his fast when she came down and excused himself to ready their carriage to return to Dublin.

How could he put what they shared behind him so easily? She glanced across the carriage at him, but he was looking out the window. After last night, Rockwell could tear her open and own her heart. Even now, her body hummed with the longing to be held in his arms once again. But it probably wasn't as special for him. He'd done that with many women and more... He was adamant they could share passion, and love was not a requirement.

Perhaps it was a requirement for her. She looked at Lucien. While he was a stunningly handsome man, she couldn't imagine wanting to share her body with him. What did that mean?

Just then, Ava-Marie, who'd been sleeping on Caitria's lap, awoke. "Are we there yet?"

Caitria murmured, "Not much longer. You've been such a good girl."

The little girl sat up and squeezed herself onto the seat between the two ladies. She started swinging her legs, banging her heels against the wood seatback. She laughed up at Farah. "I'm going on a ship, with Daid and Auntie Caitria. Isn't it exciting?"

"It is. I'm going, too. It's Lord Ware's ship."

That made her little legs stop and her eyes widen. She looked up at Rockwell. "Is it really your ship?" she asked him.

He turned to smile down at Ava-Marie and stole Farah's breath. Oh, to have him look at her like that every day. "It is. My ship's name is the *Doreen*."

"That's a girl's name."

"Sailors often name their ships after women. They like the idea that a mother figure is looking out for them and guiding them home."

"My Mama is looking after me from heaven." She stood, rocking with the carriage's movement. "Where will I sleep on the ship?"

"You'll have a cabin with a bunk to sleep on."

"Will Daid have a cabin, too?"

"Yes, we all will," Rockwell explained.

Ava-Marie asked to climb on Lucien's lap. He lifted her with ease and cuddled her tightly. She sat playing with his fob watch before she once more fell asleep.

Farah turned to Caitria. She hadn't really had time to talk with the young woman. The Irish woman was dark-haired, with blue eyes and was very beautiful. She noted that the woman had spent most of the journey peering at Lucien. Farah couldn't make out what that meant. Was she in love with Lucien? Farah could understand why. He was as handsome as sin. Lucien could definitely give Rockwell a run in the handsome stakes. Caitria had also been staring at Rockwell, too. Was she comparing Lucien's clothing and seeing it lacking?

Farah noted Caitria's gown. It was going to stand out in the wrong way when they got to London.

"If you need anything, please let me know. It's going to be a tremendous change moving to England. If you'd let me, I'd like to be your friend. And help guide you." Although the young woman may want to keep clear of Farah once her scandal broke. She'd be persona non grata.

In her heavy Irish accent, Caitria said, "Thank you. I'm not too nervous. I'll be happy becoming Ava-Marie's nanny. I'll fade into the background. Lucien might not remember, but I understand how society works. One must know one's place."

"But your place in life has changed. You have a powerful protector in Lord Furoe."

Those words didn't make her happy. "He's out of my reach."

So, Caitria *was* in love with Lucien. The poor girl. It would only end in heartache. She glanced at Rockwell, who was once more staring out the window. Farah thought the same thing applied to her, too. Rockwell would sail away and forget her.

She knew now, after sharing passion with Rockwell, that even if her brother demanded they wed, she could not. Not unless he could love her back. She'd rather run away and use her funds to find a small cottage in Cornwall.

She took Caitria's hand in hers. "You must resent our intrusion into your lives."

She shook her head. "No. He has a family who must be missing him. But it's going to be hard on them when they find he doesn't remember them."

She nodded. Hard on more than his family. Courtney kept flashing through her mind. To halt her worries, Farah asked, "Tell me about your life in Cork. Are you going to miss your family?"

Caitria stilled beside her and bit her lip. "Not really. I wanted to leave and Lucien's letter came at the right time. There is nothing left for me in Cork."

Farah got the impression that she wasn't happy discussing her previous life, so instead she said, "Well, you have a new family now. Lord Furoe's sisters, Lauren and Madeline, will welcome you like a sister. They'll be so happy to have their brother home and a little niece, too."

"I'm most nervous about meeting them. I'm just a country girl from Ireland and they are English ladies. What if they don't like me?"

"I like you and they are very kind. They will love you because you helped their brother and his little girl. You are important to him, so they will want to help you, too." She squeezed her hand. "Lucien is going to need you. He's forgotten the world he's returning to. You'll be the only person he can remember. So, he'll need you close by."

Caitria's eyes softened. "I'll be there as long as he and Ava-Marie need me." She looked at Farah shyly. "How is it you happen to be traveling with Lord Ware?" she whispered, but not soft enough.

She saw Lucien's gaze turn her way, and he frowned. He, too, must be thinking about her presence. "It's a long and silly story. Needless to say, I ended up on Lord Ware's ship by mistake."

"Isn't it likely to be…that is…you are not married?"

Rockwell stirred from his thoughts. "I've told everyone she is my sister, Ashley. And I'm hoping the news of Lord Furoe's return from the dead may distract the *ton* from discussing Lady Farah's absence. Her brother is the Duke of Blackstone and he is a stickler for propriety. Hopefully, no one will learn she has been with me all this time."

"And if they learn?" Lucien asked in a gravelly voice, his eyes piercing hers.

"Then we will be married." Rockwell's words dared her to disagree. She certainly wasn't about to do that with an audience. "It is the gentlemanly thing to do. Blackstone will demand it."

Lucien kept staring at her, as if sensing her reluctance. "As the son of an earl, I assume I'll have to marry and produce an heir."

Rockwell nodded. "Yes. Besides, your family could use a large dowry." He looked at Farah, but she shook her head, telling him not to mention Courtney just yet. Lucien had enough to take in with his family.

Lucien stretched out his legs, and he touched her foot. He looked at her with such intensity; she wondered if she had offended him. Was he judging her?

"It's funny. I have pieces of information that I never understood how I knew them. It all makes perfect sense now. I have no memory about my past life, people or places, but I seem to remember exactly what society is like. I fully understand how to behave like a gentleman and do what is expected of me. I can even picture the inside of the House of Lords. I must have visited there."

She leaned forward. "That's exciting to hear, because it means your memories might not be gone but merely trapped somewhere. Perhaps they might come back."

"Highly unlikely. It's been five years," Rockwell interjected.

Lucien smiled kindly at her. "Never say never. I never thought I'd be anything other than an honest farmer. But look at me. Overnight, I've become a peer of the realm."

Farah couldn't let that comment go. "You've always been a peer. You are returning to your rightful place. To a place you belong."

"I guess that remains to be seen," Lucien said, sinking back in the seat and looking out the window.

She flashed a look at Rockwell, but he too seemed to infer Lucien was right. Would he fit back into his old life? And what would he do if he didn't…or couldn't?

She chewed her bottom lip. For once on this trip, she wasn't concerned about what awaited her when they arrived in London. She was more worried about Lucien and how society would react to his return from the dead.

EARLY EVENING, THE group arriving in Dublin at the Twin Heads Inn garnered a bit of attention. Rockwell procured rooms for Lucien and Caitria, with Ava-Marie sleeping with her. Farah and Rockwell still had their private suite, and that was where everyone gathered for dinner.

"Look, my new gowns have arrived." Farah looked at Rockwell. "Do I have time to get some gowns made for Caitria?"

"No. We sail tomorrow."

Her face fell, but she understood Rockwell needed to get her home as soon as possible. She didn't want Caitria arriving in London and being judged. Her clothes were clean and respectable but not fit for society. She pulled Caitria into her bedchamber and held a dress up to her. "We're about the same size. Why don't you try a couple? I'm sure I can send word to Orla to send a girl to make alterations tonight."

Tears welled in Caitria's eyes as she held the two gowns. "Thank you for being so kind."

Farah hugged her. "Well, when I get back to London, society may make my life very difficult. I'll need friends. It's nice to make a new one."

"You may count me as a dear friend, and I'll always treat you as such."

She sighed and sat down while she penned a note to Orla. "You may have to stay away from me or you'll be judged. My brother doesn't let me socialize with Rockwell's sister Ashley, as she has a scandal hanging over her head. I do anyway, when I can."

"What did Lady Ashley do?"

She looked over her shoulder at Caitria. "I have no idea. She's told none of us."

"Us?"

"Say nothing to the men or Lucien, but my friends and I have formed a secret ladies' club and we invest in shares via our friend, Lady Tiffany. She's married to Rockwell's older brother, Lord Wolfarth. We even have a secret anonymous investment challenge with some of the men, including my brother. I can't wait for the sisterhood, as we call our club, to beat them." She put the quill down and said, "I'll introduce you to the club, and we can help you invest some of your pin money."

"Pin money?"

"Lucien will give you money each quarter to spend on things you want. We take some of that and invest it. I have already accumulated almost five thousand pounds."

Caitria plonked down on the bed. "Five thousand pounds," she said breathlessly. "That's a fortune."

"Well, enough to live in a little cottage somewhere if I'm ostracized."

Caitria hesitated, then bravely asked, "Why wouldn't you just marry Lord Ware? He seems a pleasant gentleman, and he's very handsome. He must be rich to own a ship. Why won't you marry him?"

She better get used to answering this question. All the ladies would ask her, too. "Rockwell's not husband material. He's known as an adventurer. He sails off around the world and is hardly ever in England. I want more than that from a husband. I don't want to be left behind, wondering what he's doing, who he is with, and bringing up children on my own. Not to mention, constantly worrying if he'll ever return."

"You're in love with him," Caitria said softly. "Otherwise you wouldn't care that he was gone."

"Love?" She shook her head. "But I could be, and that would hurt me."

Caitria nodded, and her eyes filled with tears. Farah sighed. "You're in love with Lucien."

"Yes, and I had hoped he might see me as a wife someday, after he got over Ava. He loved her a lot. I wonder if he'll feel the same about her, now he knows Ava tricked him. Still, he's Lord Furoe now, so my dream is over anyway."

Farah didn't dispute Caitria's statement. It was likely true. Besides, she hoped he would fall in love with Courtney again. However, Lucien might choose someone else. What a mess. "Perhaps there is another man out there for both of us. One that can give us his heart and love us the way we deserve to be loved."

Her new friend lifted her head and gave a shaky smile. "But it's hard to find room in your heart for another, isn't it?"

Never a truer word had been spoken. That was why Farah didn't want to lose her heart to Rockwell completely. "Let's have dinner. Orla will probably arrive soon, and then we need some sleep. It's going to be a nerve-wracking sail home."

They rejoined the men in the private sitting room and Farah loved how well-behaved Ava-Marie was. She was sitting, eating dinner with her father. Rockwell and Lucien were deep in conversation about his adventurers on the high sea. Rockwell was telling him about the trip he had taken to Brazil—one Lucien was supposed to accompany him on.

The ladies sat down to eat and it was only the arrival of Orla that broke up the happy party. Caitria took the two gowns and Ava-Marie with her to her room. Orla said she could make up a couple of dresses for Ava-Marie too, before they left in the morning. This made the little girl very excited.

Farah had asked Mrs. O'Donnell to bring up a bath and arranged one for Caitria and Ava-Marie. Rockwell might not come back before dawn, so he could arrange his own bath. She was about to stand when Lucien said, "I wonder if I may have a private word, Lady Farah."

This was not what she wanted. She was tired from last night, the long carriage ride, and the stress of not understanding what Rockwell was feeling. She wanted some alone time. But whatever she was feeling, Lucien must be feeling worse. His world had been turned upside down and his memories were gone.

Rockwell also stood. "I'm just going to the *Doreen* to ensure we are ready to sail tomorrow."

Farah found herself alone with Lucien. He rose and poured himself a drink from the sideboard. "May I get you anything?"

"A sherry would be welcome," she almost sighed. "It's been a tiring week."

Lucien set her glass on the table, then returned to stare out the window. He remained silent and the pity she felt for the man almost made tears well. What a few days it had been for him. He'd found out he wasn't who he thought he was. A woman he loved had lied and told him she was his wife, which now meant his beloved daughter was illegitimate.

"I'm in quite the pickle, aren't I," he finally said as he turned to face her. At her frown, he continued. "I'm expected to help my family, a family I don't remember, and yet I'm not sure I'll remember how to act and behave. At least I think I'll remember how to run an estate."

"You'll have an estate manager to help you too, and Rockwell and your other friends will also help."

"That's true. I actually improved the finances of our Irish family by introducing some changes. I wondered where I got those ideas from." He took a seat across from her. "But Rockwell's advice about marrying well and receiving a dowry to help my family is wise."

Well, Courtney was sitting in London but… This wasn't the man her friend fell in love with. What would happen when they met? "Perhaps it's not wise to rush such a thing. You'll be facing a lot as it is."

"From your reaction today in the carriage, I take it a marriage with Lord Ware is not something you'd look favorably on?"

Where was this conversation going? "That's rather personal."

"It's just that perhaps we could help each other. If a scandal erupts, you could marry me." Her mouth dropped open, but he continued, "As the sister of a duke, I assume you have a large dowry, and it would be a way to ease myself back into society with the backing of a duke. Especially with Ava-Marie. I know you'd be kind to her. You're a good person." He paused. "And you're very beautiful. I think we could be quite content."

"I know you're scared—concerned—at what will happen when we return to London, but I really think you should wait, before proposing to a lady you've only just met."

"You didn't answer my question. Do you wish to marry Lord Ware?"

How could she answer that question without saying too much? "Whom I wish or do not wish to marry is my concern and mine alone. I *will* deal with any potential scandal when I get home." How, she wasn't sure. She hesitated, but she didn't want to arrive in London and have Courtney believe she'd tried to steal Lucien. Courtney was going to be upset as it was.

"If you wish to marry, you had a fiancée before you went to Ireland. She's my friend, Lady Courtney Montague, daughter of the Marquess of Lorne. She loved you very much and still mourns you."

He hung his head as if she'd just piled on more guilt and she hated herself for telling him, but if he was desperate enough to proposition a woman he'd just met, then he had to know. "I can't remember her. Would she accept Ava-Marie? I won't have her shunned or set aside." He cursed under his breath.

"She would love your little girl because she is part of you." Well, Farah would. But would she, if Rockwell came home from one of his many trips with a child from another woman, love that child? At least Lucien had a good excuse. Someone had tricked him into thinking Ava was his wife.

"She's never married?" he asked.

"No. She said you were her grand love. I'm worried about how she'll react to your return. So, I'll not do anything to add to her pain."

He sighed and rubbed a hand over his face. "Another person I'll disappoint," he said.

"No!" She reached across the table to take his hand. "Courtney won't care that you've lost your memory, nor will your family. They will be so pleased you're alive. It's not every day someone you love comes back from the dead. Have a bit of faith in those who love you."

"It's hard to have faith in people I don't know. But if they are anything like you and Lord Ware, I've been very lucky in my choice of friends."

"You'll see. Everything will be all right when you get home. There are many who will rally around you and protect you and your family. Don't let stubborn male pride stop you from asking for the help you'll need."

"I think my pride fled when I found out my current life was a lie, that a woman had conned me."

"I think a woman did something she had to do to survive. But from what I've learned, I think she loved you very much and you loved her. That wasn't a lie. Was it?"

"Thank you. I will keep hold of that thought. I'm trying not to hate Ava. She nursed me back to health, and she gave me Ava-Marie, and I'll always love her for that."

"She's a lovely little girl. I don't think we need to tell anyone you weren't married, do you? It serves no purpose."

"Will Rockwell agree?"

"Of course. He loves you. You were his best friend. He was determined to find you, no matter what it cost. Rely on him if you need help."

"I will. He's already given me sound advice about my father."

She hid a yawn behind her hand. "If you'll excuse me, I'd like to retire. I've called for a bath. It's been a long day and we have an even bigger few days ahead."

Just then, the servants arrived with the tub and buckets of hot water.

As she walked toward her bedchamber, he added, "My offer stands, though. I realize I have nothing to offer you except my name. But if you find yourself in dire need, I would be honored to marry you."

CHAPTER ELEVEN

F ARAH SIMPLY SMILED at Lucien. There was no way she'd ever consider his proposal—because of Courtney. Liar—because of Rockwell. Carrying her unfinished glass of sherry, she entered her bedchamber. She waited for the servants to leave before dipping her hand in the hot water. She couldn't wait to soak away the last two days' worth of grime. It would be quite a while before she had another chance for a bath. She undressed and hopped into the water. She lay back, grabbed her glass off the stool next to the tub, and tried to empty her mind so that she might actually sleep tonight.

But, of course, Rockwell filled her thoughts. Would he come to her tonight? And if he did, how would she react? He'd ignored her today, but they could hardly talk in front of Lucien and Caitria. However, he'd also not sought her out for a conversation or more... Was he regretting what they'd shared? Was she?

No. She wasn't. If, after this scandal, she moved to her cottage in the country, then she'd unlikely experience passion and desire again. She had a few days more with Rockwell, and they might be her last. What did she want to do? Play it safe and protect her heart or let the timid mouse free. There was only one thing she craved and that was Rockwell—for as long as she could have him. To hell with anything else. The consequences were going to be the same, no matter what she did. So, she would make the most of the time she had left with him.

But how to approach the seduction of Rockwell? It was something she had no experience with. Aside from throwing herself at him, what could she do?

Luckily, a knock on her door helped her decide, especially when Rockwell walked in without waiting for a reply. He started when he saw her naked in the tub. And so she did the one thing instinct urged her to do.

Lifting her head, she squared her shoulders, put aside her sherry glass, and, with great dignity, she gracefully stood up, naked, proud and tall in the tub, as water streamed down over her curves.

There was a glorious satisfaction at the reaction her emergence from the water provoked. Longing flared across his finely chiseled features. "I was coming to tell you I don't think it's a good idea to…" Then he swore softly under his breath before flashing a mocking smile. "Farah means beautiful in old English—did you know that? You are aptly named, for you truly are a beautiful woman."

His gaze swept from her ankles, still hidden by the water, up her legs, halted at the thatch of fair curls at the apex of her thighs, continued over her stomach, and lingered again at her breasts, until finally resting on her face. Heat stole through her body and pooled in her loins. She noted his obvious arousal and the look of lust lighting his eyes. It was all she could do not to jump from the tub and flee.

Farah kept her palms flat against her thighs, willing them not to cover herself. "I think I'd like to learn more about passion." She crooked her finger. "With you."

He slowly circled the tub until she could no longer see him—he was somewhere behind her. She trembled in discomfort. It was unnerving not being able to see what he was looking at or read the expression in his eyes. With her back to him, Farah felt more exposed than ever. *Be brave. For once, be brave!*

The quiet seemed to stretch on, the water dripping off her nude body into the tub the only sound. Each passing minute increased her body's tremors.

Farah closed her eyes and took a deep breath.

He was close enough for his soft breath to caress her damp skin. "Well played, my timid mouse. I'm not sure who's seducing whom." Then she heard him curse softly, all while removing his clothes.

"What did Lucien want to discuss with you?"

She sunk back under the water. "Nothing of importance."

"Really? Or is it that you just don't want to tell me?" He slipped into the tub behind her and she leaned back on his chest.

"Would you tell me everything Lucien said to you?"

"Fair point. But I need to be prepared for what might happen when we return to London, if I'm to protect him."

She closed her eyes and considered Rockwell's words. There would probably be plenty of women willing to marry Lucien if it became common knowledge he needed money. "He offered a marriage of convenience if I found myself in need."

"Did he indeed?" Rockwell's tone was flat, as if they were talking about the weather.

"He thought we could help each other. My dowry to save me from scandal."

"And what did you say?" Again, there was a coolness in his tone.

"I told him if he wanted such an arrangement, he should wait because of Courtney. I'm afraid I told him about her."

His only response was a touch. A seductive slide of his warm finger down her spine. "I think he should be prepared before he arrives in London."

She let out the breath she was holding and sighed. "I thought so too."

He kissed her neck. "Now, what was that you were saying about passion?" He handed her a block of soap. "Turn round."

She loved the command in his voice and as she turned to face him; she lathered up her hands, eager to feel him beneath her fingers. He lifted one arm, and she washed it, marveling at the strength within the velvet steel muscles. She swapped to the other arm and gave a gasp as his soapy hands found her breasts. His fingers tweaked her nipples and heat arrowed down between her thighs.

She returned the favor, washing his nipples before leaning in and licking them. She loved the shiver that ran through him. "I can't wash the rest of you underwater." He gave her a smile that would tempt a nun and rose like a god from the water. With her on her knees, his manhood hung directly in front of her. She lathered her hands before cupping him and then wrapping her hand tightly around him. He went rock hard at her touch. He groaned and wrapped his hands in her hair.

The power she had over him in this moment would live with her forever.

He seemed to swell further into her hand. She leaned one hand on his rock-hard thigh, only to feel the tremors with each stroke of her hand on his cock.

Suddenly he lifted her, pulling her into his arms, and still dripping wet, he laid her on the bed and came down on top of her. "You're playing havoc with my honor. I want to sink inside of you so badly."

"I want that too," she said as she reached between their bodies to wrap her hand around him once again.

"So, you agree to marry me?"

She stilled beneath him. "What has one got to do with the other? I thought we agreed to sneak me home under the rise of titillation regarding Lucien returning home. There is no need to sacrifice yourself."

He pushed up onto his arms above her and looked down at their bodies. "I will not take your virginity unless we marry."

"Do you say that to all the women you bed?"

"You're not any woman, goddamn it. And I don't make a habit of deflowering young ladies. You're a young lady who is the daughter of a duke—a friend. I shouldn't be bedding you at all. But I can't seem to resist you." Then he took her lips in a searing kiss. She kissed him back before turning her head away.

"I want to marry for love. I desire a large family. I want to have the kind of relationship Tiffany has with your brother. I want it all."

Rockwell rolled off her to lie by her side, his breathing ragged. "I can't give you what you want."

She turned on her side to face him and put her hand over his heart. "Can't? Or won't?"

"Does it matter?"

He covered her hand where it lay over his heart. "I am not like my brother. I don't have it in me to be the man you want. I'm far too selfish. I have—so much I want to do with my life. How can I love you when I know I'll leave you? You'll never know when and if I'll be returning. It isn't fair to you or me." He squeezed her hand. "If we marry, I can offer you the protection of my name, my time when I'm in England, and financial security, but I can't give you anything else."

At least he was being honest with her. She felt all hope shrivel and die. He didn't want to love. Yet he knew how to. It was clear in the way he pursued finding Lucien. And in how he cared for his sisters, especially Ashley. And in the way he respected her. He just wanted his freedom more than he wanted her.

She rose from the bed and sat on the rug by the fire, a blanket wrapped around her and used her fingers to attack the tangles in her hair.

He joined her. They sat side by side, their skin drying, the heat from the fire keeping the chill at bay. The silence was not uncomfortable.

He turned to face her. "I'm sorry."

She pushed his fringe off his face. "I respect your honesty." She pressed a kiss to his lips, and he caught it and deepened it. Soon they were wrapped around each other and the kiss became almost desperate, as if they both knew this would be the last time they would be together like this.

The magnificence of his nude body took her breath away. The muscles of his chest and torso rippled and flexed, and her fingers longed to trail every inch like the shadows from the fire dancing over his naked skin.

Her eyes roamed over him in a thorough assessment, taking in the hard contours, the robust swell of his arms, the flat ridge of his abdomen, the flesh, thick and rampant between his legs—she committed it all to memory.

His mouth, hot and moist, licked the space between her breasts, sending heat searing to her very core. Farah gripped his shoulders as he licked and kissed, whipping her into a frenzy. When his delicious mouth grazed one jutting nipple, she arched more. He parted his lips and took the puckering bud into his hot, wet mouth, and she arched off the floor. Nothing had ever felt this amazing. The pleasure was almost more than she could bear. Every nerve ending screamed for more.

Turbulent emotions came bubbling to the fore. All her feminine instincts took over, and she found the courage to slide her hands over the skin she'd been hungering to explore. It was firm, hard, yet sensual.

She was conscious of his hand sliding lower. Rockwell flicked his tongue over her nipple and then drew it fully into his mouth. He sucked at her breast while cradling her mound in his palm. She didn't want to stop him.

But he broke away from her, leaving her bereft. Her breasts felt raw and ravished by his delicious ministrations. He couldn't leave her like this and she gasped into the air, about to protest. She yearned for his lips and hands on other parts of her, too.

As if sensing her every desire, he picked her up and placed her on the bed. He came over her and let her nipple slip between his teeth and turned his ravenous attention to her belly.

Hot lips pressed a trail against her taut skin, over her hips and down her thigh, branding her in the most wicked way. Her entire body trembled with the knowledge of what was to come—hoped was to come. She knew where this would end, and she couldn't regret it. Her legs parted to make his access easier—faster.

She dragged in a deep breath as his hand went between her

thighs, burning her skin.

"I want to imprint the taste of you on my brain," he ground out, his voice rough and turbulent, the tension of his restraint evident.

He parted her legs farther, the flesh tingling and exposed to him. He needed no encouragement to take eager advantage.

His fingers parting the curls at her junction, Rockwell, holding her gaze, lowered his head. The heat in his eyes blazed, and she closed hers at his first lick. *Oh, God.*

She arched and cried out as his hot, slick tongue lapped the sensitive area. Her fingers curled in the quilt, and she let out a deep and guttural groan as pleasure so intense—soul-wringing pleasure—raced over her.

His tongue moved over her dewy folds of flesh, softly, almost reverently, then flicked the tip of his clever tongue over the delicate hardened nub, causing her to sob and cry out. "Oh, Rockwell."

His lips kissed through her folds expertly in fluid strokes, stirring a welter of emotions in her belly, making her thighs flex and her hips lift in unrestrained longing.

A tight bolt of lightning unfurled in her stomach, and she couldn't help grinding herself against him. His tongue stroked faster, and just when she couldn't stand another second, he plunged his tongue deep inside her and she shattered. Shooting stars clouded her mind, and she floated in a haze of sensation.

When she finally brought her emotions under control, it was to find him leaning over her, his eyes stormy, dark and smoldering. She shivered at the intensity reflected in the deep chocolate pools.

"That was beautiful," he said. And he kissed her. She could taste herself and her desire to taste him grew.

"I'll never forget… never." She reached down and found his straining cock. "Can I do the same to you?"

In answer, he rolled onto his back and put his hands behind his head. "I'm all yours." Her heart stilled because he really wasn't. Rockwell would never be hers.

He gave a groan against her lips as she moved her hips, running her wet womanhood up and down the length of him. He could go insane if she didn't taste him soon. He couldn't wait to feel her hot mouth upon him.

Desire dissolved in his blood and spread through his veins, more potent than the brandy he'd been drinking on the *Doreen*. He wanted her. Wanted her as much as he did the first day he'd seen her in his Hessian, but she could never be his. He would only hurt her.

She pulled back and kissed down his neck, and he could not take his eyes off her. She paid special attention to his chest, nibbling on his hard nipples, causing his hips to lift. "God, this is good."

Her lips teased his senses, her hands slid down to stroke him, and his breath hissed from between his clenched teeth. She ran her nose over his skin. "I love the scent of you," she whispered against his chest. His blood pounded as she trailed those sensual, teasing lips downward toward his groin. When she finally took him in her mouth, his hips left the bed.

His deep moan filled the room. For someone who had never done this before, she had good instincts.

She gave so much pleasure. He closed his eyes and thanked God she was here with him, in this moment. The way she used her tongue, the way her hands cupped his sacs, and the sound of her mouth working him made him almost explode.

He loved to watch. But nothing prepared him for the hit of desire he got from watching her pleasure him. As she licked and suckled, taking him deep within her mouth, his eyes were locked on her face.

She could tell he was watching her. His eyes burned into her. Farah loved taking him deep into her mouth. Loved his reaction as he watched her possess him. Watching his features harden into a mask of passion. She'd never felt so powerful. The cords of his neck tightened, and his hands wound into her hair. His mouth opened. His breath became ragged. His hips rocked, pushing him farther, deeper, into her mouth. He was about to come. His eyes closed, and his head fell back. His hands dug into her scalp and his whole body trembled.

"Farah. Christ. How I love what you do to me." And then, with a series of jerks and a roar, he flooded her mouth with the very essence of him.

She drank him down, not letting him slip from between her lips until she had licked every last drop.

She crawled back up his body, showering his chest with little kisses. His skin was damp and his breathing was still erratic. She lay on top of him, savoring the feel of him beneath her.

The fire had burned low and as they lay there, she shivered. Rockwell stirred and pulled back the covers and she crawled under them. He tucked her in but didn't join her.

"I think it best I leave."

She wanted to beg him to stay, but knew it had to be this way. "I regret nothing."

"Neither do I." He hesitated. "Maybe I do. I regret I can't be the man you need."

With that, he kissed her one last time, collected his clothes and left.

Though she tried not to, she cried herself to sleep.

CHAPTER TWELVE

A S THE *DOREEN* barely moved through the waves of the Irish Sea, Farah found herself drawn to the deck, the salty air filling her senses. Rockwell, his commanding presence near the helm, oversaw the ship with practiced ease, his eyes occasionally flickering towards her, and she wished she understood what he was thinking.

He'd been very clear on his views last night and so had she. She stood watching him interact with the captain and his sailors. Rockwell belonged on this ship. Farah could see that. It was as if a sailor's life was in his blood. She understood that now. Having never seen him on board a ship before this trip, she hadn't realized what she was asking him to give up.

She stood gazing out to sea. Lost in thought, she felt a warm presence beside her. Lord Furoe approached, his daughter trailing behind him. "The sea is quite captivating, is it not, especially when it's so calm?" he remarked, his gaze lingering on her face. "It may be a longer journey home than expected with the wind so light."

"You must be impatient to get home. We have barely made it across the Irish Sea."

Just then, Rockwell joined them. "I think we should dock at Holyhead. The weather is going to be calm for several days, so the captain says, and I concur. It means a trip overland, but I still feel we'll get to London sooner."

"How long will it take?" Lucien asked.

"Roughly five days."

Farah sighed. "The same time it would take to sail if we had wind."

Rockwell turned to his friend. "You decide. We can continue to sit becalmed with a growing number of ships or we can dock at Holyhead and go overland."

"What do you think, Lady Farah?" Lucien asked.

She smiled up at him. It was so nice of him to include her. "It would be more comfortable on the ship. Ava-Marie could run around. But selfishly, I want to get home as soon as I can. The longer I'm out of circulation, the more questions might be asked, and Lord Franklin is a determined man."

"Who's Lord Franklin?" Lucien asked.

Rockwell looked at her and then said, "It's a long story. I'll tell you over a coffee, after I tell the captain to change course. Then I'll tell you how Farah came to be on my ship."

Farah crouched down to tickle Ava-Marie under her chin. "And you and I can play a little game."

The little girl giggled. "Can we play hide and seek like I used to do in the graveyard?"

"What a good idea. Shall we ask Caitria to play with us?"

"Oh, yes. Come on." Ava-Marie held her hand out.

As Farah took the tiny, outstretched hand, a pain stabbed deep in her stomach. If she remained a spinster, she would never know the feeling of holding her babe in her arms. And God forgive her, when she looked at Ava-Marie's innocent, laughing face, she had the strongest longing for a child. Suddenly, causing a scandal and fleeing to Cornwall to become a spinster no longer seemed the ideal answer to her problems.

Would that deny her the chance to marry and have children?

As she and Ava-Marie walked toward the galley to find Caitria, she watched the two men walking away. One tall and dark, the other brown-haired and tall and broad. Both had offered her marriage, but only one of them could hurt her. Or if she were brave, one of them could turn her life into something wonderful...if she was daring enough to try. Was she? Ava-Marie squeezed her hand and in that moment, her frustration with herself reached its peak.

She thought of everything Tiffany had done. Throwing caution to the wind, investing her money to make a better life, regardless of society's dictates. Then facing a man like Sprat and being brave when he'd kidnapped her. She'd managed to escape on her own.

Then there was Ashley who stuck her nose up to those who judged her because of some scandal. She still enjoyed her life and lived it to the fullest with wonderful friends and family at her side.

She was part of the sisterhood and she was strong with them at her back.

This adventure was just what she'd needed. She'd had to face the fact that her situation was of her own making. She'd been a coward, and she had to learn how to stand up to her brother and the world to get what she wanted out of her life. This time, she'd tell Lord Franklin to go to hell. In fact, she couldn't wait to see his face.

Soon she was skipping across the deck as if the weight of the world had lifted off her shoulders.

"So, PRIOR TO finding Farah in your trunk on board this ship, you didn't have any—relationship with her?"

Rockwell wondered what was behind such a question and he didn't like how it made him feel. The thought of Farah having an alternative to him if the scandal came out made him happy, but the idea of Lucien—or any man—being intimate with Farah enraged him.

"Other than as my sister's friend, no."

"May I ask why she is not marrying you, since this trip thoroughly comprised her?"

Lucien's tone told him he better have offered. "She doesn't want to marry me."

"What did you do?" Lucien growled. "She's a sensible woman. She must see that she has no choice."

Rockwell wished he knew the answer. Surely, it couldn't be that she would risk a scandal just for something called love? He thought back to Tiffany and Wolf's wedding and understood that real love existed. Maybe he was just too selfish to let it in. "She knows that a wife of an adventurer is a lonely one. I'm not great husband material."

Lucien sipped his coffee as they sat around the stateroom dining table. "And a man with little to offer in terms of financial security, with no memory of his previous life, is probably no better option."

Bloody hell, Lucien was serious about his offer. Rockwell's stomach clenched. He should be happy that his best friend found a woman he felt comfortable with, given his family's financial situation, but his brain revolted at the idea. Rockwell had the winning strategy. "Lady Courtney is still technically your fiancée, since you were never married. How are you going to approach that?"

"A part of me hopes that when I see her, it might spark a memory. But having met you, and knowing how close we were as friends, I won't get my hopes up."

"But it doesn't mean you can't start over?"

Lucien paused with his coffee cup partway to his mouth. "But, like you, is it fair to Lady Courtney? I'm not the same man."

"Shouldn't that be her decision?" Rockwell shrugged. "Besides, I think fundamentally you are the same man. You are honest, kind, loyal. You're already focused on helping your family. I think Lady Courtney will see a lot of her fiancé in you."

Lucien fiddled with his cup. "But I can't force feelings and—I like—Farah."

Rockwell stilled his features, trying not to give anything away. "You have one major problem." At Lucien's raised eyebrow, he said, "She is Lady Courtney's best friend and she won't do anything that might hurt Courtney."

Lucien said nothing. He simply sat there drinking his coffee. Finally, he muttered, "One's brain rarely rules the heart."

What the hell did that mean? Was he saying he still wanted to pursue Farah? Rockwell inwardly smiled. Of all the men in England who might court Farah, he didn't fear Lucien. Farah would do nothing to hurt Courtney, and Lucien could try all he liked. Farah would never be Lucien's wife.

But someone *would* marry Farah, and he wondered if he could stand that?

"I think you should wait to meet Lady Courtney. It is the honorable thing to do, given that she is still technically your fiancée."

"But you and Lady Farah agreed to keep the fact I never married Ava a secret."

Rockwell sighed. "I had forgotten that point."

"Is this sudden desire to point me towards a lady I previously knew instead of aiding Farah because you have feelings for Farah?"

He had feelings. If he were a selfish bastard, he'd claim her and leave her sitting at home with his children. "No." He stood up and moved round the table and placed a hand on Lucien's shoulder. "I'm saying this because I know Farah very well. If you go down this road, she will rebuff you. If you don't understand why, you don't understand Farah and you will only cause her and Courtney pain. I don't think you want to do that."

With that, he left to go back on deck, leaving Lucien to his thoughts.

As he stepped foot on deck, he almost knocked over Ava-Marie. He swung her into arms just as Caitria came running up. "Sorry, we are playing tag." Farah came puffing behind.

Rockwell tickled Ava-Marie under the chin. "Just be careful running around the deck. We don't want any accidents."

"We are about to go below for lunch and an afternoon sleep."

Farah looked over her shoulder. "The coast is nearby. I assume we'll dock tonight."

"Yes. It will take that long given we have no wind. We need the tide to help take the ship in."

"Will we be sleeping on the ship tonight?"

"Yes. We'll leave by carriage in the morning once we've arranged everything."

"Then I'm pleased we've let Ava-Marie have a run around today. It's going to be a tiring journey for her."

Was she criticizing his decision to go overland? "I thought you wanted to get home as soon as possible?"

She bit her bottom lip. "I did—I do. But…I'm thinking of the child."

Rockwell put Ava-Marie down and said to Farah, "I'm more worried about your reputation." And then a thought struck him. "And mine. If you are caught, I'll be forced to propose. I won't compromise my reputation as a gentleman, and if you refuse me… You'll be absolutely ruined," Rockwell warned.

He turned and walked away.

"Are you all right?" Caitria asked. "He seemed upset."

Farah watched him go. He did indeed look upset. He'd known this was her situation once he'd found her on his ship. She looked back at Caitria and saw Lucien leaning in the doorway, his daughter in his arms. He stared at her with an intensity that unsettled her.

Caitria slipped her arm through hers and said, "Let us take a walk, just the two of us."

She looked back at Rockwell, but he was still striding to the bow. As the ladies walked, Caitria sighed. "Lucien is interested in you and I think that has unsettled Lord Ware."

Embarrassment singed Farah's cheeks. "I'm not interested in Lord Furoe like that. And Rockwell won't care. He'll see it as a solution to my scandal."

"I wouldn't be so sure. Perhaps you could take advantage of the situation?"

"I'm not sure what you're inferring."

Caitria laughed. "Yes, you do. Make Lord Ware jealous. Make him fall in love with you and then you have the answer to your situation. If there is a scandal, you can marry the man who loves you."

"Oh, you make that sound so easy. Rockwell's mistress is the sea. How am I to compete with that?" she said sardonically.

"Easy. Make him love you more."

It was so easy for Caitria to say, but she did not know how to do that. "If it's that easy, why haven't you made Lucien fall in love with you?"

Caitria's teasing manner fled. "Because I have more to lose. I love Ava-Marie like my own child. I've raised her since she was not quite one year old. If I fail, he would likely send me home to Cork and I'd lose her too. And now…well, he's a viscount with an earl for a father, and I'm not a lady." She stared Farah in the eye. "You and I are in different places and you have nothing to lose but plenty to gain."

Her heart went out to her new friend. Caitria was right. Lucien needed to marry for money. "Are you calling me a coward?"

"Perhaps. But I'm not in a position to judge. Only you can decide if you're running away."

They walked in silence, the gulls crying overhead the only sound. If she were to win Rockwell's heart, she'd have to draw from something deep inside. She looked toward the bow and saw Rockwell helping a sailor with some ropes. Her pulse quickened solely from looking at his tousled hair and tanned muscled arms. When she thought about his naked body…she was aware of him with every nerve of her body. As if sensing her gaze, he looked her way. The very air seemed to vibrate between them. He straightened, watching her intently, silently reminding her of all the wanton things they had done during this adventure, the incredible passion they had shared.

His glance was so spellbinding, she found it impossible to tear her gaze away.

"See," Caitria whispered. "He's drawn to you, too. I don't think it would take much to make him realize he needs you more than the sea."

She continued to watch him as they walked on. She chewed on her bottom lip and thought long and hard. What *did* she have to lose?

Only her heart!

"And how on earth would I go about making a man like Rockwell, who likely has a woman in every port, fall in love with me?"

"Well, perhaps let him think you are interested in Lucien."

She shook her head. "That would not be fair to Lucien. And it might give him the wrong idea."

"Not if you told him your plan and asked him to help."

"Oh, I couldn't do that." Could she? "I suppose it would stop this silly infatuation of his if I told him I wanted to win Rockwell's heart." She rounded on Caitria. "Is that why you suggested it?"

The Irish woman shrugged. "Not solely, but it would give Lucien a chance to fit into his new life without complications. It might make him look at someone under his very nose."

Farah stopped walking and faced Caitria. "You know he needs to marry for money. Plus, he has a fiancée. Lady Courtney, my friend. She's mourned his death and has never married. She loves him."

"Perhaps she loves a ghost? Do you think he's the same man?"

"I didn't know him very well, but no. He has definitely changed. But I still think he's a good man."

"Does Lucien know about Courtney?"

"Yes."

"Yet he's still interested in you. That says a lot about where his mind is. Perhaps he wants to start anew. He's a different man and he might want to let go of his past, as he'll never remember it."

Farah sank down to sit on a barrel. That had a ring of truth about it, but he was more likely afraid of what he was about to face and she was convenient. "If that's true, Courtney will be devastated all over again." She rubbed her forehead. "Everything is getting so complicated. So many people could end up getting hurt." And now she was trapped between two friends, both wanting the same man. A part of her thought Caitria suited this new Lucien better, but she wouldn't help the family's financial position. Then there was Courtney… Courtney loved him so and could help him with her large dowry.

"I'll think about your suggestion. But I won't let him force me into a marriage if he doesn't."

"Don't think for too long. You only have a few days, a week at the most, before we reach London."

CHAPTER THIRTEEN

T HE GENTLE LAPPING of waves against the hull provided a soothing soundtrack as Rockwell stood on the deck, his gaze fixed on the brilliant stars overhead. Farah came up beside him, shivering slightly in the cool night air. They had docked in time for dinner and it had been a pleasant evening. During the meal, she was very aware of Lucien's attentions, as was Rockwell.

"You seem pensive this evening, Rockwell," she said. Perhaps Caitria was right in her assumption that Rockwell didn't appreciate Lucien's flirtation. "What occupies your thoughts under this vaulted night sky? Are you worried about the reception I may get when we return to London?"

Rockwell turned to her, his eyes alight with the passion that so drew Farah to him. But she quickly realized it wasn't a passion for her alone. He was staring at the stars above.

"Just contemplating the vast mysteries that lie beyond the horizon, waiting to be unraveled by bold explorers. I wonder if man will ever explore the heavens."

She tipped her head back. "I think sometimes it's better not to know what is out there. I prefer to bask in the beauty and not question why. Then you can't be disappointed."

"Yet the world holds such wonders, Farah—uncharted lands, undiscovered peoples and creatures, unsolved riddles of science and nature. I must seek them out and quench this thirst for knowledge within me."

"The stars have the power to make one evaluate life. I'm so

unimportant in the world's scheme. We are on this earth for such a short time. It's humbling to realize that centuries ago, the Romans and Greeks stood and looked up to this sky and saw exactly what I'm seeing now. The heavens haven't changed for thousands of years."

He reached out and stroked a finger down her cheek. "You and I are so different. You might be satisfied with simply reveling in the beauty of this world, but I see a puzzle. Man has evolved over time because men ask 'why.' If you were standing in front of a closed door, surely you'd be inquisitive enough to want to know what's on the other side?"

"I'd prefer to peer through the keyhole and not take the risk that something awful was on the other side."

He gave a rich laugh that warmed her. "What made you into this timid mouse I wonder? I *have* to walk through that door."

She shook her head slowly. "When I was ten, my mother died. A few days before her death, I'd snuck out to attend the country fair after I'd been forbidden to go. Father was very ill by then, but mother was still awake. My parents were worried about the lung disease spreading and my mother was scared I might get sick too. When she and father died, I thought it was God punishing me for being defiant. I thought my bad behavior killed her. So, I made a promise to be good and do everything I was told if God would spare my brother, who had also fallen ill. I didn't want to be alone. And when he survived, I knew I had to keep that promise. It became second nature to be docile, and I let it happen…"

He wiped the tear tracking down her face. "It's about time that little girl faced her fears. You know that it wasn't your fault. And you've become a beautiful, strong woman who knows her own mind."

Warm spread through her. Farah's brow furrowed as she studied his expression in the dim lantern light. "You speak as if your very soul depends on these voyages of discovery, this endless wanderlust." She paused, suddenly troubled. "If I were to become your wife, you would be forever leaving me behind as you sailed over the horizon in pursuit of these mysteries, wouldn't you?"

Rockwell took her hands in his, his calloused fingers contrasting with her soft skin. "You know I won't lie to you. You must understand, this need to wander is part of my very being. I could no more ignore it than I could halt the turning of the earth."

"It's your passion."

His face split into a wide grin. "If you could only see the things I've seen, you'd understand. The jungles of the south Americas are like no other place on Earth. Towering trees and dense foliage teeming with life—monkeys scampering through the canopy, brilliant birds of paradise taking flight."

Farah listened with rapt attention, imagining the exotic lands he described. "But surely the dangers are great as well? Venomous serpents and wild beasts?"

"Indeed." Rockwell nodded. "On more than one occasion, I found myself face to face with a hungry enormous cat or bloody great python. But the thrill of discovery, of being one of a few to look upon those untamed lands, makes the risk worthwhile."

His animation was infectious as the moon danced over his handsome features. "From my earliest days, I've felt a yearning to explore the unknown, to traverse the blank spaces on the maps. With each new journey, I'm plagued by more questions that can only be answered by further exploration."

Turning to face her, his expression took on a wistful aspect. "The world is so vast, so filled with mysteries, awaiting an intrepid soul. I fear I'll never be able to satiate this driving need to discover what lies over the next ridge, across the next ocean. It's an insatiable hunger. It's what I was born to do."

"It's like a calling?" When he nodded, Farah's eyes glistened with unshed tears as realization blossomed. As much as she adored the daring explorer before her, marrying him meant a life of long separations, as he indulged his thirst for adventure while she remained at home. Was that the life she truly desired? She wavered, her heart and mind engaged in a fierce debate over the sacrifices such a union would demand.

Could she go with him? Once children came that would not be ideal. But worse still, he'd never suggested it. Why?

"Would you consider taking a wife with you on your travels."

It was as if she'd asked him to sell his soul to the devil. His jaw firmed. "No. I'd never allow that."

"Why?"

He seemed to have gone to another place. He looked back out at sea. "It's too dangerous. Remember Mrs. Ahearn's talk of my fiancé Charlotte?" She nodded. "She died in my arms on my ship. I'll not suffer that again." His words were so final, she had nothing more to ask. But her heart sank. He had to love her enough to stay or she would always be left behind.

To make this man love her more than his driving need to conquer the world seemed a daunting task. She looked up at the beauty and wonder of the stars. Then looked at Rockwell. Like the stars, he took her breath away. She wondered, when he looked at her, what did he see? Whatever it was, it wasn't enough to entice him away from his mistress, the sea.

She took a deep breath. "Perhaps I should turn to Lucien should a scandal erupt upon our return. Like you say, we are so different. A marriage between us wouldn't work. We don't work."

He ran his finger over her palm. "There is one place we are very compatible."

She shivered under his light touch, noticing he hadn't blinked an eye at her suggestion. Memories of what they'd shared in bed flashed in her head. Not with Lucien. She couldn't picture giving herself to Lucien in the same way. "But is that enough?" The question was really for her, but Rockwell answered.

Rockwell turned her into his arms and drew her into the shadows. He leaned toward her and there was a wealth of restraint in his touch as he plied her mouth with soft, seductive kisses, nipping gently at her bottom lip, teasing her with light little pecks to the corner of her lips.

Even his touch surprised her. A soft hand on her cheek and another on her shoulder as he held her motionless for his tender assault. It was as if he cherished every moment with her.

She should stop him. This would not help either of them.

He coaxed her lips open. His tongue flicked to touch hers, then entered.

The invasive intimacy sent deep, visceral thrills down to her hips. It served as a stark reminder of how susceptible she was to this man's tender touch, to Rockwell's seduction.

He covered her face with soft caresses from his lips. She was glad for the brace of his arm holding her in place, keeping her from leaning into him. Her body was traitorous, yearning for something that wasn't good for her. This man knew how to strum her body, knew how to make her feel things she should only feel for a man who loved her.

And it was only a kiss.

He drew back, holding her gaze as he used his thumb to nudge her lips apart. Her blood quickened as she watched him, and without hesitation, she moved her tongue forward, sliding it against the tip of his thumb.

Her breasts rose and fell rapidly while his eyes glinted with heat.

He bent her over his arm and placed little kisses down her slender, exposed neck, making her breathing grow shallower and faster. He gently tugged at the low bodice of her gown until her breasts popped free, all the while kissing the skin of the breasts he exposed. She did not protest or struggle.

He stopped his kisses as one turgid, dark pink nipple was uncovered and it was he who suddenly could not breathe. He stared for several moments before blowing gently on it. She shivered in his arms. He could no more stop his mouth from tasting than he could stop breathing.

As he wrapped his lips around the hot flesh and suckled deep,

Farah moaned in his arms. Rockwell was not selfish. He laved each nipple separately but with equal abandon. He picked her up and carried her to a chest deep in the shadows, laying her down like the prize she was. Just then, the moon cleared the clouds, and he drank in the vision of perfection. He ran his hands down her sides and slowly raised the skirts of her gown up to her waist. She did not protest. She had a waist that required no corset to give it shape; the fair curls shielding her womanhood beckoned his fingers, and her long, shapely legs made him think of riding—her thighs gripping his hips and riding him hard.

He reached out a finger and ran it from her breastbone to her pubic bone, coming to rest in her fair curls. He kept staring, the image before him one he would never in his life forget even when he left her and sailed away into the life he wanted. Venus. She was his real-life Venus and his body longed to worship her. He cupped her womanhood, the heat from her intoxicating. His mouth watered at the idea of tasting her.

Her body tensed beneath his hands as he bent towards her womanly core, but she merely closed her eyes and moaned.

Then he let his tongue work its magic. Her hips lifted to meet his mouth, and she tasted of the sweetest nectar.

She gasped for air and could not look away from the erotic sight. He loved how her eyes darkened in her need for release.

"So responsive. So much passion we could share forever," he whispered in her ear before his lips traced butterfly-kisses down her neck.

She could not look away from the sight and she inwardly admitted watching was—arousing. Farah swallowed back a moan of pleasure. She felt as if her body were on fire. She barely noticed that her hips were moving in time to his strokes of his fingers.

His long, elegant finger entered her and made his knuckles brush her hardened nub. It was both agony and pleasure.

His fingers were moving faster, and her hips moved frantically. She watched herself riding his fingers. His eyes were hard and dark as he watched her. She could barely breathe. Her heart pounded in her chest. He pressed his thumb against her hardened nub and said, "Beautiful. Truly as magical as the stars."

All too soon, her whole body convulsed. She was flying so high, she thought she could see heaven, and she watched as her body's juices covered his hand. His fingers stilled deep within her, but his thumb kept up its circular movement until she had to close her legs to stop him. The sensations were too much.

She slumped back against the chest, breathing heavily, and closed her eyes. She couldn't imagine sharing this pleasure with anyone else. Only Rockwell. Tears slipped beneath her closed eyelids to run down her cheeks. She would lose him soon, and then what would she do? How long would the memory of the pleasure he shared with her stay in her heart and mind?

"Sharing a life of passion would be enough for me. Perhaps my trips would be shorter knowing you were waiting at home for me. But you have to decide on the life you want. I'm not selfish enough to deny you a choice when I've made mine. Exploring will always come first."

She blinked back tears. She would not cry over a man who would not let her into his heart. Farah simply nodded and pulled her bodice into place. "Let's hope that the uproar of Lucien returning means my disappearance goes unnoticed. Then I won't have to choose."

She rose to her feet and let her skirts fall. She couldn't help but notice his erection straining behind his breeches. But she turned away.

"I'm sorry," he whispered.

She frowned. "For what? You are not to blame for me being in this position."

"For not being the man you want me to be." He looked so sad. "I tried to tell you at the ball that night. I'm not looking to marry."

She sighed and stepped into the moonlight. "I could say the same to you. My actions have put you in a terrible position. You shouldn't have to choose me over your freedom." But her heart ached because, damn it, she wanted him to choose her.

Because she'd fallen in love with him.

"Just bad timing all round. Maybe if it had been in a few years…"

She turned away. "I don't have a few years. Young ladies are thought to be on the shelf by three and twenty. But at least this adventure has taught me something about myself." She swung back to face him and stood up tall and straight. "I don't want to be a timid mouse. And I shall not let my brother force me into a marriage I do not want."

"And how do you propose to do that?"

She would run. She would buy her cottage in Cornwall and live a quiet life. She might eventually find another man worthy of her love, once Rockwell was no longer in her heart. "You'll see." She added, "I must get some sleep. It's going to be a long few days of travel. Good night."

ROCKWELL WATCHED HER walk away, his cock throbbing. He shouldn't have touched her. Shouldn't have tasted her because the need to take her and make her his burned through his body. He stood breathing heavily until he got his body under control.

He knew she could stand up to Blackstone. She'd changed on this trip. Changed into a woman he admired and desired. He'd never been one to succumb to jealousy, but having to sit and watch Lucien openly flirt with her made his appetite flee. And worse, Farah gloried in Lucien's attentions and flirted back.

He looked up at the stars and cursed under his breath. Suddenly, the mystery of Farah was looking very enticing, perhaps even as enticing as exploring the Nile.

What would she do when they returned to London? How would she thwart her brother? But the worst horror of all was, would she accept Lucien's courtship? Rage built behind his eyes until his head pounded. His body screamed "mine!" But his heart's fortress remained in place. He desired her, that was all.

But the kernel of a life different to the one he'd envisioned filled his head. Sitting by the fire in winter with Farah and his children around him. But what would he do if he didn't explore the world? He was too restless to sit at home doing nothing. *You have that estate in Suffolk.* How long could he stay by her side before his need to travel saw him leave her and any family they had?

He walked to the railing and looked at the dock below. To-morrow they would head to London and both their fates would be decided by what awaited them there.

It surprised him he no longer cared if he had to offer for Farah.

But as he made his way to his cabin, he realized Farah might care more than he. It was obvious she wanted more than a seafaring explorer as a husband.

She might well choose Lucien.

Then he'd lose the best friend he'd only just brought back into his life because he couldn't watch her marry Lucien.

Thank God he'd be able to leave immediately for his African trip.

CHAPTER FOURTEEN

London—5 days later

AFTER FIVE LONG and tiring days, they thankfully made it to the outskirts of London just as night fell. Darkness would hide her arrival home. Farah's heart raced with anxiety. She stole glances out of the window as they trundled through the streets near her home, half-expecting to see curious faces peeking out from behind curtains. Or worse, society gossips ready to spread rumors like wildfire.

Ava-Marie had cried most of the day. The little girl had had enough of being cooped up in the carriage for the five days it had taken to cross England from the coast. There were only so many games of *spot the sheep* to play. As they reached Richmond, the little girl finally slept.

But it wasn't the child's sleep that muted the carriage. Those within the carriage grew quiet as the enormity of what was about to unfold grew ever closer. Rockwell and Lucien had decided to tell only Wolf that Lucien was alive, mainly to protect Farah. If everyone gathered to watch their arrival, she would find it hard to slip inside unnoticed. That was also one of the reasons they'd pushed on in the darkness. Plus, everyone wanted to sleep in a nice bed for a change—and perhaps a bath!

As the carriage rolled to a stop in the secluded stable yard of Wolf's family home, Farah's pulse quickened with a mixture of relief and trepidation. Wolf and Tiffany had done this for her, and she was very grateful. She ignored the stab of guilt that Lucian's family would have to wait a few more hours to learn the good news. This was her chance to escape unnoticed, to evade the prying eyes of society and safeguard her reputation.

She cast a quick glance at Rockwell, who met her gaze with a reassuring nod. With practiced ease, he helped her down from the carriage, his touch sending a jolt of warmth through her despite the chill of the night air.

Pulling her cape's hood over her head, Farah's heart pounded in her chest as she followed Rockwell towards the servants' entrance, her steps light and cautious. The creak of the carriage as it made its way without her to the front of the house, rung through the air. Every rustle of the wind seemed magnified in the night's stillness, heightening her anxiety.

As they reached the unassuming door, Rockwell turned to her with a whispered promise. "I'm pretty sure your secret will be safe," he murmured, his voice low and urgent. He hesitated before brushing his lips across her cheek. "I shall never forget our adventure. Send me word if you need anything or if anyone learns of your part in Lucian's return."

Nor will I ever forget. Farah nodded, her fingers trembling as she reached for the door handle. With a silent prayer, she pushed open the door and slipped inside, her heart pounding in her ears. She closed the door on Rockwell's handsome face and tried to keep the tears away. They would never again interact as they had on this trip. She would never again feel his soft touch, succumb to his sensuous kisses, or run her hands over his muscular body. Her heart clenched in her chest, the feeling of loss almost brought her to her knees.

But this was her choice. Her choice not to trap Rockwell in a marriage he didn't want. She straightened to her full height and drew in a breath.

He would be a gentleman out of her reach. They must act as society dictated. No overt familiarity. Their casual ease of address, look, and touch was gone. She prayed she could remember how to behave with him. She shuddered to think how she would behave when Rockwell took a wife, or if he flaunted a mistress in front of her.

She moved onwards, as she would with her life, whatever her future held. It wasn't marriage to a man who would rather explore on the high seas. The dim light of the servants' quarters greeted her, casting long shadows across the room. Farah paused for a moment, allowing her eyes to adjust to the darkness, before hurrying towards the staircase that led to the upper floors.

Each step felt like an eternity as she ascended the staircase, her senses on high alert for any sign of discovery. But the house remained eerily silent, its occupants sleeping soundly as Farah made her way to the safety of the bedchamber that Rockwell said Wolf had readied. It was the bedchamber she'd spent the last fifteen days in sick with woman's issues. Wolf's staff were souls of discretion.

Finally reaching her room, Farah let out a breath she hadn't realized she'd been holding, her shoulders sagging with relief. She had made it back to London without incident, her secret still safely guarded. *Then why do I feel so out of sorts?*

As she sank onto the edge of her bed, exhaustion washed over her, mingling with the lingering traces of fear and excitement. She hurriedly crossed to where Ashley had her maid leave out a nightgown and robe. She gave thanks that she'd thought to send her clothes ahead to keep up the charade of her illness.

Wolf had written that it would build her cover if she appeared with the rest of the family, surprised at Rockwell and Lucien's return. Their big concern was Ava-Marie. Would she let anything slip? They decided Caitria would carry Ava-Marie straight to the nursery and bed.

She was just struggling with the hooks of her gown when there was a soft rap on the bedchamber door. She froze before she heard Ivy say, "Can we come in?"

"Of course. I need some help to disrobe." Farah's heart raced as she prepared to face Ashley and Ivy, Rockwell's sisters, knowing she would have to navigate their questions with care and diplomacy. She straightened her posture, summoning all the poise and grace she could muster.

"Farah, my dear, you're back!" Ashley exclaimed, her eyes alight with curiosity as she all but tumbled into the room swathed in a lilac robe of heavy satin. Ivy followed suit, her expression more reserved but no less inquisitive.

"Indeed, I am," Farah replied with a warm smile, hoping to deflect questions until the men arrived. She could hear the carriage below. "It's good to see you both again."

Ashley's brow furrowed with concern. "We've been worried sick about you, Farah. And Rockwell. How on earth did this happen?"

Farah's heart skipped a beat at the directness of Ashley's question, but she forced herself to remain composed. "It's a long story. I'll explain later," she replied, her voice steady despite the turmoil raging within her. "Can you help me get changed? We will need to go downstairs soon to meet the carriage."

Ivy regarded her with a skeptical gaze, her intuition picking up on Farah's evasiveness. "I hope you weren't trying to trap Rockwell," she remarked pointedly. "While I love you like a sister, I also love my brother and do not wish to see either of you hurt." Then, having said her piece, she joined in with Ashley and the two friends helped her disrobe. Ashley held out the nightgown for her to pull on.

"It's true, I wanted Rockwell to help me with Lord Franklin, but I swear I did not deliberately set out to trap him," Farah admitted, her voice tinged with regret. "Besides, if this plan goes smoothly, no one will be the wiser."

Ashley and Ivy exchanged a knowing glance, their expressions unreadable as they seemed to silently communicate with each other. Farah held her breath, waiting for their response with bated anticipation.

Finally, Ashley spoke. Her tone softened with understanding. "Well, regardless of how it happened, we're just glad to have you are both back safe and sound, Farah," she said, her smile genuine.

"But we can't wait to hear your story. Wolf says he has a surprise for us."

With a grateful smile, she returned Ashley's embrace, her heart lighter, knowing she had the support of Rockwell's family by her side. Then it struck her. She pulled back to stare at the two women. "Wolf didn't explain who is in the carriage below?"

Ivy looked confused. "No. He explained about you and Rockwell and how we had to cover for you with Lord Franklin. Odious man. He called for the first two days until I had to tell him of your condition. It was so embarrassing. Then he's simply sending flowers every day."

She wrapped her robe tightly around her, then took both women's hands. Her eyes filled with tears as she told them. "We found him."

Ashley's mouth was the first to fall open. "No."

"Who?" Ivy asked.

"You found Lord Furoe. And he's alive?"

She nodded as she watched Ashley's eyes fill with tears. "We found him. He's in the carriage and is about to be your visitor for the night."

"What about Courtney? We have to send her a note immediately."

At Ivy's words, Farah gripped her arm as she tried to move round her to the writing desk. "No. His family first. He has no memory of anything before five years ago. He didn't remember Rockwell, or his family, and—he doesn't remember Courtney."

That made Ivy burst into tears. "Poor Courtney. To have the man you love come back from the dead, only to not know you."

"You can understand why we have told no one other than Wolf. Lucien is not the man you knew. He will need time to come to grips with this situation. Rockwell thought it best to wait until morning to meet with his family. And keep it small. Society will be aghast as soon as they learn he has returned. I suspect everyone will try to call upon him. It could be overwhelming for him."

She wanted to explain more about Ava-Marie and Caitria but thought it best not to talk longer. "Let's go downstairs and meet everyone."

"Everyone? That sounds ominous," Ashley said.

As she reached the door, she turned to them. "Remember to act surprised. You're not supposed to know all of this."

With suppressed excitement, the three ladies made their way downstairs. They met Tiffany and Wolf on the second-floor landing. "You ladies will wait in the drawing room, please. I've organized refreshments but everyone will be tired, so we mustn't keep them up long."

She felt herself blush under Wolf's gaze, but Tiffany merely hooked an arm through hers and drew her into the warmth of the fire crackling room. "Thank you for helping Rockwell. It must be hard on him. To find Lucien, but not find him, so to speak."

"You're not cross?" Farah asked.

"A woman has to do what she thinks is right for her and I understand it was an accident the way you ended up on his ship. But I was hoping there would be no sneaking home and there would be a marriage instead."

Farah searched her friend's eyes, but they held no judgment, merely disappointment.

"Rockwell is not the marrying kind."

Just then, he appeared in the doorway and his eyes sought her out immediately. Tiffany drew in a sharp breath. "I wouldn't be too sure of that." Then Tiffany stiffened as Lucien appeared. His eyes sought Farah out, too. "Oh, dear. Courtney will not like that."

Farah blushed, not even trying to deny Tiffany's implication. "He's latched on to me because I was kind to him. I'm the only lady he knows and I've accepted Ava-Marie. He's anxious about his daughter, given her start in life."

"Rockwell doesn't like it, either. So maybe that's a good thing. Might make him wake up to the fact he is going to make a mistake if he lets you..." Tiffany stopped talking and merely squeezed Farah's arm.

Farah stood back as Ivy and Ashley rushed to embrace Lucien. Farah's gut tightened as she watched the man try to cope with meeting so many people who knew him but he didn't recognize. Ivy and Ashley drew him towards the settee and were soon hounding him with questions that he obviously didn't wish to answer. And the ladies hadn't even met Ava-Marie or Caitria yet.

Rockwell gave Lucien an encouraging smile, almost as if wordlessly letting him know it would be worse tomorrow, when he met his family. Had Lucien decided what he'd tell everyone about where he'd been and how he'd been living his life?

Finally, Wolf said, "It's very late and we are all tired and emotional from such a discovery. Lord Furoe, Taylor has organized a bedchamber and my valet is ready to serve you. He's drawn you a bath."

Lucien cleared his throat and put down the glass of brandy he'd been given. "I'd like to check on Ava-Marie and Caitria first."

"Of course." Wolf nodded. He indicated the butler waiting at the door. "Taylor, show Lord Furoe to his daughter's nursery."

As soon as the door had closed and Lucien could be heard walking upstairs, Ivy and Ashley rounded on Farah and both said together, "Daughter?"

Rockwell scolded his sisters before she could reply. "This is Lucien's story to reveal. We do not involve ourselves in gossip. You'll meet Ava-Marie in the morning, but we will give our friend time to adjust. And we will support him when he meets his family."

"When will you alert Lord Danvers?" Tiffany asked.

"I sent a message that Wolf and I will call on the family tomorrow. We are going to take Lucien to his family home in the morning without Ava-Marie." Rockwell walked to the fireplace and leaned on the mantle.

"He's worried about the reception his daughter may receive," Farah explained. "Even though we've told him that his sisters will love his little girl, he can't remember them and obviously wants to protect her. Besides, it's probably best that he goes alone so he can talk to his family about what occurred without worrying about his child. Then he and his family can decide the story they wish the *ton* to learn."

"And what about Courtney? She'll never forgive us if we don't tell her. I'd hate for her to learn the news from someone else," Ivy exclaimed.

Farah silently agreed, but it wasn't really her place to dictate who and when Lucien wanted his return to become public knowledge.

Tiffany spoke up. "I think we should visit with Courtney while Rockwell, Wolf, and Lucien visit Lord Danvers and family. What do you think, dear?"

Wolf nodded. "I feel that is only fair, given she was his fiancée. But you must stress the importance of keeping the details secret until we understand how Lucien wishes to present himself to the world."

Farah couldn't hide a yawn. The past few days had been stressful, and she hadn't slept well.

Tiffany rose and gathered the other ladies. "It's been a long day. I think bed is the answer for us all. Tomorrow will be a stressful, yet such a happy day. Goodnight, gentlemen," and before Farah had time to even say a goodbye to Rockwell, Tiffany had swept her out the door and up the stairs.

ROCKWELL WARE PACED the richly appointed rug of his brother's drawing room, his boots barely making a sound because of the thick yarn. The flickering light of the fireplace created shadows that danced along the walls. His mind was a tempest of thoughts, each one leading back to Farah.

He paused, listening to the muffled sounds of the household settling down for the night. Farah was just upstairs, perhaps even lying awake, their recent escapade in Ireland undoubtedly occupying her thoughts as much as his. He could see her in his mind's eye—her delicate features framed by fair curls, her eyes alight with mischief and something more, something that called to him with an irresistible force.

He took a step toward the door, his resolve hardening. He had to see her, to speak with her, to reassure her that everything would be all right despite the scandal they had narrowly avoided.

Just as his hand reached for the doorknob, a hand landed heavily on his shoulder. Wolf. The Marquess of Wolfarth was a formidable presence, tall and broad shouldered, his expression as stern as ever. Rockwell's hand fell back to his side.

"Where do you think you're going?" Wolf's voice was low, but it carried an unmistakable authority.

"Upstairs," Rockwell replied, trying to keep his tone casual. "I need to talk to Farah."

Wolf's eyes narrowed. "No, you don't. You have both clarified that a marriage is not your preference. Continuing behavior that is as familiar as it is scandalous will cause just that—scandal. Isn't that what you are trying to avoid? Tiffany and I didn't partake in your lies to fool society, only to be undone at the last hurdle. Blackstone would never forgive me."

Rockwell bristled at his brother's words. "We avoided the scandal, didn't we? No one knows we were together in Ireland."

Wolf stepped closer, his expression hardening. "And you want to risk it all now by sneaking into her room in the dead of night? You need to keep your distance, Rockwell. For her sake and yours. Unless you wish to marry the chit."

Rockwell clenched his fists, frustration bubbling up inside him. Deep inside, he understood he had a wonderful brother, but the pressure of being the spare and making a life of his own, proving he was just as good as his older brother, meant Wolf's judgment over something that wasn't his fault was a kick in the guts. "I can't just leave her alone, Wolf. She needs to know she's not alone in this."

Wolf's gaze softened slightly, but his tone remained firm. "She's not alone. She's under our roof, and we're going to do everything in our power to protect her reputation. But you need to stay away from her, at least for now."

Wolf was taking charge once again, as was his right. This was his house. He was the head of the family. Rockwell's shoulders sagged, the fight draining out of him. He knew his brother was right, but that didn't make it any easier to accept. He looked toward the staircase, the urge to run up those steps and see Farah nearly overwhelming.

"Just for the next few weeks," Wolf said, his voice gentler now. "Stay away. We'll handle this, but we need to be smart about it. I think it best you return to your bachelor quarters and you're not seen to be staying under this roof while Farah is here. She'll likely go home tomorrow."

Rockwell nodded reluctantly, stepping back from the door. "Please let her know that I'm here if she needs me."

Wolf gave him a brief, approving nod before turning and leaving the room, his footsteps echoing down the hall.

Rockwell stood there for a moment, staring at the closed door, his heart heavy with longing and frustration. He would respect his brother's wishes. What irked him was why it was so important for him to see her, talk to her. He didn't want her as his wife. But he couldn't ignore the part of him that couldn't stay away from Farah. She had become a part of him, and he wondered if he could let her go.

CHAPTER FIFTEEN

THE FOLLOWING MORNING, after some semblance of sleep, Farah sat in the sunlit parlor, her hands tightly clasped in her lap. The delicate China teacup in front of her remained untouched. Across from her, Ashley, poised and elegant, studied her with a mixture of curiosity and concern.

Farah took a deep breath, steeling herself. She knew she had to be honest with Ashley, despite the fear that twisted her insides. "I need to talk to you about something important," she began, her voice wavering slightly. "You may be the only person who will understand."

Ashley raised an eyebrow, her curiosity piqued. "Understand what?"

"Don't blame him for any of this. Should the scandal leak, it wasn't Rockwell's fault." Farah hesitated, her heart pounding. "But whatever happens I… I can't marry him. I don't want to marry him."

Ashley leaned back in her chair, her expression unreadable. "May I ask why? It's clear that Rockwell cares for you. And I'm sure you feel something for him as well. It would be an excellent match. One even your stuffy brother would approve of."

Farah swallowed hard, her mind racing. How could she explain the myriad fears that plagued her? "It's not that I don't care for him," she said slowly. "But… I've spent my entire life being the timid mouse, doing everything my family and society expected of me. Marrying Rockwell because we have to… No.

For once, I want to choose the path of my life."

"What if Rockwell is your path?" Ashley listened intently, her gaze unwavering. "What is it you're really afraid of, Farah?"

Farah's eyes filled with unshed tears. "I'm afraid of losing myself, Ashley. Of being trapped in a life where I have no control, no say in my future. I've been living my life for my brother as a penance, thinking my ten-year-old behavior killed my parents. Marrying Rockwell would mean trading one prison for another, even if it's gilded. He would sail off around the world and I would sit at home being the demure wife. I would be alone. I feel as if I've been alone my whole life. I've never had a sister; our sisterhood is the closest I've had to being a part of something. I'm an afterthought for my brother, who just wants to see me married off. I'd rather face a scandal and take my chances than live a life that's not truly mine."

Ashley sighed softly, her expression softening. "I understand. More than you might think."

Farah looked up, surprised. "You do?"

Ashley nodded. "You know about my scandal, don't you?"

Farah bit her lip, nodding. "Yes, but not the full story."

Ashley took a deep breath, her eyes distant as she recounted her past. "I tried to help a friend who fell for a totally unsuitable man. But my help backfired in the most horrendous way and I… Needless to say, I was ruined, through no fault of my own. The scandal nearly destroyed my brothers. As you know, I lost my standing in society, and my family was shamed."

Farah's heart ached for her friend. "I'm so sorry, Ashley. That must have been terrible. But you are so strong. You look society's scorn in the face and don't cower."

"Because I did no wrong. But I'm judged, anyway. And it still hurts," Ashley admitted. "But it taught me something important. It taught me that living authentically, being true to oneself, comes at a price. Sometimes, that price is steep. Only you can decide if it's a price worth paying. With experience and age, I understand I would do it all again. Is loving Rockwell worth a risk? Or will you be happier alone? Rockwell may settle down at some point."

"I have feelings for him, but we want different things out of life, out of a marriage and family." Farah looked into Ashley's eyes, seeing the strength and wisdom there. "Do you regret what you did?"

Ashley shook her head. "No. My actions saved my friend. Men place such value on honor. Women do too, but we are then scorned for it. I learned who I truly am, and I live on my own terms. It's difficult, and it's often lonely, but it's honest. When, or if, I decide to marry, it will be to a man worthy of such love and he will love me back, regardless of any scandal."

Farah felt a weight lift from her shoulders. Ashley's words gave her the courage she needed. "Thank you, Ashley. Your story means more to me than you know."

Ashley reached across the table, taking Farah's hands in hers. "Whatever you decide, know that you have a friend in me. And if facing a scandal is what it takes to live the life you want, then face it with your head held high. You're stronger than you think. You can stand up to Blackstone. Under his gruff exterior, I believe the man is as soft as wool."

Farah squeezed Ashley's hands, a new determination filling her heart. She knew the road ahead would be fraught with challenges, but she was ready to face them. For the first time, she felt a glimmer of hope that she could determine her future, no matter the cost. And as soon as they returned from their visit to speak with Courtney, she'd send for Lord Franklin and give him her answer.

The sound of hurried footsteps and the light laughter of a child interrupted the drawing room's warmth. Farah and Ashley looked up just as the door opened to reveal a small, vibrant girl with curly black-as-coal hair and bright blue eyes, clutching a stuffed rabbit. Beside her stood a serene woman with a gentle smile, holding the child's hand.

"Good morning," the woman said shyly. "I hope we're not interrupting."

Farah smiled, her tension easing at the sight of the newcomers. "Not at all, Caitria. Come in. Ashley, this is Caitria."

Ashley rose gracefully from her seat, her eyes softening as she looked at the child. "It's a pleasure to meet you both. And who might you be, young lady?" she asked with a kind smile.

Ava-Marie looked up at her aunt for reassurance before answering shyly. "I'm Ava-Marie. Caitria is my second cousin."

Ashley knelt down to the child's level, her smile widening. "Hello, Ava-Marie. I'm Ashley. It's lovely to meet you. You look just like your father."

Before Ava-Marie could respond, the door opened again, and Ivy entered the room. "I hope I'm not too late for tea," she said, her eyes lighting up when she saw the little girl. "I've been longing to meet you. Your auntie Lauren is my best friend."

Ava-Marie's face brightened as she ran to Farah, who scooped her up into a warm hug. "Who is Aunt Lauren?" she exclaimed, her earlier shyness forgotten.

Farah bit her lip. Ivy had put her foot in her mouth. As Ivy settled into a chair with Ava-Marie on her lap, the child looked around the room, her expression turning curious. "Where's my daid?" she asked, her pronunciation of "dad" bringing a smile to everyone's face.

Caitria exchanged a glance with Farah before answering gently. "Your father is out meeting your grandfather and your other aunties, sweetie."

Ava-Marie's brow furrowed in confusion. "I have a grandfather and other aunties? Why couldn't I go to meet them too?"

Ashley leaned forward, her voice soothing. "Your papa needed to talk to them about some important grown-up things, Ava-Marie. Sometimes grown-ups have to do things that aren't very fun for little ones."

Ava-Marie pouted, her lower lip trembling slightly. "But I wanted to go, too."

Farah hugged her tighter, brushing a kiss against her forehead. "I know, darling. But these ladies wanted to meet you too."

The little girl considered this for a moment, then nodded slowly. She said to Ivy, "I like your house and my bed is so comfortable. My room has a rocking horse in it too. Can I stay here? With Caitria and Daid and Farah?"

"Your daid has a house just like this up the street. You'll be moving there with him and Caitria."

"Will my room have a rocking horse too?"

"I'm sure that can be arranged," Farah laughed. If only she could brush off the changes in her life as easily as an innocent child.

"Will you be living with us?" the child asked Farah. "My Daid likes you, I can tell."

Silence settled on the room and three pairs of womanly eyes turned her way. "No. I live with my brother and must return home. Besides, your daid and I are just friends."

Ava-Marie seemed to accept this, but Farah noted the concern on Ivy's face. All of them were likely thinking about Courtney, and what Lucien's return would mean to her. Did Ivy think she'd made a move on Lucien? How could she think that? Courtney was her friend, too.

Ivy addressed Caitria. "Will you and Ava-Marie be all right here while we pay a visit to Lady Courtney? There are plenty of toys in the nursery, and the garden is extensive. She might wish to play outside after being in a carriage for so long."

"Of course. A picnic lunch in the garden might be nice."

Farah watched the exchange with a soft smile, grateful for the distraction Ava-Marie provided. It was a reminder of the simpler joys in life, even amid the complexities and fears she faced. She caught Ashley's eye and saw a flicker of understanding there, a silent acknowledgment of the shared burdens and the strength found in family and friends.

"While we wait for Lady Tiffany, how about we have some tea and cakes?" Ashley suggested, answering for the little girl who was facing such an upheaval in her life. "I know there's a delicious lemon cake in the kitchen, and it's just waiting for us to enjoy it."

Ava-Marie's eyes lit up at the mention of cake. "Yes, please!"

As they settled into a more relaxed atmosphere, the tension of the earlier conversation ebbed away. Farah concentrated on entertaining Ava-Marie so that Caitria could talk with Ashley and Ivy. To Farah's relief, the three ladies seemed to be on the road to becoming firm friends.

Halfway through Ava-Marie's second piece of cake, Tiffany arrived with gloves and hat on, ready for them to depart. Farah could see the concern etched on her friend's face. Their visit to Courtney was going to be difficult.

As they entered the carriage, Ashley turned to her and asked, "What went on between you and Lucien to make him interested in you?"

She would not feel guilty about this. It wasn't her fault. "He learned I did not wish to marry Rockwell, even if I faced a scandal. He also knew I was the daughter of a duke and had a large dowry. He decided I might be the answer to his problems. I had accepted his daughter and I'm the only woman of quality he knows whom he can be himself with. He is not in love with me or anything like that. I'm merely convenient."

"Convenient? Oh, goodness, did he ask you to marry him?" Ivy's face went pale as Farah remained silent.

Ashley nodded. "I can see how it makes sense to him."

"There is no need to tell Courtney anything about his offer of marriage. He didn't even know at that point about Courtney. He knows about her now though, because Rockwell told him."

"Rockwell? That's interesting. I wonder why he felt the need to reveal Lucien's engagement to Courtney?" Farah tried to ignore Tiffany's knowing smile. Rockwell might have feelings for her, but it wasn't enough. It wasn't love.

It was only a few minutes' ride to Lady Courtney's house. As the ladies gathered outside the building, none of them were looking forward to this conversation. It should be a happy visit sharing good news, but Lucien's lost memory changed everything.

The ladies were shown to the drawing room while they waited for Courtney. Everyone fell silent as Courtney entered, her eyes quickly scanning their solemn faces. Farah's heart ached, knowing the news they were about to deliver would at first answer her prayers, but then just might shatter her friend's world.

"What's happened?" Courtney asked, her voice trembling slightly. "You're all looking at me as if someone has died."

Farah stepped forward, taking Courtney's hands in hers. "Courtney, my dear friend, please sit down. We have some rather shocking news to share with you."

As Courtney sank into the nearest chair, Farah could see the fear building in her eyes. Tiffany moved to sit beside her, while Ivy and Ashley hovered nearby, their faces etched with concern.

Farah took a deep breath, steeling herself. "Courtney, it's about Lucien. He's... he's alive."

The color drained from Courtney's face. For a moment, she sat perfectly still, as if frozen in time. Then a small, choked sob escaped her lips. "Oh, that's...that's... Alive? But...how? Where? I don't understand." But her mouth couldn't smile any wider. "I knew if I waited..."

Tiffany wrapped an arm around Courtney's shoulders as Farah continued, her voice soft. "Rockwell found him in Ireland. He's been living there for the past five years, but Courtney, there's more you need to know."

She watched her smile die. "He's been living there for five years?" Courtney had quickly worked out that if he were alive, he'd left her and everyone he supposedly loved. Courtney's eyes, brimming with tears, met Farah's. "Why didn't he come home?"

Farah swallowed hard, feeling the weight of her next words. "Lucien suffered a head injury during the rebellion. He...he has no memory of his life before waking up in Ireland. He doesn't remember any of us, or…or you."

A heart-wrenching cry tore from Courtney's throat. She crumpled forward, her body shaking with sobs. Tiffany held her tightly, tears streaming down her own face.

"Who found him? How did this happen?" Courtney asked through sobs.

"When Rockwell went to Ireland to retrieve my money, he thought he saw Lucien. So a week ago, he sailed back to Ireland and found him. They arrived home last night. Lucien's meeting his family right now. It's all overwhelming for him. We're all strangers to him," Tiffany ended softly.

"It's not fair," Courtney wailed between gasps. "All these years, I've mourned him, loved him, waited for him. And now he's back, but he doesn't even know who I am?"

Ashley knelt before Courtney, taking her hands. "We're here for you, Courtney. We'll help you through this, whatever you decide to do."

"Do?" Courtney rose and began to pace. "The timing couldn't be worse. Just as I'd started to let someone else in… Is he expecting me to honor our engagement? I think it might be too late. What can I do? The man doesn't know who I am. It's not fair…"

Ivy added softly, "He may not remember, but he's still Lucien. The man you fell in love with is still in there somewhere."

Farah felt tears prick her own eyes as she watched her dear friend's world crumble and reshape itself in a matter of moments. The joy of Lucien's return warred with the pain of his lost memories, and she could see that battle raging in Courtney's eyes.

"What do I do now?" Courtney whispered, looking up at them with a vulnerability that broke Farah's heart. "How do I face him? How do I start over with a man who doesn't even know me? Do I want to start over? I've just put it all behind me and finally managed to move on."

"Perhaps you'll know when you meet him?" Ivy said softly.

"You will know if he's the man you want to fight for or if you should walk away. But at least you have a second chance to find what you've lost. How many women can say that?"

Courtney wiped the tears from her face with the handkerchief Tiffany gave her. "He deserves more than my tears. I will, of course, see him and take one day at a time!"

Farah bit her lip. "There is one more bit of information you must know." The other ladies looked away. They couldn't look at Courtney. "He has a daughter, Ava-Marie. She's three years old. His—wife—is dead. But her cousin Caitria has looked after the child for most of her life. She is here, too."

Courtney sat still for one moment and then burst into tears again, and they gathered around her, offering what comfort they could.

CHAPTER SIXTEEN

T HE DRAWING ROOM was abuzz with excitement and whispers as the sisterhood gathered at Valora's home the next day. The only person missing was Lauren, who didn't wish to leave her returned-from-the-dead brother's side.

The group of ladies, led by the ever-poised Tiffany, sat in a circle, their expressions ranging from curiosity to concern. Farah took her seat, noting how this was the first time they were all together since her foray to Ireland and Lucien's unexpected return.

Tiffany began the meeting with the usual formalities, but it was clear everyone wasn't thinking of shares or their wager with the men. They were too eager to discuss the latest developments regarding the man who had returned from the dead, as well as Courtney, and her predicament with Lucien.

"Have you talked with him yet?" Ivy said softly, breaking the tension. "What will you do now that Lucien is back?"

All eyes turned to Courtney, whose usually vibrant demeanor was now shadowed with uncertainty. She sighed, her fingers nervously twisting a handkerchief in her lap. "He's calling on me this afternoon," she admitted. "I thought I had lost him forever, and I'd finally accepted that. In fact, oh, never mind… But now he's back…it's like a dream. A dream that I don't know the ending of. Everything has changed. He doesn't remember me. Is he even the same man I remember? How am I supposed to deal with that? Where do I start?"

The room fell silent, the weight of her words settling over them. She watched Courtney closely, empathizing with the turmoil her friend was experiencing.

"He is a man in need of a wealthy wife. You would seem the logical choice given your previous relationship. Is that something you'd consider?" Tiffany said.

Courtney nodded at her friend's words. "Part of me wants to remind him of everything we had, to make him remember our love. But from what I have heard, he will never remember. He didn't know Rockwell, and they were best friends since childhood. Can I endure watching him live a life with no recollection of me? Worse still, what if he no longer finds me attractive? What if the attraction we felt for each other is no longer there?"

"It's a difficult situation. His father will want him to marry quickly because of their financial situation. Lucien may not have time to find a love match. He might wish to honor your contract. Have you thought of that?" Tiffany acknowledged.

Valora snorted. "He would be stupid to not consider you, because he knows he loved you once before. What if he wishes to hold you to the contract? Would you cry off?"

"But I'm just a stranger to him, as everyone is. Besides, he married. That nulls our betrothal."

Farah spoke up. "He will consider you because we have all spoken so highly of you. But what about you? He will look like the man you loved," she said with a sigh, "but he's changed. You must also consider what's best for you, Courtney. Can you marry a virtual stranger in the hope he learns to love you again? Don't lose yourself in trying to reclaim the past."

Courtney nodded, but her eyes filled with unshed tears. "I just… I don't know if I can risk my heart with him again. But I still love him so much. But I love who he was… What if I can't love who he is now?"

Farah nodded. "Yes. He's confused and frustrated by his amnesia. I just wish his father wasn't so concerned with money. He needs time to find his way back into this world without having to worry about marriage." She reached out and squeezed Courtney's hand. "We'll be here for you both." Courtney smiled.

The other ladies murmured softly, their expressions a mix of sympathy and encouragement. Courtney wiped a tear from her cheek, a small smile breaking through her sadness. "Thank you. That means more to me than you can imagine."

"What are you going to do?" Ivy asked gently.

Courtney straightened, a new resolve in her eyes. "I'm going to help him. I'll be patient and give him the time he needs to decide what he wants and if we are still suited, but I will think of myself this time. I've waited long enough."

They all knew Lucien had little time. Creditors were at the door.

Tiffany smiled warmly. "That's the spirit, Courtney. Rockwell says he's still the same man underneath his new persona. If that's the case, there's every possibility he will come to love you again."

"And what are you going to do about Lord Franklin?" Valora asked Farah as she poked her in the arm.

"I am politely, but strongly, declining his offer. He is calling on me this afternoon, too. And I now know I don't need to create a scandal to do that. The timid mouse is finally standing up for herself."

"Is Blackstone back from his hunting lodge?" Tiffany pressed.

She shook her head. "Tomorrow or the next day. I'll deal with him too." She wasn't about to tell them she had a plan, should her newfound strength falter under her brother's rule. "I'm trying to think of a way to show my brother that I'm a grown woman capable of making her own decisions. If not for the anonymous wager with the men, I'd show him how much I'd earned. But then he would likely guess who his challengers were."

Tiffany clapped her hands together. "I know. Blackstone and Lucien used to be close. And given Lucien's money situation and the rumor mill surrounding his return, it would be a kindness for the Duke of Blackstone to be seen supporting his return. Why don't you get the Blackstone to hold a welcome home ball for Lucien? You could hold it in four days' time on his return and have it all organized before your brother gets home, proving your capabilities to him."

Courtney excitedly leaned forward. "I'll help you. We could do it together. That should get the *ton* talking."

"There would certainly be no problem in getting society to attend at such short notice. Everyone wants to see the man who came back from the dead," Valora said dryly.

"Don't you think we should ask Lucien first?" The excitement died away at Ashley's words.

"I'm sure Lucien, or at least Lord Danvers, will think it a fine idea. He wants his son to find a wife." Courtney's words were filled with resentment. "And the mothers of young ladies will throw their daughters at him."

Farah wished she could offer some advice to her friend, but nothing came. Farah really did not know what Lucien would do. Would he decide Courtney was for him? Or would she merely be an easy option? Farah wasn't sure what Courtney would do if that were the case. But Courtney had loved him so deeply, many thought she'd never get over his death. That might make her settle, and she deserved more. But then if she still loved him…

The meeting continued with a renewed sense of purpose. While the challenge against the men and their shares was important, the ladies were firmly in the arena on two separate missions. One, to see if Lucien could fall in love with Courtney once more. And two, to help Farah stand up to her brother and thwart Lord Franklin. Farah felt a swell of pride and gratitude for her friends. Never had she felt so lucky to have these women by her side.

THAT AFTERNOON FARAH sat in her drawing room of her home in the Blackstone townhouse, the sparkling sunlight filtering through the lace curtains, casting delicate patterns on the plush carpet. She'd tried to ignore Mrs. Thompson, who refused to let her greet Lord Franklin alone. She clasped her hands tightly in her lap, willing them to stop trembling. The past weeks had been a haze of fabricated ailments and lies, but the time had come to face her unwanted suitor.

There was a clearing of a throat at the open door and Howard, the family butler, announced, "Lord Franklin, my lady," and Lord Franklin stepped in, his tall, thin frame casting a long shadow across the room. His face, usually so composed, was now a mask of concern. He approached her with determined strides, his boots echoing ominously on the wooden floor.

"Lady Farah, my dear. How good it is to see you fully recovered. Recovered enough, in fact, to be hosting a large ball in four days' time. And Blackstone is not yet home."

She motioned him to sit. She hated how he towered over her. At least while sitting, she wouldn't feel intimidated by him. "Would you like some brandy, perhaps? Or tea?" He nodded to indicate tea. She took a deep breath. Might as well get this over with. "I'm well recovered, thank you. Lady Tiffany and Lord Wolfarth have looked after me well."

"So, are you feeling strong enough to discuss our marriage? I was thinking of an October wedding."

"I do not believe I have accepted your proposal, my lord."

He sat back in his chair and gave her a smile that seemed to say, *don't be so foolish, it's a forgone conclusion.* "Come now. Your brother welcomes the match, and I am rather wealthy."

This was going to be painful, and she willed her backbone to stiffen. "You are indeed a fine man. However, I'm not sure we would rub along together at all well. So, I've made my decision. I regretfully must decline your generous offer."

"Lady Farah," he began, his voice filled with anger, "I have waited patiently, endured your endless postponements, but I will not allow you to make a fool of me any longer. Is there another suitor?"

How she wished she could say yes. "No. It's just I am content to wait until I find a match I feel I'm better suited to."

He jumped to his feet. "Better suited to. What nonsense is this? Your brother is quite in agreement as to my suitability. I'm a wealthy earl who would make you a fine husband. I think we should have this conversation after your brother returns."

"My brother's presence would make no difference. My answer would still be no." Farah stood, smoothing her skirts with a nervous hand. She met his gaze, her chin lifting defiantly. "Lord Franklin, I appreciate your patience, but I cannot accept your flattering proposal. My feelings for you do not extend beyond friendship, and that is not enough for me. There is no need to wait for my brother's return. I shall not be persuaded."

"Obviously, your illness has robbed you of your reason." His eyes flashed with rage, and he took a step closer, his voice dropping to a dangerous whisper. "You think you can reject me without consequence? Your brother, the Duke of Blackstone, will hear of this. He will make you marry me."

Farah's heart pounded, but she stood her ground. "My brother may be a duke, but he does not control my heart or my decisions. I refuse to be coerced into a marriage I do not want."

Lord Franklin's jaw tightened, his fists clenching at his sides. "You are making a terrible mistake, Lady Farah. You will regret this. I won't let you walk away so easily."

She took a deep breath, drawing on every ounce of her courage not to step back as he crowded her. "That may be, but I would rather live with my choices than be shackled to a man who resorts to threats. I will not marry you, Lord Franklin. That is my final word."

"How dare you?"

He reached for her just as a loud, deadly voice spoke from the doorway. "Step away from the lady immediately or I shall have something to say about it."

Farah's gaze flew to Rockwell standing in the doorway, his face a mass of fury. She had never been so thankful to see him. "Lord Ware, Lord Franklin was just leaving. Is Howard there to show him out?"

"I'll see him out," was Rockwell's reply.

"There is no need. I can find my way." Lord Franklin swung to face him. "I see how it is. I shall speak with your brother on his return. A second son is not nearly as good a match as an earl. I'm sure he'll agree."

"I'm sure His Grace would prefer a second son of a marquess over a bully. Perhaps we should continue this discussion outside."

"That won't be necessary," Lord Franklin said, sneering at Rockwell. "I'm leaving. For now."

The tension in the room was palpable, a silent battle of wills. Lord Franklin glared at her, his eyes dark with fury and frustration. Finally, with a sharp exhale, he turned on his heel and stormed out of the room, Mrs. Thompson chasing after him. Rockwell closed the door after them.

Farah collapsed into her chair, her composure crumbling as the tears she had been holding back spilled down her cheeks. She had stood her ground, defied him, but at what cost? Only time would tell. For now, she could only hope that her brother would understand her decision and support her in the storm that was surely coming.

"He will not stop, will he?" she whispered, almost to herself. "I do not know why he's so obsessed with a marriage to me. Can it simply be that I'm a duke's sister?"

Rockwell crouched before her. "He's a man who usually gets what he wants. He desires a duke's sister as his wife to elevate his position within society. There are few daughters of dukes looking to marry and no father who would consider Franklin. The man has a mean temper. I don't understand what Blackstone is thinking."

Farah knew. Farah's brother was so worried about the timid mouse being led into a scandal that he thought to save her. He just didn't understand her. Mainly because he'd never taken the time to get to know a sister seven years younger. He'd been seventeen when their parents died, and sick too. When he recovered, he was lost in learning to become the man of the house and she was too young to be of any help to him.

"He thinks this is protecting me. He thinks Franklin's feelings are genuine. But I won't marry him."

"That's my girl. No more timid mouse. Show Blackstone the woman you've revealed to me over the past weeks. Make him see you, then he'll understand."

Rockwell was right. She wiped her eyes. "I will not shed another tear over that man, and I swear I'll run away before I marry a man like him. Can you imagine sharing myself..." She did not hide her shudder, and she noted Rockwell's lips firm. "I could use a sherry right now."

Rockwell walked over to the sideboard and poured them both a drink. Once he sat down, she looked at him quizzically. "Has something happened?" Why else would he call?

Rockwell settled into the chair across from Farah, his expression grave. "I'm afraid I have some concerning news about Lucien," he began, his voice low. "His fascination with you seems to have grown, and I fear it may lead to trouble."

Farah's brow furrowed. "What do you mean? Surely, he understands that I have no interest in him romantically."

He sighed, running a hand through his hair. "I'm uncertain he does. He's been asking questions about you, about your relationship with your brother. I'm worried he might..." He trailed off, seemingly reluctant to voice his concerns.

"He might what?" she pressed, leaning forward.

"He might reveal the truth about our journey to Ireland," Rockwell said quietly. "He seems to think that if a scandal breaks out, you will be forced to marry. And he believes you would choose him."

Farah gasped, her hand flying to her mouth. "But that's absurd! I would never... And what about Courtney? Surely he wouldn't hurt her like that?"

His expression darkened. "I'm not sure he fully understands the ramifications of his actions. He doesn't remember Courtney, doesn't feel the connection they once shared. In his mind, you're the woman who's shown him kindness and understanding since his return."

She stood abruptly, pacing the room. The tension between them was palpable, crackling in the air like electricity before a storm. "This is a disaster," she muttered. "If word gets out about our journey, we'll both be ruined. My brother will insist on a marriage, and I'll lose any chance of finding a love match."

Rockwell watched her, his eyes following her movements. The air seemed to thicken with unspoken emotions, desires they both tried desperately to ignore. "We won't let that happen," he said firmly. "I'll speak to Lucien, make him understand the consequences of his actions."

"And what of Courtney? How will she react if she learns of Lucien's infatuation?" Farah turned to face him, her eyes shimmering with unshed tears. "She's already heartbroken that he doesn't remember her."

He stood, closing the distance between them. She longed for him to take her in his arms, to comfort her, but he held himself back. "There's another possibility we need to consider," he said softly. "Courtney might see this as an opportunity, too."

Farah's eyes widened. "What do you mean?"

"If word of our journey gets out, there will be pressure for us to marry," Rockwell explained. "Courtney might see that as a way to remove you as a potential rival for Lucien's affections."

Her heart raced at the implication. "She'd never do that. No. I won't believe that of her." The idea of marrying Rockwell sent a thrill through her she tried desperately to suppress. "But you don't want to marry," she whispered. "Your travels, your adventures—they mean everything to you."

Rockwell's gaze softened as he looked at her. "Sometimes life doesn't let us follow the path in life we would choose. But we only have to face this issue if and when it happens." The words hung between them, heavy with meaning. "I mean to do everything in my power to persuade Lucien it's not in his best interests to pursue a match with you. What I'm asking is that you do the same."

Her eyes flashed to his. Was that jealousy she heard? "Who are you trying to protect—me or Courtney, or is it yourself? This possessiveness you are showing can't possibly be simply about desire?" *Can it?* she asked herself. She held her breath while waiting for his answer.

He simply stood looking at her as if she were all he really wanted. But she knew that wasn't true.

The air between them seemed to crackle with unspoken emotions. Farah stood, drawn to him despite her best efforts to resist. "Rockwell," she began, her voice trembling, "I won't ask you to give up your dreams for me. Your travels, your adventures—they're part of who you are. That decision has to be made by you freely. But I won't marry a man who will be away from home more than he will be there."

Rockwell took a step closer, close enough that she could feel the warmth radiating from his body. "And what if my dreams have changed?" he asked, his voice low and intense.

Farah's heart raced. She wanted nothing more than to throw herself into his arms, to forget about Lucien and Courtney and the impending scandal. But she held herself back. "Have they?" she asked, searching his eyes. "Or are you just saying that because you see a rival for my affections?"

Rockwell reached out, cupping her face in his hand. She leaned into his touch, unable to help herself. "Farah," he said, his voice rough with emotion, "you know if I thought I could make you happy, I'd suggest marriage immediately."

Farah felt tears prick her eyes. "But your wanderlust—you said it was part of who you are. I don't want you to resent me for tying you down."

Rockwell's thumb brushed her cheek, wiping away a tear that

had escaped. "I could never resent you," he said softly. "Yes, I love to travel, to explore. But the selfish part of me still wants you. And you're right. I hate the idea of you being with any other man. And that's not fair—to either of us."

"I deserve a man who loves me above all else. Like Wolf loves Tiffany," she whispered. Farah felt herself wavering, torn between the desire to give in to her feelings and the fear of getting hurt. "When you can give all of yourself to me, then I would consider marrying you. Not before."

"You're forgetting one thing," he whispered as pulled her tight into his embrace. "You may have no choice. You might have to marry me."

She closed her eyes and lay her head on his chest, listening to his strong heartbeat. Oh, she had a choice. He didn't know that she was financially secure. She didn't need her brother's money or his protection. Her adventure in Ireland had awakened the timid mouse. She'd even had the nerve to invite Mrs. Ahearn, a woman who'd been Rockwell's mistress, to dinner while pretending to be his sister. She'd given in to passion with Rockwell and to hell with the consequences. She'd turned into a lioness who would fight for every piece of the life she wanted.

She sighed and said, "Then best we ensure Lucien and Courtney find each other again and don't destroy us in the process."

She gazed up at him. She drew in a sharp breath and stared at his sensual, inviting mouth. As if he could feel the sudden flare of awareness in her eyes, a low groan issued from deep in his chest and suddenly, Rockwell's lips crashed onto hers. The possessiveness of the kiss almost destroyed her will to keep him away. Desire did not equal love. Could she make him love her?

His tongue swept into her mouth like a conquering hero, and she reveled in the taste of him. She'd missed him these past few days. Missed this connection that they undeniably had. She encouraged his ravishing and loved when his hand sought her breasts and pushed her gown down until they sprang free.

This time, it was her that moaned as his mouth left her lips to suckle one turgid nipple. Her head fell back, and he bent her over his arm to gain better access to her breasts. His thigh slipped between her legs and he encouraged her to ride him. Soon she was panting with need, her climax so close…

Thankfully, Rockwell still had his head about him and heard the commotion below.

He drew back immediately and helped right her gown while she ran her hands over her hair. They barely had time to take a few calming breaths when the door crashed open and her brother stood in the doorway.

He saw Rockwell immediately…and the fact that they were unchaperoned. "What the hell is going on here?"

CHAPTER SEVENTEEN

ROCKWELL KEPT HIS cool while Farah unfortunately looked as guilty as sin. Her flushed face and the wisps of hair escaping in little tendrils sent a clear message that her brother was not slow in picking up on. "Blackstone, you're home. I was told not to expect you so soon," she said.

The duke stalked further into the room. His eyes bore into Rockwell's, his fists clenched at his sides. "I repeat. Why are you here with my sister—alone?"

"I'm here at Lady Farah's request. Since I found Lucien in Ireland, she wanted my opinion on how to ensure I helped her with Lucien at the ball she's hosting in two days. What to expect from him and how best to protect him from the savages of the *ton*, considering society knows he needs to marry, and he's a widower with a young child. As you can imagine, he's not too keen on stepping back into society, so Lady Farah sought my advice on how to announce him."

That seemed to take the immediate wind out of Blackstone's sails. "So, it's true. You found him in Ireland. And he has amnesia?" The duke walked over and pressed a kiss to Farah's cheek, ignoring Rockwell. "You should have waited for my return before volunteering to organize such a momentous ball."

"I'm quite capable of organizing a ball, Blackstone. In fact, we've already made all the arrangements for the event. Lady Tiffany, Lady Courtney, and Lady Lauren have helped."

His head turned away from where he was pouring himself a

drink to gaze at her in surprise. It wasn't often she answered back to her brother. "Perhaps we could relieve some of Lord Furoe's pressure by using the ball to announce your engagement."

"That won't be happening. I have already declined Lord Franklin's offer."

Rockwell cleared his throat. "Do you mind if I pour myself a drink? I believe Lady Farah just needs to go over a few more details with me—"

"I think it's time you left. My sister and I have things to discuss. I'm quite capable of advising her as to anything around Lord Furoe. How is he, by the way?"

Farah stepped forward as if about to speak, when Rockwell shook his head. How would she know how he was? He answered for her. "He is handling his return remarkably well, all things considered. Already he's organized the creditors and been given some relief."

"It's a pity he married the Irish lass or else his engagement with Lady Courtney would still stand."

They looked at each other. How had he heard so quickly?

Obviously, he knew what they were thinking. "I called on Wolf briefly and saw a little girl who was obviously Lucien's child. Wolf told me of the situation. That Lucien had married in Ireland."

Blackstone didn't know the truth, and it was probably a good thing.

Farah cleared her throat this time. "Lady Courtney is meeting with him today. Perhaps something will come from that."

Blackstone nodded. "Now, if you would mind leaving us, Rockwell. I have some business to discuss with my sister."

Rockwell looked at her as if asking should he stay, but she merely gave a slight shake of her head.

"I shall see you tonight at the opera, Lady Farah. I'll be with Lucien and his family." He silently wished her success with her brother. He was proud when he saw her head lift and she squared her shoulders noting the defiant slant of her chin. Blackstone was in for a surprise and a part of him wished he could stay to watch.

As soon as Rockwell took his leave Blackstone sat in his large-backed chair by the fire that looked like a throne and indicated she should sit. Rather than taking her seat on the chaise lounge, she took the other high-back chair opposite him and noted with satisfaction as his eyebrow rose.

"I realize Lord Ware is a friend of this family and his sisters are your acquaintances, but you know better than to be in a closed room with him without a chaperon. I would at least have expected your lady's maid to be with you. You know how rumors start and tarnish reputations."

The lady's maid you have spying on me? Not likely. "I didn't notice it was closed. Lord Franklin must have closed it on his way out when R—Lord Ware arrived. And Lord Ware is a man of honor. He would do nothing to harm me or my reputation."

Blackstone seemed to accept that, as he said no more. "What makes you think you know better than me as to if Lord Franklin is suitable? As your elder brother, I have your best interests at heart."

"Do you? How is it that most other guardians know that Lord Franklin has a mean temper? How is it you seem unaware he merely wants a marriage to elevate his social status and an ornament on his arm? He has no genuine regard for me at all. Is that the type of married life you want for me—your beloved sister? Loneliness and fear?"

"Don't be hysterical. Lord Franklin would treasure you. He knows he'd have to answer to me if he didn't."

She bit her cheek to keep from screaming. "I am not being hysterical. I'm merely trying to have an adult conversation with you. I've reached my age of majority and I will have a say in my future, and brother dear, Lord Franklin is not in it. Do I make myself clear?" She ignored the look of surprise and pressed on despite the anger that edged into his face. "Deep down I know you love me, but you don't know me." He was about to object when she asked, "What are my favorite hobbies? What do I enjoy doing? Do you know what charities I'm patron of?"

She sat staring at a brother who was so different from the youth he'd been before their parents died. As she'd grown older, she hated that she didn't know him as well as she'd like to. He kept everyone at bay. He wore the mantle of ducal responsibility, as if it were the weight of a stone bridge on his shoulders. No time for joy or fun. He had suffered from their parents' early demise as she had.

"I'm responsible for your safety and well-being. Know that I'd not let anything hurt you."

"You're the one hurting me if you think I'd be happy, or safe, in a marriage to Lord Franklin." Her whispered words were not to shame him, but to make him understand.

He looked at the floor. "Why didn't you tell me before that you didn't wish to marry him?"

She sighed and shook her head. "I told you the minute you said he'd approached you about a match, but you wouldn't listen. He is a humorless man, much like yourself, and my life with him would be suffocating."

His head jerked up. "Humorless like me?"

The hurt in his expression made her move to crouch at his feet and take his large hands in hers. "I know Father dying young made you face a life of responsibilities far too soon. I cannot even imagine what you've had to deal with. But you used to laugh and tease me when I was little and I don't think I've seen you laugh since Father's funeral. What joy do you find in life?" When he didn't reply, she added, "What's the point of living if you're not happy? Are you happy? I certainly want to be happy. But Franklin would make my life miserable."

"Happiness? Responsibilities leave little room for happiness. I'm unsure what that feels like." He gave her a wry smile and sat staring at her for a long moment. "You've grown up and I've missed it."

She could let him off with that almost apology, but she wasn't going to because he needed to hear how he'd changed. "You really hurt me when you wouldn't let me clear Mother's things."

"I thought it would upset you too much."

"It upset me more that I could not go through my mother's belongings and remember her. Look at me. Really look at me. I'm stronger than you know. I'm capable of many things. I've organized this very special ball, for one." She rose and straightened her gown.

He, too, rose to his feet. "Perhaps I should go hunting more often. What has occurred while I've been away that has made you suddenly speak up like this? What have you been doing while I've been away?"

Her face heated. She hated lying to him. "I have been a tad unwell, actually. Women's problems again." At his look of concern, she quickly added, "I was fine. Lady Tiffany and Lord Wolfarth took me in, and I stayed with them. I didn't alert you because I didn't want to ruin your hunting excursion. You needed to take some time from your duties. Being unwell, I had the time to think about my life and what I wanted. I want to be happy like Mother was. She loved Father. I quickly realized I'd never love Lord Franklin...or even like him." She hung her head. "I think Mother would be ashamed of how I have not stood up for what I want and how I let you decide everything for me."

"Mother would never have been ashamed of you." His voice lowered. "Of me—perhaps. I have been a bully, haven't I?"

She nodded. "Perhaps we could make some changes in both our lives. We should agree to break the fast together each morning and converse. And we should attend events and social activities together. Become a brother and sister again. I'm not the only one who should look to marry. You need an heir. But most of all, I want you to find a special woman who can help you carry the weight of all your responsibilities. Or perhaps I could help you find a woman suitable to be your duchess."

He moved and drew her in for a hug. "You're right. We both need to find someone we want to share our lives with. If not Franklin, do you have anyone in mind?" She tried not to stiffen in his arms. "Do you have your eye on Rockwell?" His voice held concern once more.

She shook her head. "The wanderer explorer?"

"I can see I shouldn't have worried about you. Yes, he would not be a good choice if you want a loving family man. While I'm sure he'd treat his wife well, he'd not be home. Always off on some adventure."

Deflecting was her only option. "You almost sound like you envy him."

He laughed. "Maybe I do a bit. But I love this country. I love my estates and looking out for our tenants." He paused. "And I love you. I'm sorry if I've been the overbearing big brother. It will not be easy to stop, but I promise I won't force a marriage on you. It's just what happened to Lady Ashley…"

"She was much younger than I am now. Besides, we ladies talk. Ashley's experience has helped all of us. I don't understand why they didn't tell us about these things when we were younger, so we could have been prepared.

"We men think we know best and are protecting you, but I'm seeing the so-called fairer sex has some backbone. You are smarter than we give you credit for."

She inwardly smiled. If only her brother knew. He had no idea that in a few months' time, he was about to be beaten in an investment wager by a bunch of women. She pressed a kiss to his cheek and said, "I must get on and finish some last-minute tasks before the opera tonight. Would you care to attend with me?"

"As much as I'd love that, I've been away so long, the correspondence almost fills my study. Shall we have a late breakfast tomorrow?"

She loved that he'd asked, not commanded. "I'd like that." At the door, she turned to him. "By the way, I'm taking over the running of our household. Mrs. Thompson and I shall work well together. At least that's one burden I can take off you." She sailed out the door before her brother could respond.

CHAPTER EIGHTEEN

T HE ROYAL OPERA House glittered with candlelight, the air thick with anticipation and the heady scent of perfume. In the Wolfarth box, Farah sat rigidly, acutely aware of the tension surrounding her. To her left, Rockwell lounged with deceptive casualness, his knee occasionally brushing against hers. To her right, Ivy sat occasionally talking with Tiffany on her other side. Wolf sat behind them with Lucien and Courtney. Courtney sat like a statue, waiting to be knocked over.

"Can you remember attending the opera?" she heard Wolf ask.

"I'm sorry to disappoint you all, but I don't," Lucien replied. The silence was deafening. Then he gave a loud sigh. "My apologies," he said, then looked at Courtney, who simply smiled at him, but she saw the worry deep in her eyes.

Wolf replied, "No. It's I who should apologize. It was a silly question. But I suppose we all live in hope."

This time, Lucien looked directly at Courtney. "I suggest everyone forgo the idea of a miraculous remembrance. I can't and won't remember."

Farah squeezed Courtney's hand but she merely shook it off. Her friend's opera glasses were trained on a box across the way and she appeared not to be listening to the men.

Ivy tapped her fan on Farah's arm to get her attention, and Farah leaned in to hear her words. "Tiffany's hunch about the Armley shares has paid off. Our investments are booming. I can't

169

wait for the next meeting of the club. I'm sure we will beat the men."

"Valora is hosting the meeting, isn't she? She used to prefer to head to Claire's townhouse to see if she could catch a few minutes with Claire's brother, Fane. I wonder if this means she's given up the dream of taming the rake."

Ivy nodded. "I even saw her flirting with Lord Norton at the ball and look—" Ivy pointed across the theatre to the box across from them. "She's sitting in his box with his mother. Claire's with them." Ivy waved and watched Claire wave back.

"That is interesting. Do you think this is Claire's doing? She's tried to get Valora to understand her brother is not the man Valora thinks he is for a long time. Claire has always opposed Valora's infatuation with Fane."

"Well, he is a rake of the first order," Farah said. "He goes through mistresses like he goes through handkerchiefs. But I'm not sure who Claire is protecting, Valora or Fane." And the two women laughed.

"Valora doesn't need any protection. She always does as she pleases. She's the *ton's* darling, breezing through society like an exotic butterfly, all of her sins forgiven due to her beauty. Perhaps Claire *is* more concerned for Fane. I think that's what makes them a good match, if Fane would only stop and take notice."

Farah laughed in agreement. "Valora will make him take notice. You wait and watch."

"Either way, I can't wait for our next meeting so we can learn what is afoot. Surely Valora is not so cruel as to lead Lord Norton on. He's a nice man, although his mother seems to have him under her tight control." Ivy shook her head. "She's turned down numerous proposals and is getting quite the reputation."

Before Farah could reply, the music began, and soon the ladies were engrossed in the story unfolding before them.

As the opera progressed, the skin at the back of Farah's neck prickled. She glanced behind her to find Lucien sitting ramrod straight, his gaze flickering between the stage and her with unsettling frequency. Worse still, Courtney appeared to notice Lucien's stare.

Rockwell sat up straighter and seemed to sense the tension. "How did Blackstone take your refusal to marry Lord Franklin?" Rockwell's question made her relax.

"We had a pleasant talk. He's accepted that I wish to select my husband and he will help me if I need it."

"That's wonderful. No need for you to create a scandal now. What persuaded him?"

She smiled at him. "Speaking up. It sounds so simple, doesn't it? But I didn't have the confidence before to challenge him. Our trip helped me. You helped me. I guess I grew up."

He pressed his thigh against her leg. "You *have* grown up. Into a beautiful woman."

She looked away. Why did he keep confusing her? But at the moment, she'd accept his attention because Courtney was looking at her and Lucien.

Farah could feel Courtney's eyes boring into the back of her head from the row behind. She resisted the urge to squirm, focusing instead on the opera unfolding before them. Puccini's *Madame Butterfly* had never felt quite so tragic.

As Cio-Cio San's heartbreaking aria filled the air, Farah felt a gentle touch on her shoulder. She turned to look behind her only to find Lucien leaning close, his breath warm against her ear.

"Beautiful, isn't it?" he murmured. "Though not as beautiful as present company."

Farah's cheeks flamed. She was acutely aware of Rockwell stiffening beside her, of Courtney's sharp intake of breath. "Yes, quite," she managed to reply, her voice barely above a whisper.

The rest of the first act passed in a blur of music and mounting tension. When the curtain finally fell for intermission, Farah felt as though she might snap from the strain.

"Farah…" Courtney's voice rang out, overly bright, "would you accompany me to the ladies' retiring room?"

Farah nodded, grateful for the excuse to escape. As she rose, she caught Rockwell's concerned gaze. She gave him a small, reassuring smile before following Courtney out of the box.

The ladies' retiring room was mercifully empty when they arrived. Courtney immediately rounded on Farah, her eyes shimmering with unshed tears.

"What's going on, Farah?" she demanded, her voice trembling. "Is there…is there something between you and Lucien?"

Farah's heart clenched at the pain in her friend's voice. "No, Courtney, I swear it. There's nothing between us."

Courtney's lower lip quivered. "But I've seen the way he looks at you. The way he leaned in to whisper in your ear. He never looks at me that way anymore. He is so reserved and awkward with me. It's as if he feels obligated, and I don't want that for him, or me."

"Oh, Courtney." Farah reached out, taking her friend's hands in hers. "Lucien is…confused. He's latching onto familiarity, that's all. You know I would never…"

"But that's just it"—Courtney interrupted, a tear slipping down her cheek—"I know nothing anymore. The man I loved, the man I mourned for five years, is sitting right there in that box and yet he might as well be a stranger. And now he's looking at my best friend the way he used to look at me."

Farah felt her own eyes welling up. "I'm so sorry, Courtney. I can't imagine how difficult this must be for you."

Courtney pulled away, pacing the small room. "Is he interested in you, Farah? Be honest with me, please. I need to know."

Farah hesitated, torn between honesty and the desire to protect her friend's feelings. "I…I think he might be," she admitted softly. "But Courtney, you must believe me when I say I have no interest in him. My heart belongs to Rockwell."

Courtney stopped pacing, turning to face Farah with red-rimmed eyes. "And what if Lucien decides his heart belongs to you? What am I supposed to do then?"

The raw anguish in Courtney's voice broke something inside Farah. She crossed the room in two quick strides, enveloping her friend in a tight embrace.

"Then we'll face it together," she whispered fiercely. "You're my dearest friend, Courtney. Nothing and no one will ever change that. If Lucien can't see what an amazing woman you are, then he doesn't deserve you. But I'm sure if you give him time, he'll see the woman he fell in love with."

Courtney clung to Farah, her body shaking with silent sobs. "I just want him to remember me," she whispered brokenly. "To remember us. Is that too much to ask?"

She had to lie. It was too much to ask, because Farah doubted Lucien would ever remember. Farah stroked Courtney's hair, her own tears falling freely now. "It's not too much at all," she soothed. It appeared lying came so easily now. "And who knows? Maybe his memories will return. But even if they don't, that doesn't mean you can't build new ones together."

Courtney pulled back slightly, wiping at her eyes. "You really think so?"

Farah nodded, managing a watery smile. "I do. The Lucien I've come to know may not remember his past, but he's still kind and honorable. Give him time, Courtney. Can you imagine what it's like for him? To have all these people around him who say they know him, but he cannot remember. That is why he's become a bit fixated on me. I helped him in his hour of need and he feels safe with me. He doesn't have to pretend. I know his story and I've accepted him and his daughter."

Courtney nodded and dried her eyes. "I'll have patience. But if he and you want to be together..."

"I don't want him like that, Courtney. Be patient. Let him get to know you again. And in the meantime, I'll do everything in my power to discourage any misplaced affections."

Courtney let out a shaky laugh. "What would I do without you, Farah?"

"Let's hope you never have to find out," Farah replied, giving her friend another squeeze. "Now, what do you say we fix our faces and go show those gentlemen what they're missing?"

As they turned to the mirror, repairing the damage done by their tears, Farah caught Courtney's eye in the reflection. "I love you, you know," she said softly. "No man will ever come between us. I promise."

Courtney's smile, though tremulous, was genuine. "I love you, too. Thank you for being my friend and being honest with me."

Arm in arm, they made their way back to the box, their bond stronger than ever despite the emotional storm brewing. As they took their seats, Farah caught Rockwell's questioning glance. She gave him a subtle nod, silently communicating that all was well.

The curtain rose on the second act, the tragic tale of love and loss unfolding on stage. But in the Wolfarth box, Farah thought a very different kind of drama was playing out. How was she to tell a man who was adrift in a world he couldn't remember that she was not for him before he caused irreconcilable damage?

Farah settled back in her seat, acutely aware of Lucien's presence behind her and Courtney's fragile state. What could she do to bring the couple together? She would ask the rest of the women at the next shareholder meeting.

⁂

ROCKWELL HUNG BACK after the opera had finished and detained Lucien with him. He waited until the women were out of earshot, well down the stairs.

"What the hell are you doing?" Rockwell growled as he rounded on his so-called friend. "That was not well done tonight, with Courtney sitting there. You're putting a friendship at risk."

"Finally, a reaction. When are you going to realize that Lady Farah deserves more from you?" Lucien poked him in the chest with his finger. "I may have lost my memory. I may have lived the past five years as an Irish peasant, but I know the rules of society. You took liberties with her in Ireland and seem to think you can walk away when it's obvious the woman holds a tendre for you. Now who's being cruel?"

"So, you're saying your behavior tonight was to make me jealous?" Rockwell scoffed.

"It was, and it worked. You're not angry at me coming between friends. You're angry that I'm showing interest in Farah."

"Well, your plan backfired, because you hurt Courtney. She doesn't deserve that. And who is not being honest with whom? You have feelings for Farah. I can see it."

Lucien hung his head and cursed. "It's not that I have feelings for Farah exactly. It's just that my father has made it clear I should find a wealthy wife and quickly. I like Lady Farah and she is kind and accepting of Ava-Marie. I have little time, and I'm unsure of Courtney. I can't connect with her the way I have with Farah."

Rockwell paced the box, trying to get his jealousy under control because Lucien was right. He was jealous. And obviously selfish. He didn't want to marry her, but he didn't want her marrying anyone else either.

"You need to apologize to Courtney and explain what is going on. You need to be honest with her so she can decide whether she wants you back in her life." He looked at Lucien. "Don't give her false hope. She's been pining for five years. If you think nothing will come of your relationship, set her free."

Lucien nodded. "You're right. I've been putting off this conversation because I didn't want to hurt her, but I'm hurting Courtney more by not being honest. Tell me. Do you think I can ever go back?"

Rockwell thought about the question for a moment. "But it's not really going back because you can't remember her." He paused before asking, "What do you think of Courtney?"

Lucien shrugged. "I feel trapped. Everyone expects me to just resume my life as if nothing happened, but I can't recall how it was. Courtney looks at me with such expectations in her eyes and it kills me I can't be the man she remembers, because I don't know who that man is. It's draining and I...I resent her for it, even though it's not her fault."

"Have you talked to her about how you feel?"

Lucien tossed his head back and laughed. "No. We are chaperoned every minute of our time together and she is so scared I'll shatter if she says the wrong thing."

"Will you? Shatter? You've been through a lot in such a short time."

He slumped into a seat. "Perhaps."

"Do you find her attractive?"

"Courtney?" He nodded. "Yes. She's beautiful. But until you found me, I was in love with Ava. I've thought a lot about what Ava did to me, but I can't find it in me to hate her. I understand her reasons, and I can't simply turn my feelings off."

Rockwell sat down next to him, relieved it wasn't Farah Lucien loved. "What a mess. If Farah would just have let me offer for her…"

"Woo her then. Surely a man like you knows how to seduce a woman?"

"The thought had crossed my mind, but our feelings for each other don't change the fact that we're not suited. I want to explore the world and she wants the happy family at home. I can't give her what she wants."

"Can't or won't?"

"Does it matter?" Rockwell stared at his friend. "I'll only end up hurting her either way."

Lucien stood and rested his hand on Rockwell's shoulder. "Then perhaps you don't love her. Because genuine love isn't selfish. That's why I question Ava's love. If she really loved me, she would have told me the truth. Because you would do everything not to hurt those you truly love. You put their needs before your own. Ava didn't."

"Maybe she died before she got the courage to tell you."

"Perhaps. But I sat with her for two days while she was dying of the infection ravaging her body and not once did she confess what she'd done. It's hard to forgive that."

"Still, I can understand how she might be scared to die with you hating her for what she'd done. I think she couldn't bear that thought."

"I hadn't thought of it like that, but it's likely. She also probably worried about Ava-Marie if I came back to my old life."

Like the ghost of his old friend, Lucien left and walked down the stairs to join the rest of their party.

Rockwell ran a hand through his hair and took a deep breath. Did he love Farah? They'd only known each other in a grown-up sense about a month. Not enough time to fall in love, or was it?

He marveled at how his life had changed in a few short weeks—finding Lucien, almost creating a scandal with a stowaway on his ship, and then the unexpected desire that had flared between Farah, the timid mouse, and himself. But then, he knew the moment he'd seen her in his Hessian boot in his bedchamber that she was all fire and heat under that quiet exterior she showed the world.

He'd wanted her from that moment on and a part of him knew he'd taken advantage of her on their travels. Because he wanted her. And God damn him to hell, he still wanted her.

But what ate him up inside was, did she still want him? What did he offer her?

I want my husband to love me. Those were the only stipulations she'd expressed in a husband to be.

If she loved him as she said, then perhaps she'd be content if he traveled.

As he walked slowly down the stairs, he cursed under his breath at why loving anyone, let alone only one woman, was the hardest thing for a man to do.

CHAPTER NINETEEN

I T HAD BEEN four days since Lord Lucien Cavanaugh, Viscount
Furoe's return to London, became common knowledge, and
tonight she would host the event of the season to welcome him
home. People said that his father, the Earl of Danvers, was so
happy, he immediately stopped drinking and gambling.

Lucien settled in with his father and family and was taking
each day as it came. Society had already started gossiping about
his daughter and his "marriage"—the lie all of them had agreed to
honor to protect Ava-Marie. But all in all the *ton* welcomed him
home as the injured war hero. Wolf and Rockwell rallied around
him, too.

What set the *ton* titillating more was the rumor, or was it a
truth, that Lucien needed a rich wife.

As she sat letting her lady's maid, Theresa, put the finishing
touches to her gown, Farah couldn't worry about her chat with
Courtney at the opera last night. She'd confessed to Courtney
that she loved Rockwell. But she hadn't told Courtney the truth
that Rockwell didn't love her, nor did he wish to marry her.

She pushed all the conflict from her mind. All she wanted to
do was get through this ball and prove to everyone, most of all
her brother, that she wasn't a hopelessly fragile woman.

Half an hour later, Farah stood at the top of the stairs to the
ballroom next to her brother. The receiving line had finished, and
their guest of honor had descended into the ballroom. Now, he
was surrounded by people he did not know, most of them

mothers with marriageable daughters. She sighed and wished she could help Lucien through this ordeal.

Courtney stood by his side, but the tension between them could fill the whole ballroom. Her heart bled for her friend. She turned to her brother and took his proffered arm to descend the stairs. She couldn't believe how well Blackstone had taken her refusal to marry Lord Franklin, but since their talk, he was trying not to be such an overpowering elder brother. It was an uneasy truce, helped by the fact he and society still did not know she went to Ireland with Lord Rockwell.

As she stepped down the stairs, she viewed her success. The grand ballroom of Blackstone House sparkled with candlelight, the soft glow reflecting off crystal chandeliers and polished marble floors. She herself felt quite resplendent in a gown of emerald silk, and as she stepped onto the floor, she ensured she moved gracefully among the guests, playing the perfect hostess alongside her brother, the Duke of Blackstone. To all outward appearances, she was the picture of poise and elegance. Inside, however, she was a bundle of nerves, her stomach tied in knots that would put a sailor to shame. Her brother might judge her and be less accommodating if she failed tonight.

"Smile, sister dear," the duke murmured in her ear. "Stop looking so scared. I'm proud of you. This ball will be the social event of the season."

"Only because everyone is here to see what a dead man looks like."

His family surrounded Lord Furoe and she could see the strain on Lucien's lips from across the ballroom. Rockwell was also by his side, and she could feel his eyes upon her. She couldn't resist glancing his way. The heat and desire flashing in his gaze would ruin everything. It had to stop. She let go of her brother's arm. "I just wish to ensure Lady Courtney is supported."

Her brother's face for once showed emotion—pity. "You are a good friend." Without a backward glance, he turned to talk with the prime minister and forgot all about her.

She made her way toward where Rockwell stood, his eyes tracing her every step. She squeezed Courtney's hand when she reached her friend's side, and Courtney gave her a grateful smile. "Get a servant to come and fetch me if you need a break from your guard duty," she whispered to Courtney. "How is he doing?"

Courtney leaned her head sideways and whispered, "His father and sister are doing most of the talking. Lucien is—that is, he's—it's almost as if he's detached from what is going on around him. But he squeezes my arm now and then."

"And how are you doing?" She watched Courtney fight back tears.

She glanced briefly at Lucien, and her face softened. "I'm fine." But her voice wavered. "He's trying. We will try together, and if it's not to be, then… At least I know he's alive."

Before she could reply, Farah's skin prickled with awareness. Rockwell was beside her.

She turned to face him and tried to maintain her composure and not let the world see how much his smile made her knees give out. "Good evening, Lord Ware. Our thanks for the safe return of Lord Furoe." When he stepped nearer, she stepped back.

But he just kept coming until she noted they were in the shadows. She stiffened as he leaned towards her and his arm reached behind them and unlatched the door that was there, almost pushing her into the servants' corridor and closing society out when the door closed behind him.

She was about to remonstrate with him when he pulled her against his hard, lean body and his mouth took hers in a kiss meant to stir her senses—and it did. Her body clung to his, desire flared, heating her blood and she remembered the taste of him with a hunger that burned in her soul.

But he didn't want to marry her…

She put her hands on his chest and pushed him away. Anger replaced the desire. "You can't keep doing this. The way you were looking at me in that ballroom… If not for all eyes on Lucien, someone would pick up on your interest. And everything we've done to keep the scandal at bay would be for nothing."

He ran a hand through his hair as he leaned back against the wall. "You're right. I'm sorry. It's just… It's just that I miss you, and you look so beautiful tonight. Almost regal. Your confidence is dazzling."

She swallowed her anger at his honesty. "You can't miss me. You can't want me. Do you want to create a scandal? I don't need one. Blackstone has agreed to allow me to select my own husband."

He stepped back toward her. "That's good." He looked as if he wanted to say more, but he didn't.

She sighed and placed a hand on his chest. "You need to leave me be. You'll be leaving soon, I assume? For Africa?"

He cleared his throat. "I've put that on hold until Lucien no longer needs me." He shrugged. "I brought him home. It's only fair I stay to see it go as smoothly as it can." He took her hand from his chest and raised it to his lips. "Is there a man present tonight who you would consider marrying?"

You, you idiot. "Why is that of interest to you?"

"I might offer you advice on the man. Tell you things you might not know about or see."

"That won't be necessary. Blackstone will do that. Besides, I'd like to marry a man who is in love with me. I hardly think there is a man at the ball who fits that description." She held her breath and hoped for just one second that he'd profess his love for her. And then the seconds passed. "If that's all, then I shall return to the ball. Wait several minutes and then reenter but from the other end of the corridor. I haven't worked this hard to avoid a forced marriage to you, only for you to unravel everything."

She made to move round him, but he grabbed her arm and her heart jumped into her throat when it looked as if he wanted to say something. But he simply stood looking at her with the saddest look in his eyes. She shook her arm free and slipped through the door back into the crowded, heated ballroom and refused to let the tears that were building come.

Rockwell slid down the wall until he hit the floor. *What are you doing?* He hid his face in his hands and cursed. Farah was right. He didn't want to marry her and he definitely was not out to ruin her, so why could he not leave well enough alone?

It was because she made him think of a different way of life. Or was it the visit from Scot Armley yesterday? He and two other newly created mill owners had asked to meet with him. As he was already a shareholder—and Rockwell held quite a large share-holding—they'd approached him with an idea to help them meet the growing demand for Merino textiles. They needed a landowner to start a rapid breeding program to farm the sheep for their wool.

They wanted to know if he'd buy a large estate and begin the breeding program to supply these mills. They didn't know he already had a large estate. He'd bought it over two years ago in Suffolk when he'd had a wonderful investment year and his friend's family was in trouble. He liked the idea of being at the forefront of new farming.

It would also add to his profits by increasing the mill's out-puts. It was a long-term investment and when he saw Farah tonight, the idea of becoming a pioneering sheep breeder held several attractions.

Being at the forefront of a new industry and breeding pro-gram held appeal. But it would mean his travels would be curtailed. But not totally. Maybe just shorter trips.

When he held Farah in his arms, suddenly that didn't seem to be so terrible.

He stood up and turned to walk down the corridor. Rockwell knew he'd better get his head sorted out before he did something stupid like ruin Farah. He needed to decide what he wanted from his life, and soon. Farah shone like a priceless diamond tonight. The timid mouse was all but gone and every man in that ballroom had taken notice. She was beautiful, composed, and the daughter of a duke with a sizable dowry. Blackstone would be fighting her suitors off.

Suddenly, it was imperative for Rockwell to return to the ballroom and protect what was his. He made his way round to the terrace and entered from there so no one could link his disappearance to Farah's. He'd been out for a cheroot. That was all.

He'd only just stepped onto the terrace when the sight before him made the blood run cold in his veins.

"Lord Ware, I wondered if I'd see you here tonight. I thought it most likely, given you were the one who found Lord Lucien and brought him home. I cannot believe it."

"Mrs. Ahearn, what a surprise to see you here in London," he uttered as he bent low over the gloved hand she'd extended.

"May I introduce you to my sister, Lady Hampton? I didn't have time to inform you when I saw you in Dublin that I would be visiting."

Blast he'd forgotten her sister was married to Baron Hampton. He had to warn Farah and Ashley. Mrs. Ahearn could ruin everything. She thought Farah was Ashley and if that was revealed, all would be ruined.

"Lady Hampton, you look as lovely as ever. However, I think the chill of the night, while refreshing, is a little brisk for my liking. Shall we go back inside?"

"You are quite right, Lord Ware. But Fiona thought I looked a tad peaky and the fresh air has helped." She patted her stomach and Rockwell understood. She was with child and the heat in the ballroom was a tad overbearing.

He ushered the ladies back inside and scanned the room. He stayed talking for a polite minute before he really had to find Farah.

Farah plastered on her brightest smile, all the while scanning the room for any sign of disaster. And by disaster, she meant one very specific person: Mrs. Ahearn from Ireland.

When Rockwell had informed her that the spirited Irish widow had arrived with her sister to tonight's ball, Farah had nearly fainted dead away. It was bad enough that she'd had to pretend to be Ashley during their impromptu Irish adventure, but now she had to somehow prevent Mrs. Ahearn from meeting the real Ashley while simultaneously keeping her brother in the dark about the whole sordid affair.

"It's simple," Ivy had assured her as she gathered Ivy and Ashley to her side and told them the disturbing news. "We just need to keep you and Ashley on opposite sides of the ballroom. What could possibly go wrong? If she meets Ashley, we will introduce her as you, and vice versa."

Farah had given her friend a look that could have curdled milk. "Have you met us? We don't look alike and we are in different colored gowns. Plus, I'm the hostess. She's likely to want an introduction." She'd added drily, "Besides, what if she's with someone who knows who we are?"

Now, as she navigated the crowded ballroom, Farah felt like a character in one of those ridiculous farces her brother so enjoyed at the theater. All that was missing was someone losing their trousers.

She spotted Ashley across the room, looking radiant in a gown of pale blue. Their eyes met, and Ashley gave an almost imperceptible nod before turning in the opposite direction. So far, so good.

"Lady Farah!" a familiar voice called out, nearly causing her to jump out of her skin. She turned to find Lord Lucien approaching, a tired smile on his handsome face. "Thank you for holding the ball for me. But I hope you'll not be offended if I beg off early. I know I'm the guest of honor, but it has been rather overwhelming."

Farah felt her cheeks warm as all eyes turned their way. "I

hope Lady Courtney and your family were adequate support? And I'm sorry I haven't been by your side most of the night, but as the hostess…"

"I'll forgive you if you indulge me for a moment." His eyes bored into hers and then lifted to scan the room, noting the attention they were receiving. "I may not remember much, but apparently my feet still know how to dance. Could I beg a dance before I retire? I suspect the crowd is waiting to see me take to the floor." He held out his hand in invitation.

For a moment, Farah was tempted. But then she caught sight of a flash of red hair near the refreshment table—Mrs. Ahearn. "Oh, I'd love to, truly," she said quickly. "However, don't you feel your first dance tonight should be with Lady Courtney?" She gestured towards the far side of the room. "She is more deserving."

Lucien's brow furrowed, but before he could respond, Farah had already darted away, weaving through the crowd like a hunted rabbit. She would not embarrass Courtney like that, and she needed to escape Mrs. Ahearn.

She nearly collided with Rockwell, who steadied her with a hand on her elbow. "Easy there," he murmured, his eyes sparkling with barely suppressed laughter. "One might think you were running from something."

"Or someone," Farah hissed, glancing over her shoulder. "It's not funny. Why are you taking this so casually? Your friend Mrs. Ahearn—Fiona—is here, and she's headed this way!"

Rockwell's eyes widened. "Quick, behind the potted palm!"

Without thinking, Farah allowed him to steer her towards a large decorative plant. It was only when she found herself pressed rather intimately against Rockwell's broad chest, peering out between the fronds, that she realized the absurdity of their position.

"This is ridiculous," she whispered, trying to ignore the warmth of his body against hers. "We can't spend the entire evening hiding behind shrubbery. Can't you think of some way to make her leave? She was your paramour once. Can't you seduce her into leaving?"

"I'd rather seduce you," Rockwell replied, his breath tickling her ear. "I find it rather cozy here. There's a thought though. Fiona's here with her sister, Lady Hampton who is newly with child and feeling unwell. Perhaps I could persuade Lady Hampton to leave early." His hand slipped to her waist and squeezed.

Farah elbowed him sharply in the ribs, eliciting a satisfying grunt. "Focus, please. How could you make her leave early? We need a plan."

Just then, they heard Mrs. Ahearn's distinctive laugh nearby. "Oh, but you must introduce me to your sister Ashley, Lord Wolfarth! I've been simply dying to meet her again."

Farah and Rockwell exchanged panicked glances. "Distraction," Farah mouthed silently.

Rockwell nodded, a mischievous glint in his eye. "I'll guide her to her sister and suggest she looks unwell and to think of the baby." Before Farah could stop him, he'd slipped out from behind the palm and approached Mrs. Ahearn with a flourish.

"My dear Mrs. Ahearn!" he exclaimed, perhaps a touch too loudly. "I wonder if you'd let me introduce you to some friends of mine." As Mrs. Ahearn sputtered in surprise, Farah took the opportunity to escape from her leafy hideout and make her way across the ballroom. She caught sight of Ashley and made a series of frantic hand gestures she hoped conveyed *Danger! Red-haired Irish widow approaching! Retreat!*

Whether Ashley understood the message or simply thought Farah was having some sort of fit was unclear, but she turned and head towards the terrace, which was good enough for now.

Farah breathed a sigh of relief, only to nearly jump out of her skin when a hand touched her shoulder. She whirled around to find her brother, the duke, regarding her with a mixture of amusement and concern.

"Are you quite all right, sister?" he asked, raising an eyebrow. "You seem rather…jumpy this evening."

"Jumpy? Me?" Farah let out a high-pitched laugh that sounded unhinged even to her own ears. "Don't be silly, brother. I'm as calm as a…a very calm thing."

The duke's other eyebrow joined the first. "Indeed. Well, in that case, perhaps you'd like to join me in greeting some of our guests? There's a delightful Irish widow I'd like you to meet, Mrs. Ahearn. She met with Ashley and Rockwell while in Ireland and helped them so she's part of the story I believe."

Farah felt the blood drain from her face. "Oh, I'd love to, truly," she said, frantically searching for an excuse. "But I'm afraid I must… that is there is an issue with the punch. I'll seek you out later."

Before the duke could respond, Farah had darted away, leaving him staring after her in bewilderment.

She made it halfway across the ballroom before disaster struck. In her haste, she failed to notice a rather rotund gentleman backing up from the refreshment table, his attention focused on the plate of canapés. They collided with all the grace of two drunken elephants attempting a waltz.

Farah let out a most unladylike yelp as she stumbled, her arms pinwheeling wildly. She might have maintained her balance had her foot not caught in the hem of her gown. Instead, she fell backwards, arms flailing, directly towards the punch bowl.

Time seemed to slow as Farah saw her life flash before her eyes. She could already imagine the mortification, the scandal, the way the red punch would clash horribly with her emerald gown…

And then, miraculously, she felt strong arms catch her just before impact. She looked up into the concerned face of Lord Lucien, who had apparently materialized out of thin air to save her from a watery and fruity doom.

"Are you all right?" he asked, helping her regain her footing.

Farah nodded, too breathless to speak. She was acutely aware of every eye in the ballroom upon them, and she could practically hear the gossips sharpening their tongues.

"Oh my," a familiar voice rang out. "Is everything all right, dear?"

Farah turned, her heart sinking, to find Mrs. Ahearn approaching, the Duke of Blackstone on her arm. This was it. The moment she'd been dreading all evening. There was nowhere to run, nowhere to hide. She was about to be exposed as a fraud in front of the entire *ton*.

Mrs. Ahearn's eyes lit up with recognition. "Why, Lady Ashley! How wonderful to see you again! I was just telling your brother, Lord Wolfarth, before, how much I enjoyed our time together in Ireland."

The silence that fell over the immediate vicinity was deafening. Farah could practically hear the gears turning in her brother's head as he processed this information. His eyes narrowed dangerously.

"Ireland? Lady Ashley?" he drawled, his gaze burning into Farah. "This is my sister, Lady Farah."

"But that can't be right. Oh…" Mrs. Ahearn's words trailing off as she finally understood.

"How fascinating. I wasn't aware you'd been to Ireland recently, sister dear."

Farah opened her mouth, though what she planned to say, she did not know. Before she could utter a sound, however, Lord Lucien stepped forward, a beaming smile on his face.

"I believe there's been some confusion," he said smoothly. "You see, Mrs. Ahearn, this isn't Lady Ashley at all, but rather her dear friend, Lady Farah. A simple mistake to make, I'm sure, as they look quite similar."

Mrs. Ahearn's brow furrowed in confusion. "But…but I could have sworn…"

"And I'm afraid Lady Farah couldn't possibly have been in Ireland recently," Lucien continued, "as she's been on her sickbed for over two weeks. But she's recovered beautifully to host this event for me—for us. In fact—" He paused for dramatic effect, taking Farah's hand in his. "She's only just accepted my proposal of marriage and we'd hoped to announce it tonight after I'd spoken to His Grace."

The ballroom erupted in a flurry of gasps and excited whispers. Farah stood frozen, her mind reeling as she tried to process what had just happened. She was vaguely aware of her brother's thunderous expression, and of Mrs. Ahearn's bewildered congratulations, and the curious stares from all around.

But mostly, she was aware of Lucien's hand holding hers, warm and steady, as he smiled down at her with a warning to keep quiet.

Well, at least no one lost their trousers, Farah thought.

As if on cue, there was a commotion near the entrance, and Lord Franklin came stumbling in, his face red with drink and his breeches noticeably askew. "I thought it was Lord Ware you're marrying. The chit can't seem to decide who she wants. It certainly wasn't me."

Farah closed her eyes and silently prayed for the floor to open and swallow her whole.

It was going to be a very long night.

The Duke of Blackstone, his face a thundercloud of barely contained fury, grabbed Farah's elbow and began steering her towards a secluded corner of the ballroom. "A word, sister dear," he growled through clenched teeth.

Lucien, still holding Farah's other hand, cleared his throat. "Perhaps we should discuss this privately, Your Grace. After all, we wouldn't want to cause a scene."

Blackstone's glare could have melted steel, but he nodded curtly. "My study. Now."

As they made their way through the crowded ballroom, Farah caught sight of Rockwell's worried face. She gave him a small, reassuring smile, though she felt anything but reassured. This was going to be an absolute disaster.

Once inside the study, the duke rounded on them, his face purple with rage. "Would someone care to explain what in the blazes is going on?" he thundered.

Farah opened her mouth to speak, but Lucien beat her to it. "It's quite simple, Your Grace. I've asked for Lady Farah's hand in marriage, and she has accepted."

The duke's eye twitched. "Is that so? And when, pray tell, did this miraculous courtship occur? Don't take me for a fool. How is it you were in Ireland with Lord Ware?"

"Ah, yes, about that," Farah began, finding her voice at last. "It was all an innocent mistake. A funny story actually... I got locked in Rockwell's trunk and thrown on his ship without his knowledge."

If possible, her brother's face grew even redder. "You did what?"

Farah felt her heart racing. This was it. The moment of truth. She squared her shoulders and lifted her chin defiantly. "I was with Rockwell and we found Lucien together."

The silence that followed was so thick, you could have cut it with a knife. The duke stared at her, his mouth opening and closing like a fish out of water.

"You...what?" he finally sputtered.

"I went to Ireland with Rockwell," Farah repeated, her voice growing stronger. "It was an accident, truly. By the time he realized I was on his ship... But the point is, the adventure helped me. I'm not the weak-willed lady you think I am, brother. I can make my own decisions, including who I will or will not marry."

The duke collapsed into a nearby chair, looking shell-shocked. "But...but what about the scandal? If word gets out..."

"That's where I come in," Lucien interjected smoothly. "By announcing our engagement, we've neatly sidestepped any potential scandal. The *ton* will be far too focused on our upcoming nuptials to worry about any rumors of impropriety. If I say I fell in love with her as soon as she found me in Ireland, the scandal will be embraced."

Farah turned to Lucien, her eyes wide. "But...we're not really engaged," she whispered.

Lucien merely looked at her. "We could be," he murmured

back. "If you'll have me, that is."

"You'll have to marry now. I will not let you be ruined," her brother all but roared.

Farah's head was spinning. This was all happening so fast. Courtney—Oh my God, what must her friend be thinking? And then she did the only thing a woman caught up in a situation like this could do… she gained time by pretending to faint dead away.

CHAPTER TWENTY

ROCKWELL TOOK THE stairs two at a time, his heart hammering against his ribs like a caged beast. *What the hell had just happened?*

He arrived outside Blackstone's study just in time to see Farah's limp form being carried up the stairs, her face as pale as moonlight. "Farah," he called, but Blackstone emerged like a storm cloud from the study and pulled him inside, slamming the door after him.

"I should beat you to a pulp…" But Lucien materialized between them, pulling Blackstone off him.

Rockwell stepped back, his fingers trembling slightly as they smoothed his ruffled clothes. He addressed Lucien. "Is Farah all right?"

Blackstone's roar filled the study. "No, she bloody isn't all right. She's ruined. Or she will be once Mrs. Ahearn talks. I should call you out. Regardless of how she ended up on that ship of yours, you should have come to me and offered for her immediately."

"She wouldn't let me."

The duke scoffed. "Let. Let!" His fist crashed onto the desk, making the crystal decanters jump. "She doesn't understand what her life will be like if she's ruined. You, of all people, should know because of Ashley. How could you not protect her? Your brother must be ashamed of you."

"I gave her my word." Rockwell's voice roughened with

suppressed emotion. "I gave her my word that we would try to return home, and if there was no scandal, I'd respect her choice. *Her choice.* But if word got out, then of course we would have to marry."

That seemed to take the wind out of the duke's anger.

"Well…" Lucien's smooth voice cut through the tension, "you don't have to marry her, anyway. As I've offered for her."

Rockwell swung round to face his—*friend.* "You're taking advantage of the situation. Farah would never consider you if not for the revelation of this scandal."

"You seem rather upset at my offer? For a man who told me, and Farah, you didn't wish to marry, you seem awfully upset at my honorable proposal to save her from ruin."

Lucien's smug smile made Rockwell's fingers itch to rearrange his face. "Has Farah even said yes to you? I doubt it. She doesn't love you and you are her friend's former fiancé. Courtney's heart still beats for you, and Farah would never hurt her. What must Lady Courtney be feeling standing in the ballroom downstairs with all of society watching her abandonment?"

"God damn it." Lucien's face twisted with guilt. "That's a low blow."

Rockwell walked over and stood toe to toe with Lucien. "Just because you don't like the truth, don't get angry with me."

Blackstone agreed with Rockwell, and he rounded on Lucien. "While I thank you for coming to Farah's rescue with your very public offer, Lady Courtney doesn't deserve this treatment from you. She's in the ballroom facing this alone. Please explain yourself to her."

Lucien hung his head and sighed. "I didn't ask for this. It's not my fault I lost my memory."

"But the way you've been behaving towards Courtney since you've been back is your fault."

Lucien didn't refute Rockwell's words. "I'd best sort out my mess." Lucien turned before leaving the room. "My offer stands if Farah needs me."

"She won't need you," Rockwell almost growled.

Once the door closed behind him, Rockwell faced Blackstone. "Do you love Farah?"

Rockwell sunk into the nearest chair and tried to get his emotions under control. "Lucien is not marrying her."

"Well, someone bloody has to." He poured Rockwell and himself a drink. "I won't have my sister ruined. She believes the world is a forgiving place because she thinks Ashley got away relatively unscathed. What she doesn't see is how society and men in particular treat Ashley and why it's unlikely she'll ever find a husband."

"I have feelings for Farah, but even you must see, I wouldn't be a good husband."

Blackstone shrugged. "Throughout life, our priorities change. Look at me. Over the past few years, I've consolidated the estates and investments while trying to find my sister a husband. Once Farah is married, I too will then turn to finding a wife to ensure I provide the next heir. That's my duty."

"I don't need to provide an heir. As a second son, I have no duties." He closed his eyes and let that thought settle over him. "I'm not needed for anything."

"Farah needs you." Blackstone's words sent a jolt through his body. Did she? She'd seemed to manage on her own quite nicely up until the scandal.

"You don't know your sister very well. She can be a force to reckon with. If she doesn't want to marry either of us, she won't. And right now I'm not her favorite person. But she'd never marry Lucien and hurt Courtney."

"Don't be ridiculous. She's ruined and I shall make her—"

"Good luck with that. She didn't marry Franklin, did she?"

Blackstone was suddenly standing and pacing. "She can't just disobey me. She has no money, nowhere to go."

Rockwell inwardly laughed. He'd learned that Farah had plenty of money from the ladies' investing, but he wasn't about to tell Blackstone that. The duke might guess what the ladies were up to and he wanted both Fane and Blackstone to lose to the women. Those men needed to be brought down from their high lofty positions.

Blackstone looked incredulously at him. "What about your reputation? If you walk away, Farah tarnishes you as well. Society would never forgive you."

"Then I'll be free to sail around the globe." Rockwell stood to take his leave. "I'll come back in the morning and I will marry her if she'll have me. But don't be surprised if she tosses me out on my ear." He looked at his friend. "I'm sorry for all of this, but it's really your fault. If you hadn't tried to force her to marry Franklin, she would never have ended up in my trunk and on that ship. It's ironic, really."

"If she won't marry you or Lucien, then it will be Franklin. I'll not see her ruined."

"Good luck with that edict. Just be careful what you wish for. If you push her too hard, you'll lose your sister forever. Is that what you want? I know that I've never regretted standing by Ashley. She's still in my life and safe. How do you think Franklin would treat Farah after this?"

The fire died in Blackstone's eyes. "What a bloody mess. I've made this mess."

"Yes, you have."

Rockwell turned to leave. "Let's work together to try to sort this situation out before all our lives are ruined. I'll see myself out. Best you go back and ensure the worst of the gossip is contained and you end the ball."

The evening's revelations sat heavy in Rockwell's chest as he made his way home. He prayed he could convince Farah to wed. He was right when he said to Blackstone too many people would be hurt if they didn't.

But the thought of how to win her trust back made his head spin. He tapped on the roof of the carriage. "Actually, can you take me to Wolfarth House, please?" Perhaps Wolf might have some words of wisdom.

WOLF WAS ALREADY waiting up for him in the library. "Tiffany's gone to bed, which is just as well, as she's really upset with you."

He plonked himself into a chair by the fire and accepted the drink his brother handed him. "There is a long line. What have I done wrong according to your wife?"

"As soon as you knew Mrs. Ahearn was at the ball, you should have gone to Blackstone and announced your engagement to Farah, instead of trying to hide the fact she was with you in Ireland. Not well done of you."

He hung his head. Wolf was right. He didn't want to face the fact he hadn't acted that honorably.

"I think you're using Farah's reluctance to wed you as an excuse for not having to do your duty." He hesitated before adding, "And I think this reluctance is because you're afraid to marry her because you have feelings for her and this realization has you running scared."

He swallowed back a denial because his brother was right. She'd slipped into his heart with little fanfare. It wasn't like with Charlotte, where with one look, he'd fallen head over heels in love. No, his timid mouse had awoken his desire first and then had put his broken heart back together.

His brother continued. "When I offered a marriage of con-venience to Tiffany, I did not know how important she'd become to me, and how much I would grow to love her. Love isn't anything to be afraid of, if it's the right person. Is Farah the right woman for you?"

"I think she could be." He sighed.

"Then what is stopping you from committing?"

He sat in silence for a moment, his thoughts all jumbled. "I think Father prepared me to be the spare by instilling in me the excitement of travel. He knew what it would be like for me. What was my purpose? What could I do with my life? I fixated on it after he died and thought that was all I could do with my life."

"I sense you might be rethinking that…"

"My trip with Farah has made me question what I want out of my life. I loved being with her. I loved her company, and she is so…desirable. Armley has approached me with an idea to set up a Merino breeding farm to supply their mill and I've also been thinking about crossbreeding with our native sheep. What wonderful things we could develop, maybe even become world leaders? Could we lead the textile revolution? I now realize travel is not all 'the spare' can do."

Wolf smiled. "I'm sure Father didn't think that's all you could do. He merely loved talking about the world and all the wonders that it held. He wouldn't have expected you to spend all your life traveling. Father, of all people, understood the joy of building a family and having children."

"I believe you could be right. Now I only have to convince Farah to marry me and all will be well."

Wolf frowned and twirled his brandy in the glass. "I thought she was in love with you?"

"I think she is, but she doesn't believe I'm in love with her."

"Are you?"

"I don't know. I know I don't want any other man touching her, looking at her, or bloody marrying her. But I fell in love once before." He waved his brother to silence. "It ended badly. But I don't feel the same with Farah. It's different."

"I suspect it's because you've known her all your life and she's our sisters' friend. Your relationship is bound to differ from that of a woman you've never had in your life before. I would suspect your relationship with Farah would be deeper because you are not strangers. Do you want children?"

Did he? He thought about his relationship with his father. He'd like a son to teach and nurture. He could picture a blond boy who looked exactly like Farah. If he had a daughter, he would treat her better than Blackstone treated Farah. He'd ensure she was fully aware of the dangers in this world.

"I believe I do."

"Can you imagine having children with anyone other than Farah?" Wolf's questions pierced through his carefully constructed defenses.

Rockwell closed his eyes, memories washing over him like waves: Farah's sleepy smile in the morning light, her cold feet seeking his warmth at night, her brilliant mind challenging his own, her laugh that could brighten the darkest day. She knew his world as he knew hers. His heart swelled with the realization that had been growing all along—she wasn't just in his life, she was essential to it.

"No," he whispered, the truth finally breaking free. "But is that love?"

"I agree this is all very sudden," Wolf added. "However, whether you love her matters little because you have to marry her. You can't taint the whole family with this scandal and walk away. Ashley is already under a cloud. If you disgrace the Wolfarth name, Ivy will have very few chances of a good marriage. And I can't see Blackstone letting Farah remain unwed."

He took a long swallow of the fiery liquid. "It's funny. I don't feel at all upset that I must marry Farah."

"That speaks volumes. She's a beautiful woman and you'll have a good life with her by your side. Ivy and Ashley will be very pleased to welcome her into the family, as will my wife."

"Then best I work out a way to ensure Farah agrees to marry me. Blackstone will help because he's determined she marries someone and that will only be me."

"That's easy, brother. Simply give her your heart. You know you want to."

THE PREDAWN DARKNESS wrapped around Farah like a conspirator's cloak as she slipped out of the servants' entrance. Trying to get into the Marquess of Lorne's townhouse to reach Courtney without being seen was much harder. If one of Courtney's brothers or her father caught her, her desperate bid for freedom would crumble like a house of cards.

When she'd roused herself from her fainting episode and realized her brother would make her marry either Lucien or Rockwell, she'd done the only thing a lady could do. She'd run. And who better to aid her escape than Courtney? The woman who understood better than anyone how love could turn to ashes in your mouth.

She'd found a pair of trousers and a boy's outfit in Blackstone's old wardrobe, relics of his own youth that now served as her armor against society's demands. The rough wool scratched against her skin, so different from her usual silks, but it was a small price for freedom. The masculine attire made scaling the tree outside Courtney's window possible, though her arms trembled with each reach upward, as she was unused to such exertion.

She pulled herself onto the window ledge and pushed up the sash window. Thankfully, it opened easily, and she tumbled into the room landing in an ungainly heap of borrowed clothes. She put her arms up and cried out, "Don't hit me. It's me, Farah."

"I should hit you over the head with this lamp anyway. Friend indeed. You stood there and let Lucien announce your engagement when it should have been Lord Rockwell."

Farah scrambled to her feet, her borrowed boots scuffing against the fine carpet. "Yes, well. It should be Rockwell, but I'd prefer it to be neither gentleman. That's why I'm here. I need your help."

CHAPTER TWENTY-ONE

ROCKWELL STRAIGHTENED HIS cravat and smoothed down his jacket as he stood before the imposing doors of the Duke of Blackstone's townhouse. The sleepless night clung to him like a shroud. He'd spent a restless night tossing and turning, his mind churning over how to convince Farah to marry him. Should he lay his confused heart bare before her and pray she would see the genuine feeling beneath his clumsy words? Now, in the harsh light of morning, he felt woefully unprepared. But he knew he had to convince her that his feelings were indeed genuine.

Taking a deep breath, he raised the brass knocker and rapped sharply. It wasn't every day a man called to offer his hand in marriage just to avoid a scandal, but then again, nothing about his relationship with Farah had ever been ordinary. Yet he didn't know what her answer would be. After a moment, the door swung open to reveal Blackstone's butler, his expression as impassive as ever.

"Good morning, Lord Ware," the butler intoned.

"Good morning, Howard. So sorry to call so early—"

"His Grace alerted me to the fact you might call early. He's in the drawing room. I'll announce you."

"I know the way, Howard. Perhaps you could let Lady Farah know I'm here." His hopes for a private moment with Farah crumbled like sand upon learning His Grace was awake so early. He'd have to convince him to leave him alone with Farah. A wry smile touched his lips. It wasn't like he could damage her reputation further.

"Of course, my lord."

Rockwell entered the drawing room to see Blackstone pacing the floor.

"Ah, you've arrived. I sent a servant to alert her to your presence and she should be with us shortly. I thought while she's getting presentable, you and I could go over the marriage contract."

His Grace was getting ahead of himself. "I'm sure I'm happy with whatever you feel is appropriate. Her dowry I'd like to put in trust for her to use should something happen to me or for any daughters we may have. I want her to know she'll always be taken care of." His voice softened with genuine feeling. "As you know, I have considerable wealth and an estate in Suffolk. I will, of course, have to purchase us a London townhouse."

The men sorted out the details rather quickly. "I'll have my lawyer send the contract to you."

Rockwell merely nodded, his stomach churning as he waited to see Farah.

"Where is the girl?" her brother said for about the hundredth time. He walked toward the door as if to go fetch her himself when Howard entered. His face was white. "Where is she?" His Grace demanded.

The butler's face remained carefully blank. "I'm afraid I couldn't say, my lord. Her ladyship's whereabouts are unknown to the staff at present."

Rockwell closed his eyes, a groan escaping him as his worst fears took shape. She wouldn't...

"What do you mean her whereabouts are unknown? Where is my sister?"

A horrible thought struck him. What if she had run away to avoid marrying him? She had threatened to do so, but he'd thought she was being fanciful. The idea carved a hollow in his chest that he refused to name as heartbreak.

Well, there was only one way to find out. If Farah had fled, she would have gone to one of her friends for help. The ladies were a tight-knit group, a sisterhood really—surely one of them would know where she was.

"Maybe she's gone to speak with one of her friends. She was a tad upset last night."

His Grace swung to face him with relief, clearly evident. "Yes. That is what she's done. I'll send word to you once she's home."

"I'll speak to my sisters to see if they know anything. If you'll excuse me, I have a fiancée to find." And he knew where he'd start.

Decision made, Rockwell strode purposefully down the street. His first stop would be his brother's house to talk with Tiffany. As his sister-in-law, she was the most likely to have aided Farah in any escape attempt, given she held the finances for the women.

But when he arrived at Wolfarth House, Tiffany became most distraught at the news Farah was missing. Farah had not contacted her, and she knew nothing of any plan to run away. "We must alert Wolf and talk to Ashley and Ivy." But they too knew nothing, either.

"Who would she go to for help if not us?" Ivy asked.

"Lauren is unlikely to be the one, given she's Lucien's brother."

"Or Courtney," Ashley added dryly.

Rockwell turned to leave and called over his shoulder, "Then I shall have to visit Claire and Valora."

"Surely Claire wouldn't aid her. She's far too sensible. But Valora… That's a possibility," Tiffany added.

"Of course, we're assuming she didn't just simply run." Everyone turned to stare at Ashley. "I'm just saying…"

He too had considered that, but his stomach heaved at the idea of her on the road in the dark—alone. "Let's not panic just yet until I've spoken to Claire and Valora. I'll send word as soon as I've found her."

A half-hour later, Rockwell's frown deepened as he left his

meeting with Claire. She was beside herself with worry and was heading to Tiffany's to meet with the rest of the ladies. Something was definitely afoot, and he didn't like it one bit.

By the time he reached Lady Valora's townhouse—and his last hope—Rockwell was seething with barely contained anger and worry. He'd wring Farah's pretty neck for putting him through this, but then again, he'd given her no reason to believe he held strong feelings for her. If anything happened to her, it would be on his head.

He paced Lord Vale's drawing room, waiting for Lady Valora. "Is Farah here?" he demanded as soon as the door opened.

"Good morning to you too, my lord." Lady Valora said. "And why on earth would Farah pay me a visit so early after her ball last night? Especially as it is the talk of the *ton*."

"Don't play games with me, Valora," Rockwell growled. "Farah is missing. Yours is the last place I've sought her out. She must be here." Because if she weren't... God, she was alone and if anything happened to her... That familiar pain of not being able to do anything hit him. He'd lost Charlotte. He wouldn't lose Farah before he'd even told her he loved her. God, he did love her.

Valora's expression hardened. "I'm sure I don't know what you mean, my lord. And I'll thank you not to barge into my home making wild accusations."

Rockwell ran a hand through his hair in frustration. "Damn it all, Valora! This isn't some game. Farah could be in real danger if she's run off on her own. Tell me where she is."

For a moment, Valora's mask of indifference slipped, revealing genuine concern. "I'm sorry, Rockwell, but I do not know what you are talking about. Farah isn't here. Are you telling me she's missing?"

Rockwell opened his mouth to argue further, but the genuine concern in Valora's eyes told him it would be useless. With a muttered curse, he spun on his heel and stormed out of the house.

He stood on the pavement for a long moment, at a loss. He had been so sure that one of Farah's friends would give him answers. Now what was he supposed to do?

As much as he hated to admit it, there was only one option left. He would have to go back to Blackstone and confess that Farah had disappeared. Together, perhaps they could find some way to locate her before it was too late.

With a heavy heart, Rockwell made his way back to Blackstone House. This time, when he knocked, the door opened immediately to reveal the duke himself. The look on Blackstone's face indicated Farah's brother knew what he was about to reveal. "I have some disturbing news," he said, pushing past Blackstone and into the house.

"ARE YOU SURE this is a sensible plan? Apparently, everyone is frantic, thinking you've run off on your own." Farah looked up at her friend from where she was lying in a bath in Courtney's dressing room. She'd slept with Courtney last night and was feeling rather tired and put out.

Courtney continued to pace. "Apparently, Rockwell is beside himself and is hunting for you across London."

"I know what I'm doing. This is the only way to make everyone understand that this is my life and I shall decide whom and when I marry. Scandal or no scandal."

Courtney pulled up a stool next to the tub. "Don't get angry with me, but I think you're being foolish. You don't know what it's like to be alone, thinking that you'll be a spinster for the rest of your life. When I heard Lucien had died, my heart died with him. I thought I'd not want to marry any other man. I was happy to stay a spinster." She flicked a guilty look at Farah and licked her lips. "But five years is a long time, and I came to understand how lonely and unfulfilled the rest of my life as a spinster would be. In fact, just recently I'd made the decision to marry. I may not find the enduring love I felt—feel for Lucien, but I would have children and a family and a life." When Farah remained silent, Courtney added, "This scandal is far worse than Ashley's, and I don't know if your reputation would ever recover. You must see that you might never find a man who would marry you. Will you still feel satisfied with a spinster's life as you get older?"

She slunk further under the water and tried to stop the fear that crept over her skin. What if Courtney was right? Could she be alone and content when all her friends would marry and have families? Would she be able to mix with her friends or would doors be closed to her like they were on Ashley?

Courtney pressed on. "Lord Ware is certainly upset. Isn't that a good sign? Perhaps his feelings run deeper than you thought."

"It's probably guilt. Or he's worried about his family's honor."

"That's a tad unfair. Lord Ware is a fine man. He'd never lie to you."

Farah picked up a towel and stood to exit the tub. "That's why I know he doesn't love me. He told me he doesn't."

"Did he?"

She hesitated. "Well, not in exact words, but he told me he didn't want a wife because his first love was travel. Marriage to him would be lonely. Is sitting at home waiting for a husband who is hardly ever home any better than sitting alone but having my heart free to find someone else?"

"I suppose it isn't."

Just then, a little girl came barreling into the dressing room and skidded to a halt. "Farah's here, too," Ava-Marie called as she flung herself into Courtney's arms. "Farah! Are you playing hide and seek? Everyone's looking for you!"

Farah exchanged a worried glance with Courtney before smiling down at Ava-Marie. "Something like that, sweetheart."

Ava-Marie clapped her hands, dancing on the spot. "I want to play too."

Lauren popped her head in the door and gasped as she saw Farah standing there. She held out her hand to Ava-Marie. "Come, Ava. Let's find some of Lady Courtney's dolls and let Farah get dressed. I think we ladies need to have a chat."

"Can we play hide and seek once Farah is dressed?" the little girl asked.

Farah smiled at her. "If you play quietly with the dolls while the ladies talk, we'll play hide and seek before you go home."

"Auntie Lauren gave me my doll. It's at home with Daid, but I suppose I can play with your dolls too." With that, Ava-Marie happily let Lauren guide her out of the dressing room.

Courtney shrugged at Farah's exasperated sigh. "I forgot they were coming to visit this morning. My maid will help you dress, and I'll order some food. Come to my sitting room when you're ready."

A half hour later, Lauren raised an eyebrow as Farah joined the ladies in the sitting room off Courtney's bedchamber. "So this is where you've been hiding. Rockwell and your brother are frantic."

"I know," Farah sighed as she took a seat. "But I needed some time to think."

As Ava-Marie continued to play on the floor with Courtney's childhood dolls, the women discussed Farah's situation in hushed tones.

"You can't stay here forever," Lauren pointed out. "Rockwell will find you. He's like a man possessed."

Courtney nodded in agreement. "Maybe you could stay with your aunt in the country?"

Farah shook her head. "Blackstone would look there first. I was thinking of going to Bath, actually."

"Who do you know in Bath?" Courtney asked.

"No one. But a Mrs. James lives in Bath and she is selling a cottage near Clevedon on the coast. The staff she employs at the cottage wishes to stay. A maid, a cook and a groom. It's well within my budget."

The two other women shared a look. Lauren said, "But you'll need a lawyer to ensure everything is in order."

Farah nodded. "Mrs. James has recommended one."

Another concerned look was shared. "You can't trust a woman you don't know." Lauren shook her head and added, "This is all so rushed. I don't think you are thinking clearly. What would Tiffany say?"

"I was hoping she would go with me and then we can assess Mrs. James and her offer."

"But that is unfair. Asking her to help you puts her in a terrible position. Rockwell is her brother-in-law," Courtney exclaimed.

"Besides, Tiffany would tell Wolf and he would get involved," Lauren added.

"Well, I didn't say my plan was perfect, but if you have a better idea on how I can live my life out from under my brother's control and not end up married to a man I don't want, then by all means let me know."

This outburst of Farah's was greeted by silence.

Finally, Courtney spoke up. "Perhaps it would solve a lot of problems if you simply married Lucien."

Lauren gasped while Farah's mouth dropped open.

Lauren turned to Courtney. "You don't mean that. You can't mean that. He's your Lucien."

Courtney shrugged. "The man who returned from Ireland is not my Lucien, and the way things are going, he never will be."

"But he could be," Lauren insisted.

"I'm not sure he even wants to try," Courtney whispered.

"While that is a very kind offer, Courtney, I don't want to marry Lucien. He's not in love with me either. And you, of all people, having experienced love... How can you recommend marrying without it?"

"I told you why. Being alone for the rest of my life is something I know I no longer want."

Lauren looked confused. "Did I miss something?"

Courtney tuned to her and said, "Before I knew Lucien had been found, I was considering marriage. In fact, I had thought about Mr. Axton Fancot, Valora's brother."

"But what about Lucien?" Lauren spluttered. "He's home, and he needs a wife."

"But does he want me and are we still suited? He is not exactly clamoring to woo me back. While I accept I can marry for respect and friendship, I can't marry your brother while I love him and he doesn't love me. That would be torture."

Lauren sat back, biting her lip, looking like the world was ending. Farah understood her need to see Lucien settled not just financially with a good marriage but settled back into society. Farah was sure she'd counted on Courtney being the key to everything.

"I'm not going to discount Lucien immediately, but I won't sit around and be embarrassed or ignored for long."

"That's fair," Farah said and hugged her friend.

"My brother is just confused and struggling with all that has happened to him." A wobble entered Lauren's voice. "I just want him to find happiness after all that has happened, and I think he can find that with you."

"I hope so, too," Courtney replied.

Ava-Marie interrupted their conversation, tugging on Farah's skirts. "Can I play hide and seek, too? I'm good at hiding!"

"I know you are," Farah said, laughing. "All right, why don't I go hide and you all have to find me?"

"I bet I find you before my auntie. But Lady Courtney knows this house best."

She tapped Ava-Marie's nose. "Then the ladies will give you a head start. Once I've hidden, Ava-Marie gets a lead of twenty counts. How is that?"

"That's fair," the little girl said, nodding.

Farah knew she could only hide in these two rooms, or Courtney's father or brother might see her. She moved quietly and hid in one of Courtney's armoires pushing her gowns aside.

It took Ava-Marie only fifteen minutes to find her. "You didn't hide very well. I would have gone up to the attics. I almost started there. I'll teach you one day at my Daid's house. I'll tell him how I found you so quickly."

The women shared a look of concern before Courtney knelt to Ava-Marie's level. "Sweetie, this is a special game. You can't tell anyone that Lady Farah is here, okay? It's a secret."

Ava-Marie's eyes widened with excitement at being entrusted with a secret. "Are you hiding from someone?"

"Yes. I'm playing a game with Lord Ware. An important game that I must win. Will you help me by keeping my secret?"

She nodded solemnly, though the women weren't entirely convinced she understood the gravity of the situation.

As Lauren prepared to leave with Ava-Marie, Farah hugged the little girl goodbye. "Remember, not a word to anyone," she whispered.

⫸⫸⫸⫷⫷⫷

LATER THAT EVENING, as Lucien tucked Ava-Marie into bed, she looked up at him with bright eyes. "Papa, I know where Farah is hiding. If I tell you, will I win the game?"

Lucien's eyebrows shot up in surprise. "What game, sweetheart? Where is Farah?"

Ava-Marie seemed to hesitate, as if she knew she wasn't supposed to tell him. But the temptation to win was too strong. "She's at Lady Courtney's house. Did I win?"

Lucien's mind raced with this new information. He kissed Ava-Marie's forehead, his voice soft. "Yes, darling. You won the game. Now, time for sleep."

As he closed the door to her room, Lucien debated what to do with this newfound knowledge. Should he tell Rockwell, or keep Farah's secret?

At least she hadn't run off on her own and the worry eating at his stomach eased. He felt responsible for Farah's situation and if anything happened to her... Well, he carried some of the blame.

He understood what Rockwell would be going through, not knowing where she was. He'd be going out of his mind with worry. As would Blackstone.

He summoned a servant and sent a missive for Lord Ware. He thought Rockwell would likely be at Wolf's house. He would let Rockwell know first, to give him time to go and talk some sense into Farah. Then in a few hours, he'd have to send the same note to Blackstone.

Once his task was completed, he sat in his study wanting time to himself. He loved his two sisters even though he couldn't remember them. Lauren and Madeline fussed over him and he knew Lauren was desperate for him to marry and help the family's financial situation. He also knew Lauren expected him to marry Courtney.

Everyone expected him to marry Courtney.

She did, too.

He wasn't opposed to that idea. She was a beautiful, intelligent, and obviously a loyal woman. But was that fair to her? He was not the same man she'd loved, and he wouldn't hold her to an obligation just because they were to be married before.

Maybe he could find something more than a marriage of convenience with her, but it would mean letting Courtney get close. And his heart just wasn't ready. Ava filled his mind, his soul, and his heart. He didn't know if he loved her, or hated her, or probably a bit of both. Until he could get some clarity, he didn't know how to let anyone else in.

But he didn't have time to wait for his heart to heal. Farah would be the perfect choice as his wife, because he liked her. He knew her better than any other woman, and he admired her. But her heart belonged to Rockwell. Could he marry her knowing that?

Lucien sat back in his chair and closed his eyes. Maybe a marriage of convenience with a woman who didn't have any expectations of him, who didn't know him from before he lost his memory, would be better.

But then a picture of Courtney's face when she'd seen him alive and well swam into his mind. The love shining in her eyes, the joy, the happiness... Oh, to have a woman look at him like that again was intoxicating.

He'd shared his life with Ava and loved her and it had been wonderful even as a poor country peasant. Could he do a marriage without love? His heart clenched in his chest at that idea.

No. He selfishly wanted it all.

CHAPTER TWENTY-TWO

ROCKWELL WALKED TO the Marquess of Lorne's townhouse to talk with Farah. The crisp morning air did little to cool his temper. How could she put them all through this? She must really want to punish him. And punish her brother.

His cravat constricted like a noose, far too tight around his neck. How was he to convince her to marry him when she thought so little of him?

Wolf had said to be honest with her, as it had worked with Tiffany.

Rockwell's mind raced. The events of the past day played repeatedly in his head—Farah's pale face at the ball as scandal circled like sharks, Lucien's impulsive proposal, and now her disappearance. With each step, his frustration mounted. Did she not understand the consequences of her actions? What about the scandal that would erupt if she weren't found?

And yet, beneath the anger, a deeper truth whispered through his bones. Had he not felt the same urge to flee, to escape the constant intrusion of society? The weight of disappointment that clung to him like a second skin—the wastrel life of a second son. Was that not what had driven him to travel the world all these years?

As he approached the Marquess of Lorne's impressive townhouse, Rockwell slowed his pace. His reflection in a window caught his eye—disheveled hair, burning eyes, a man on the edge of something momentous. He needed to approach this calmly, rationally. Charging in like a bull would only drive Farah further away. And despite everything, the thought of losing her for good made his chest tighten painfully.

Taking a steadying breath that did nothing to calm his thundering heart, Rockwell smoothed his disheveled hair and straightened his jacket. He had come here to convince Farah to marry him, to show her he truly cared for her. That their marriage could be more than just a solution to a scandal.

Rockwell rapped sharply on the door. As he waited for a response, the words he'd rehearsed a hundred times on his walk dissolved like morning mist. He'd lay his heart bare, pride be damned. It was time to stop running—from his feelings, from commitment, from the future that had been staring him in the face since the day he'd found her on his ship.

The door creaked open, and Rockwell steeled himself. This was his chance to make things right. To prove to Farah, and to himself, that love was worth fighting for.

"I'm here to see Lady Farah, and don't tell me she's not here. I know she is," he growled, shouldering past the startled servant.

The commotion in the front foyer saw Courtney come running. She took one look at Rockwell's thunderous expression and fled back up the stairs.

"Tell Farah I'll meet her in the drawing room when she's ready," he called after Courtney's departing back.

"Rockwell, what brings you here this early, causing a stir?" Tarquin, Courtney's brother, strolled towards him.

"I came to speak with Farah, who is hiding here with your sister in the last place I thought to look."

"I think you need a drink," Tarquin replied and added, "Let's give the ladies time to gather themselves and we'll meet them in the drawing room shortly." He spoke loud enough for the house to hear.

"I think I'd like that drink," Rockwell replied.

As the two men walked toward the library, Tarquin said, "And you can tell me what excitement I appear to have missed while I have been away at our country estate."

A few drinks later, Rockwell took a deep breath as he was shown into the drawing room where Farah waited. Tarquin and Courtney had given them some privacy, and he was grateful. She stood by the window, her back to him, tension evident in the rigid set of her shoulders. His heart ached at the sight of her.

"Farah," he said softly.

She turned, her eyes wary. "Rockwell. I guess I shouldn't be surprised you found me," she said, her eyes wary. "I assume little Ava-Marie let my location slip."

"I'm very glad she did." He stepped closer, fighting the urge to pull her into his arms. "Did you really think I wouldn't find you? That I wouldn't move heaven and earth? Do you know I almost went crazy thinking you'd run off alone? Anything could have happened to you."

A flicker of emotion passed across her face before she schooled her features. "I needed time to think. To consider my options."

"And have you?" he asked. "Considered your options? After putting your brother and me through hell, I hope you'll be sensible. I should put you over my knee and spank that perfect bottom." Damn. The image of his words sent blood fleeing south. It was the most inconvenient time to get an erection, but he saw her face redden and knew she was picturing the same image. *Promising.*

Then tension crackled between them like lightning before a storm.

Farah lifted her chin. "I have. I won't be forced into a marriage, Rockwell. Not even to save my reputation."

He nodded, unsurprised by her declaration. It was one thing he admired most about her—her new strength, her determination. She'd blossomed on their trip. "I understand. But what if I'm not here to force you into anything? What if I'm here because I want to marry you? What if I confessed that I'm jealous of the way you appear to be happy without me? Because, I have to say,

I'm not happy without you!"

She eyed him skeptically. "Can you tell me you love me?"

"No," he said with a sigh. "But my feelings are complicated. This has all happened so fast. I can confess that I can't imagine letting you marry anyone else."

Farah's eyes widened, a mix of hope and disbelief swirling in their depths. "You know what I'm looking for in a marriage. Can you give me your heart?"

"I believe I can—with time. I refuse to lie to you and tell you something you want to hear, just to make this situation easier for everyone."

"Believe you can? That's not very persuasive, but I admire your honesty."

He moved to stand directly in front of her so she could see his eyes and he hoped everything he was trying to convey was shining deep within, as he wasn't very good with the words. "I've known you since you were a little girl. Yet, when I saw you dancing around my bedchamber in that Hessian, I didn't see you as a little girl anymore. You were a very desirable woman full of fire. But I had other plans for my life and marriage wasn't in them." He reached out and cupped her cheek. "It's funny how plans can change so suddenly. If you give me a chance, I believe what I feel for you could be love."

In the deafening silence, he swore he could hear his own heart thumping.

"It's a risk for me to hope that your feelings deepen. A lady only gets to marry once."

He leaned in and pressed a kiss to her lips and loved the shudder that ran through her. When he drew back, he saw desire swirling in her eyes. She wanted him. He could work with that. He decided to try a different track. "Aren't you suggesting to Courtney that Lucien could fall in love with her again? Why would I not fall in love with you when we already share so much—friendship, respect, and desire?"

As if sensing he was going to seduce her, she put some distance between them, taking a chair across the room.

"Lucien and Courtney are facing a different situation, and you know it. They can try, but she can still walk away if things don't work out. If we marry, I'm trapped."

He ran a hand through his hair, willing his temper to remain locked away. "If I could, I'd give you time but this scandal… You are utterly ruined and your brother is not happy. Do you think you could come to love me?" At her nod, he said, "Then why is it so hard for you to believe that I could come to love you?"

SHE BIT HER lip. He made a good point. She'd always been infatuated with him, but since their trip to Ireland, she'd fallen completely in love with him. Women tended to open their hearts easier than men. He did desire her. He was jealous of her attracting other men, including Lucien. Weren't these all examples of a man falling in love? He could have, for instance, simply let her brother force her to marry Lucien.

She thought about what Courtney had said about living her life alone. Denying society dictates and riding the waves of the scandal was just as risky as tying herself to Rockwell when he didn't love her, because she may well end up a spinster and she wanted children. Longed for children—with Rockwell. It was a little girl with his coloring and twinkling eyes she had always envisioned.

Life with Rockwell, even if he never came to love her deeply, would be preferable to being alone. Was it her silly pride holding her back? Deep inside, she understood she'd run out of time. Run or marry. What a choice. If she ran, she would lose everything— her brother, her friends, and her heart would be broken.

The tension clear in Rockwell's jaw told her he was only just holding back his temper. If she put her sensible hat on, she had no choice but to marry. Was his tension because he was worried she would pick Lucien?

She sighed and smoothed down her skirts. "I will allow you to escort me back to my brother's townhouse—" She paused, her eyes searching his face. "Where we will announce our engagement." Her statement saw him breathe a sigh of relief, but it was the smile that curved his lips that undid her completely.

She beckoned him with her little finger. He needed no further encouragement. He was by her side in a flash, lifting her out of the chair and into his arms. His lips found hers in a searing and possessive kiss that set her toes curling.

When he drew back, she giggled. "I suppose marriage to you won't be all bad." His answering laugh was light and breathless, warming her from the inside out.

His thumb traced the curve of her lower lip, his eyes darkening with possession. "I'll have to rename you spicy vixen. The timid mouse is long gone."

She laughed delightedly. "I wouldn't mind that name. And I'll only ever be spicy with you."

"God help me," he groaned, his forehead dropping to rest against hers. The sandalwood scent made her head spin. "I wish we were married already. I want to take you to bed and do all manner of wicked things to you."

She felt heat bloom on her cheeks, but her eyes held his boldly. "I'd like that too. How long before we wed?"

"My eager little vixen," he murmured, his hands tightening possessively at her waist. "Haven't you changed their tune?" At her embarrassed squirm, he added, "I will get a special license and we can marry as soon as it is arranged, perhaps in your brother's drawing room?"

She traced idle patterns on his lapel and loved how he shivered. "Where will we live?"

"With Wolf and Tiffany for now, and you can help me purchase a London town home for us. Then we could take a few weeks and visit my estate in Suffolk."

Her fingers stilled against his chest. "What estate?"

"I bought the Spencer's estate in Suffolk, mainly to help the family who found themselves in financial difficulty."

Her eyes narrowed suspiciously, though her lips twitched with amusement coupled with surprise. "What are you doing with an estate if you are sailing away?"

He captured her hand and pressed a kiss to her palm, seemingly delighted in her sharp intake of breath. "Didn't I say sometimes the adventure you had planned changes?" His voice dropped lower, intimate. "Do you remember my investment in Armley Mills? Well, someone approached me about starting a Merino wool breeding program. I can't breed sheep without an estate. The land runs right down to the coast. It would mean settling on my estate in Suffolk, working to revolutionize the textile industry. It's a chance to make a real difference to the economy of England, to build something lasting."

She couldn't hide the wonder from her face as her heart stuttered deep in her chest. Gosh, that *was* a change. He used the word *settling*. He must be serious. "I can't wait to see it—with you."

Still carrying her, cradling her precious weight against his chest, he opened the door. "Do you want to say goodbye to Courtney?"

They looked up the stairs and saw Courtney standing there, her face glowing with vicarious joy. "I gather it's to be a wedding."

"She said yes," Rockwell replied, his voice rough with emotion and pride.

Farah squirmed in his arms. But she really didn't want to escape. "You can put me down. You can't carry me home, that would be scandalous." Turning to Courtney, her eyes bright with unshed tears of happiness, she said, "Thank you for letting me invade your house. I won't forget your kindness. If you need anything, please let me know."

When Rockwell finally put her down, she walked over and hugged her friend, whispering in Courtney's ear, "Is Lucien worth fighting for? That's the question only you can answer."

As they prepared to leave, Rockwell's arm remained firmly around her waist, as if he feared she might still slip away. But Farah leaned into his touch, her heart too full of joy to care about propriety.

It was like a dream. Shortly she'd be Lady Farah Ware. As they walked back towards her family home, she said to her husband-to-be, "You do know I'll have to tell Tiffany about your plans with Armley Mills. This could really increase the profit in our challenge if news of your venture got out. Don't you dare tell anyone else. Wolf already knows who my brother and Fane are being challenged by, but they don't. Please help us win."

He slipped her arm through his. "I've known from the beginning that the sisterhood were the ones challenging the men. Wolf needed my help with stopping Sprat. He confessed all about Tiffany's skills and that her stockjobber, Sprat had stolen the money. But as for Fane and Blackstone, they both could do with being taken down a peg or too, so your secret is safe with me." He paused, then squeezed her hand. "You're safe with me. I'll never do anything to hurt you."

She merely nodded. He probably meant that, but when you love someone who doesn't love you back, the opportunities for being hurt are endless.

"If you don't wish to see me hurt, then I hope you know how to handle my brother. He may very well kill me when we arrive home."

Rockwell laughed. "I suspect he'll be so pleased to hear of the engagement that all else will be forgotten."

Blackstone came bounding down the stairs at their entrance and what he saw made him slow down and smile. "I see you've come to your senses, Farah. Good girl."

"I'm not a dog, brother dear," she replied tartly.

"It's me that has come to my senses. I suddenly realized I can't see her marry anyone else," Rockwell said.

Farah tried to ignore the brief stab of doubt at Rockwell's

words. What she really wanted him to say was he realized he loved her. One day—perhaps.

"Regardless, I'm pleased to see you together. I think you'll have a wonderful life as man and wife." Blackstone reached out his hand. "Welcome to the family, Lord Ware."

Rockwell turned to Farah. "I'll be on my way. I have a special license to organize and I think you'd like to summon the ladies to go over your wedding dress and things. Shall we marry the day after tomorrow? Will that give you enough time?"

Her head was spinning. In two days, she'd be Lady Ware. Gosh, that sounded so soon. Was she really doing this? But she hid her thoughts and smiled up at her fiancé. "When you get to Wolf's, could you ask Tiffany, Ashley and Ivy to attend me? I'll send notes to Lauren, Courtney, Claire, Serena, and Valora." And before her brother could utter a sound, she rounded on him. "Yes, Lady Ashley too. She will be my sister-in-law, and I insist she be present."

Blackstone held up his hands in defense. "I'm not saying anything."

"Very wise, brother dear." She turned and pressed a kiss to Rockwell's lips. "Will you dine with us tonight?" she asked Rockwell. Her head swam with doubts, but her heart sang loudly. Thankfully, she had a lot to organize because she would leave her brother's house after the wedding breakfast. She would only take what she needed for the immediate future and then collect the rest at her leisure.

"I'd like that," he replied. "Until dinner then."

"And bring the rest of the Ware family," she called after him. She'd finally have sisters—Ashley and Ivy.

As she watched him leave, she couldn't help feeling like this was all a dream.

LATER THAT EVENING, after enduring Wolf's knowing smirks and Tiffany's tearful embraces, they announced their engagement to a relieved household. The family's exuberant celebration had left Farah's cheeks aching from smiling and Rockwell's hand warm from countless congratulatory handshakes.

The garden welcomed them like a secret sanctuary. At last, they were alone. Night-blooming jasmine perfumed the air, its sweet fragrance mingling with the earthy dampness of the evening.

Rockwell settled onto a stone bench, drawing Farah between his legs until she melted against his chest. The steady thrum of his heartbeat against her back anchored her to this perfect moment. They gazed up at the stars, diamond-bright against the velvet sky. "I still can't quite believe this is real," she murmured, her fingers intertwining with his where they rested at her waist.

He nuzzled the sensitive spot behind her ear, his breath warming her skin. "Which part? The engagement or the fact that I located you so quickly?"

She shifted against him, delighting in his sharp intake of breath. "Both, I suppose. Though I should have known better than to think I could outwit you for long."

"Mmm, I wouldn't be so sure about that," he said, his chest rumbling with appreciation against her back. "You're far cleverer than I am, my dear. I simply had the advantage of being utterly desperate to find you."

Farah twisted in his embrace, studying the play of moonlight across his beloved features. "You really were worried, weren't you?"

"Terrified," he confessed, his arms tightening possessively around her. "The thought of something happening to you... it was unbearable."

She traced the worried line between his brows with gentle fingers. "I'm sorry for putting you through that. I just felt so trapped, so powerless. I needed to prove to myself that I could make my own choices."

Rockwell caught her wandering hand and pressed a kiss to each fingertip, sending shivers down her spine. "I understand. And I admire your strength, your determination to chart your own course. It's one of the many things I respect about you."

"Even when it leads me to do foolish things?" she asked, her lips quirking.

His chuckle vibrated through her body. "Especially then. Though perhaps in the future, we could face our challenges together? I rather like the idea of being your partner in crime."

Farah's eyes sparkled with mischief in the starlight. "I think I'd like that too."

They fell into a comfortable silence, broken only by the distant chorus of crickets and the whisper of leaves in the evening breeze. Then Farah spoke again, her voice carrying the weight of dreams finally within reach. "Tell me more about this life you envision for us. I want to hear everything."

Rockwell's hand drew idle patterns on her waist as he spoke, his arm secure around her. "It's a grand old place with bones as strong as its history—in need of some care, like all precious things, but with endless possibility stretching before us. I thought we might split our time between there and London, at least initially, while we get the breeding program off the ground."

"We'd need to buy a London town home," she said, already picturing their life together.

"I've already started looking. I want to be close to Wolf and Tiffany."

Farah turned fully in his arms, her eyes bright with purpose. "I'd like that. And I've been thinking… Perhaps we could set up a school on the estate? For the tenants' children, and maybe even some from the nearby village. Education is so important, and it could make such a difference in their lives."

"God, you're magnificent," Rockwell whispered against her hair, looking at her with such intensity, it stole her breath. "See? This is exactly why I need you by my side. You think of things I never would have considered."

She preened under his praise, warmth blooming in her chest. "We *will* make a good team, don't you think?"

"The best," he agreed, his voice rough with emotion. "And speaking of teams… I hope you know I'm serious about wanting children with you, Farah. Not right away, of course—not unless you want to. But someday…"

Farah's eyes softened. "I want that, too. A little boy with your curls and mischievous smile. A girl with your sense of adventure."

Rockwell's eyes welled with emotion. "They'll have your intelligence, your compassion. Your ability to see the best in people."

"And your courage," Farah added. "Your integrity."

A small frown briefly creased his forehead before he smiled once again. "How did I get so lucky?"

Farah stretched up to kiss him softly. "I think we both got lucky."

CHAPTER TWENTY-THREE

T HE FOLLOWING AFTERNOON, the drawing room was full of laughter and chatter as all the ladies attempted to voice their opinion on which gown she should wear for her wedding tomorrow.

She'd had a few glasses of sherry, needing the courage. She was marrying the man of her dreams, except for the fact that she was not the woman of his.

The feminine goings on at least kept Blackstone well away. He had, however, been gracious enough to welcome Ashley back to his home. Ashley hadn't stepped foot in the house since her scandal more than two years ago. Farah noted Ashley's head lifted higher and her shoulders squared under his welcome. It had meant a lot to her friend and for the first time in a while, Farah could have kissed her brother.

The room was a mess. Gowns in various shades of cream and ivory were draped over every available surface.

"You must wear this one," Tiffany insisted, holding up an empire-waist gown with delicate pearl beading. "The cut is perfect for your figure."

Valora shook her head emphatically. "No, no—the one with the lace overlay is far more romantic. It's your wedding day, Farah. You should look like you stepped out of a fairy tale."

"I still think the silk with the ribbon trim would be lovely," Claire added, fingering the material thoughtfully. "Simple but elegant."

Farah sat amid the whirlwind of fabric and opinions, feeling somewhat overwhelmed. Just yesterday, she'd been hiding at Courtney's house, determined to avoid marriage altogether. Now here she was, preparing to wed Rockwell tomorrow morning. Her heart fluttered at the idea of becoming Lady Farah Ware.

"You're awfully quiet," Courtney observed, settling beside her on the settee. "Having second thoughts?"

"No," Farah replied quickly—perhaps too quickly, given the knowing look Courtney gave her. "It's just…everything is happening so fast."

"That tends to happen with special licenses," Ivy remarked dryly. "Though I must say, my brother seems remarkably eager to get you to the altar."

The ladies exchanged meaningful glances and knowing smiles that made Farah's cheeks heat.

"Can you blame him?" Valora asked with a wicked grin. "After that scandalous journey to Ireland together…"

"Nothing scandalous happened!" Farah protested, though her blush deepened at the lie.

"Of course not," Tiffany agreed, her eyes twinkling. "I'm sure you were the very model of propriety while alone with my devastatingly handsome brother-in-law."

The other ladies dissolved into giggles, while Farah buried her face in her hands. "You're all terrible," she mumbled.

"We're just happy for you," Ashley said, giving Farah's shoulder a squeeze. "Even though he's my brother, Rockwell is a good man. You'll be very happy together."

Lauren nodded in agreement. "And you've already proven you can handle his adventurous spirit. Not many ladies would take so well to being accidentally shipped off to Ireland."

"Speaking of adventures," Ashley said, rising to her feet, "we should check your wardrobe for any other potential wedding gowns. Lauren, will you help me?"

As the two women headed upstairs, Farah made to follow them, but Valora caught her arm, her eyes bright with wedding fever. All the ladies and their brothers and parents would wish to attend. Several minutes passed as they debated who to seat with whom.

Finally, extracting herself from Valora's enthusiastic clutches, Farah made her way up the stairs toward her bedchamber. The thick carpet muffled her footsteps as she approached, and she heard voices drifting through the partially open door.

"...had no choice really," Ashley's voice carried clearly through the gap. "Wolf was quite adamant about it."

"Well, of course he was," Lauren replied. "The family couldn't risk another scandal, not after..."

"After my disgrace, you mean." Ashley's voice held the weight of old pain. "That's exactly why Wolf insisted Rockwell had to convince her to marry him. He told him in no uncertain terms that the Wolfarth family name couldn't withstand another ruined reputation."

Farah's world tilted sideways, her hand half-raised to push open the door. Ice seemed to spread through her veins as Ashley's words echoed in her head like a death knell.

"At least Rockwell seems to have done a good job of it," Lauren continued, oblivious to the fact that her heart was breaking mere feet away. "She seems happy at the idea of marrying him. And as you say, he is a good man. They will be happy, won't they? And I'm not just saying that because I was hoping she'd pick Lucien." A pause, then more softly, "He is running out of time to find a rich wife."

"Well, my brother has always had a silver tongue when he wanted something," Ashley remarked, each word another dagger in Farah's heart. "But I saw him send a missive to Lady Mary."

Lauren sighed. "His mistress?"

"Well, the lady he was seeing prior to going to Ireland the first time. Though I do think he cares for Farah in his way."

"But not enough to have offered for her if Wolf hadn't forced his hand?"

"Probably not. You know how he is about his freedom. But

he'll do his duty to protect the family name."

Farah stumbled backward, the world swimming before her eyes as tears burned hot trails down her cheeks. Everything—all of Rockwell's beautiful words, his begging for her to give him a chance to learn to love her, his promises for their future—had been a lie. A masterful performance by a man who knew exactly how to manipulate her heart. Oh, she was so stupid. He'd danced around her questions about love like a practiced courtier, never quite lying but never telling the whole truth, either. She hadn't even thought to ask him about a mistress. She wouldn't make that mistake again.

She pressed trembling fingers to her mouth to stifle a sob. How could she have been so foolish? Of course, he didn't truly love her—how could she have believed otherwise? She was nothing more than a duty to be discharged, a problem to be solved.

The thought of their intimate moments in the garden made her stomach turn. Farah couldn't go through with it. She couldn't bind herself for life to a man who saw her as an obligation. What if he met someone who stirred his heart the way she never could? The thought of watching him grow to resent her, of living with the knowledge that he'd rather be anywhere else or with someone else…

But what choice did she have? Her reputation hung by a thread. If she didn't marry Rockwell, she'd be ruined. Her brother would be furious if she cried off—might even force her to marry Franklin, bringing her full circle to where this nightmare began. Running away wasn't an option either. Not really. Not if she wanted children.

Unless…

Lucien's proposal floated to the surface of her troubled thoughts like a lifeline. Lauren was right. He needed her help. He'd proposed marriage in front of the *ton*. It would be a neat solution to both their predicaments—her scandal and his need for a wealthy wife. At the time, she'd refused, believing she had another choice. But now…

Perhaps a marriage without love's illusions would be kinder than one built on beautiful lies. At least with Lucien, they both knew exactly where they stood. It was more bearable than living with the constant hope that Rockwell might one day love her truly. And Courtney certainly didn't seem so enamored of her returned-from-the-dead fiancé.

Drawing in a shaky breath, Farah gathered her skirts and quietly made her way down the back stairs. Each step felt like both an escape and a betrayal, but she had to protect what was left of her heart. She had to find Lucien before it was too late. Before she made the biggest mistake of her life by marrying a man who could trample her heart to pieces because he saw her as nothing more than a duty to be fulfilled.

She slipped out of the house while the other ladies were still distracted with wedding preparations. The afternoon sun seemed to mock her with its cheerfulness as she made her way toward Danvers House, where Lucien was staying with his father. No one gave her a thought and with her eyes swimming in tears, she'd not recognized anyone, anyway.

Each step felt heavier than the last, her heart pounding in an erratic rhythm. Was she making another rash decision? But surely, any port in a storm was better than drowning in false hopes. Lucien freely chose to do so, and Courtney had essentially given her permission to accept Lucien.

The butler at Danvers House seemed startled by her appearance but showed her into the library where Lucien sat reading to Ava-Marie. The little girl's face lit up when she saw Farah.

"You found me!" she exclaimed. "Are we playing hide and seek again?"

"Not today, sweetling," Farah replied, forcing a smile. "I need to speak with your father about something important."

Lucien studied her face for a long moment before turning to his daughter. "Why don't you go find Caitria and see if she'll take you to feed the ducks in the park?"

Once they were alone, he gestured for Farah to sit. "What's wrong? You look upset."

"Your offer," she blurted out. "Is it still open? The one about marriage?"

His eyebrows rose in surprise. "Lauren informed me you were marrying Rockwell tomorrow."

"I can't," she whispered, tears threatening again. "I just... I can't."

"What happened?"

Haltingly, she explained what she'd overheard. With each word, fresh pain lanced through her heart. "So, you see," she finished, "he was just doing his duty to protect the family name. I'm not sure he has any feelings for me at all."

"I'm totally confused. Are you saying you have feelings for me then? Because you state you want love in a marriage. I don't love you. I barely know you, but we could make a fine marriage. I like you. I am attracted to you and you dote on Ava-Marie. You know the truth about her lineage, and yet you care about her." He shrugged. "Besides, perhaps love can grow."

Rockwell had said exactly the same thing, but did he mean it? Lucien obviously did.

"I think you should talk to Rockwell before making any rash decisions," he said.

She scoffed. She didn't trust herself. If Rockwell spoke more pretty words, would she believe him? Could she believe him? She shook her head. "Is it possible for you to get a special license by tomorrow?" Lucien sat silently, contemplating her. "I have a very large dowry. My brother is a duke and he will be very pleased to see me wed. He won't care who I marry, as long as I marry."

"You're serious, aren't you?" Lucien said something else under his breath.

"Can you imagine marrying a woman who loves you, but you wonder if you'll ever love her back? I know you understand because that's why you haven't offered for Courtney. It wouldn't be fair to her. Well, marrying Rockwell is not fair to me. Will you help me and let me help your family by giving you my dowry?"

Slowly, a smile crept over his face and her heart froze as she realized she was about to get what she asked for. "I *will* meet you at the altar tomorrow morning at your brother's house."

A part of her died inside. "How am I going to tell Rockwell?"

Lucien stood suddenly all businesslike. "Leave everything to me. I'll deal with Rockwell and your brother. You return home and continue your preparations for tomorrow as if nothing is amiss." He drew her into his arms and hugged her. Nothing lit up in her body at all. She closed her eyes against the pain. Lucien wasn't Rockwell and he never would be. But at least he could never break her heart.

She pushed out of his hold. "Thank you. I hope you're sure about this."

"Oh, I'm very sure."

THE DOOR HAD barely closed behind Farah before Lucien called for his coat. His heart raced with a mixture of sympathy and exasperation—he'd seen that look of devastation in a woman's eyes before, in Courtney's, and he'd be damned if he let another couple's happiness shatter due to a man's stubborn blindness. He had to find Rockwell before it was too late, and bloody well knock some sense into the man. How could someone so clever be such an utter fool when it came to matters of the heart?

Yanking on his coat with more force than necessary, Lucien shook his head at the absurdity of it all. Worse still, Rockwell seemed to have no idea that he was already head over heels in love with Farah.

The way he'd stormed into Blackstone's study the night he'd offered for her and almost roared at Lucien for even thinking of marrying Farah. That was when he knew Rockwell was a man in denial. He was in love but was fighting it for some reason.

The signs were there for anyone with eyes to see—the way Rockwell's gaze followed her across every room, how his entire demeanor softened in her presence, the possessive tension in his jaw whenever another man spoke to her. He'd behaved the same with Ava. But he'd been the fool that time.

If Rockwell didn't sort this mess out, he'd lose the love of his life to his own damned pride and stubborn refusal to recognize what was right in front of him.

The irony wasn't lost on Lucien—here he was, racing to save another man's romance when his own lay in shambles. Because one way or another, either Lucien or Rockwell would be at the altar tomorrow morning. He'd already failed one woman he cared for; he would not stand idle and see Farah ruined.

His fingers curled into fists as he strode purposefully toward the door. Time was running out like sand through an hourglass. He just prayed Rockwell loved her enough to do anything to secure her hand in marriage. And more importantly, that the fool would finally realize it before it was too late.

"Have my carriage brought around immediately," he barked at the footman. Every second counted now—every moment Farah spent believing herself unloved was another crack in the foundation of what could be a magnificent love story. If only Rockwell would get out of his own bloody way.

CHAPTER TWENTY-FOUR

FARAH'S HEART THUNDERED against her ribs like a caged bird seeking escape as she stood at the entrance to Blackstone's drawing room. Blackstone had transformed the familiar space into something out of a dream—with flowers adorning every surface and chairs arranged in neat rows. Morning sunlight spilled through the tall windows like liquid gold—making the scene appear almost ethereal.

She gripped her brother's arm tightly, fighting back the tears that threatened to shatter her carefully constructed composure. This wasn't how her wedding day was supposed to be. Everything felt wrong. The ivory gown that had seemed so perfect yesterday now wrapped around her like chains, each breath a struggle. Her bouquet of white roses trembled in her hand, the petals threatening to fall like her own tears.

"It's not too late." Blackstone's whisper carried a weight of understanding that nearly broke her. "If you truly don't want this…"

She shook her head quickly. "No, I made my choice."

Now here she was, about to seal her fate, by marrying Lucien because she'd convinced herself it was the safer choice. Better a marriage of convenience than risking her heart on a man who might never truly love her. The thought sat bitterly on her tongue. She was such a coward.

But oh, how her heart cried out for Rockwell, each beat echoing his name.

The first notes of music swelled through the room like the death knell, and Blackstone patted her hand. "Ready?"

No. She wasn't ready at all. She'd never be ready to say goodbye to love. But she forced herself to nod.

As they started down the makeshift aisle, Farah kept her eyes fixed on the polished floorboards, watching her white slippers peek out with each step. She knew they were all there—the sisterhood with their concerned faces, Courtney's presence, a particular weight, Rockwell's family, her friends. What tales would they whisper at their tea parties about the girl who jilted Rockwell to marry Lucien instead?

She could feel their stares prickling along her skin. Let them talk. She was doing what was best for everyone. Wasn't she? The question echoed hollowly in her chest.

Her vision swam with unshed tears as they approached the altar. She blinked rapidly, determined not to let them fall and betray her heart to all of London. Just a few more steps and it would be done. She would be Lady Furoe, and she would learn to be content with her choice. She would learn to live with the ghost of what might have been.

But then something—fate or providence or her own treacherous heart—made her look up, and her heart stopped.

It wasn't Lucien waiting for her at the altar.

It was Rockwell, standing tall and proud, like something from her deepest dreams. He stood there in his finest morning coat, so handsome he could make a nun weep. His dark eyes were fixed on her with an intensity that sent flames dancing along her nerves. A small smile played about his lips as he watched her reaction, as if he'd been waiting forever for this moment.

"What... how..." The words tumbled from her lips. "No. No. Absolutely not."

Rockwell stepped forward, his warm hands enveloping hers. "Did you really think I'd let you marry another man?" he asked softly. "Especially after Lucien told me why you went to see him yesterday?"

Heat bloomed across her cheeks, staining them rose as she became acutely aware of their audience. "But... You are doing this out of duty not because you really love me. Wolf ordered you to marry me. To save the family name."

A ripple of gasps and whispers swept through the assembled guests. Rockwell didn't seem to notice them. His entire world had narrowed to her face, as if memorizing every detail. "Is that what you think?" he asked, his voice carrying a note of tender amusement. "That I'm only marrying you out of duty? As if anyone could force me to do anything I didn't want to do."

"What about Lady Mary? I'm not enough for you, am I? I heard Ashley and Lauren talking... You sent her a note..."

"Ah. It was to decline an invitation and to inform her I was to marry, and I would not see her again." His thumbs traced soothing circles on her palms. "Plus, you didn't hear the actual conversation I had with my brother. The part where Wolf told me I was being a fool for letting my fears keep me from admitting how much I love you."

Fresh tears sprang to her eyes, turning Rockwell into a beloved blur. "But..."

"Let me finish," he murmured, his voice as gentle as his touch. "Yes, Wolf insisted I do something about the scandal. But do you know what he actually said to me? He said, 'For God's sake, Rockwell, stop being such a coward and marry the woman you love before she comes to her senses and realizes she could do better.'"

A laugh bubbled up through her tears like sunshine through rain. "He did not."

"He did. And he was right." Rockwell's chest rose with a deep breath, his words ringing with truth through the now breathless room. "I've been a coward, Farah. I've been so afraid of losing my freedom, of risking my heart again, that I almost lost the best thing that's ever happened to me."

He reached up, his thumb catching a tear as it traced down her cheek. "When I thought you'd run away, I realized something. My greatest adventure isn't exploring distant lands or making scientific discoveries. It's loving you. It's building a life with you. It's waking up every morning knowing that I get to spend another day making you smile."

More tears fell as Farah's heart swelled with hope. "Do you really mean that?"

"With all my heart." His own eyes were suspiciously bright now. "I love everything about you, Farah. I love your brilliant mind and your gentle heart. I love how you challenge me to be better, how you see the best in everyone. I love that you're not afraid to stand up for what you believe in, even when it means defying convention."

His smile softened with tender memories, eyes dancing with mischief. "I love how you tried on my Hessian boot and danced around my bedroom, showing me that the timid mouse everyone thought you were had a passionate heart underneath. I love how that moment revealed the real you—brave and playful and utterly enchanting. I love that you accidentally stowed away on my ship and turned my entire world upside down in the best possible way."

Someone in the audience—probably Valora—let out a dreamy sigh that echoed through the hushed room.

"I love that you're willing to help me build something new with the breeding program." Rockwell's voice grew thick with emotion. "That you immediately started thinking of ways to improve the community with schools and projects? You don't just share my dreams—you make them bigger, better, more meaningful than I ever imagined."

With trembling fingers, he reached into his pocket, pulling out a small velvet box. Farah's breath caught in her throat as he sank to one knee before her.

"I got the stone in this ring on one of my trips. The color captured my heart because it reminds me of your sparkling eyes."

Farah's hand fluttered like a nervous bird as she reached out to touch the ring with an enormous emerald in the middle, surrounded by diamonds. "It's beautiful," she whispered.

"Not half as beautiful as you." Rockwell's voice rang with conviction. "I know I've given you reason to doubt me. But I swear to you, on everything I hold dear, that I love you. Wholly, completely, with every fiber of my being. You've awakened parts of my soul I never knew existed. You challenge me, you inspire me, you make me want to be a better man."

He drew in a shaky breath, his eyes never leaving hers. "I want to build a life with you. A family. I want to see your smile first thing in the morning and last thing at night. I want to watch our children inherit your quick mind and gentle heart. I want to grow old debating politics and literature by the fire."

Tears spilled down Farah's cheeks. "Rockwell…"

"I'm asking you to give me a chance to fulfil your dreams…" His voice roughened with emotion. "No, I'm asking you to let me be a part of them. To let me support you, encourage you, stand by your side as you take on the world. No more hiding in shadows, my love. I've seen you shake off that mantle and grow into this amazingly strong woman. My brilliant, fearless Farah."

The ring caught fire in the morning light as he held it up. "So, what do you say? Will you marry me? Not out of duty or obligation, not to stave off the scandal, but because we love each other and want to face life's adventures together?"

Farah's lips trembled as she looked down at him. "You really mean it? All of it?"

"Every word," he vowed, his voice rough with naked honesty. "I love you, Farah. More than I ever thought possible."

"Why do you suddenly know you love me?"

"Because when I thought I'd lost you, the world lost all its color. Only love can hurt like this. Please marry me and end my suffering."

For a long moment, she simply stared at him, searching his eyes. Then, slowly, a radiant smile spread across her face. "Yes," she whispered. "Yes, I'll marry you. I love you so much."

Joy exploded in Rockwell's chest. He slipped the ring onto

her finger, then surged to his feet, pulling Farah into his arms. Her laughter rang like silver bells as he spun her in a circle.

When he set her down, Farah's eyes shone with happiness. "I love you too, you know," she said softly. "So very much."

Rockwell's heart soared to impossible heights. He leaned down, capturing her lips in a tender kiss. When they parted, he rested his forehead against hers. "I promise you, Farah, every sunrise will bring fresh proof of my love for you."

She smiled, her fingers threading through his silken hair. "I like the sound of that."

Lucien gave a discreet cough. She turned on him. "You knew about this?" she demanded.

He shrugged, grinning. "Who do you think told Rockwell you were at Lady Courtney's? And helped him plan this little surprise?"

"You're supposed to be my friend!"

"I am your friend," he replied. "That's why I couldn't let you settle for a marriage of convenience when true love was right in front of you." His eyes drifted to where Courtney sat beaming at them, and his expression softened. "Sometimes we all need a little help to see what's right in front of us."

The bishop cleared his throat pointedly. "Shall we proceed with the ceremony, then?"

Rockwell took Farah's hand, pressing a kiss to her knuckles. "What do you say, my love? Ready to begin our greatest adventure?"

She smiled up at him, her heart so full it felt like it might burst. "With you? Always."

As they turned to face the Bishop, Farah couldn't stop smiling. This was how her wedding day was supposed to feel—full of joy and love and promise. She'd nearly let fear keep her from this happiness, but Rockwell had fought for her, had laid his heart bare in front of all their friends and family to prove his love.

Through the ceremony, she couldn't take her eyes off him. Every time their gazes met, she saw the same wonderful truth reflected there. This was real. This was love. This was forever.

When they were finally pronounced man and wife, Rockwell pulled her close, his forehead resting against hers. "I love you," he whispered. "No more doubts?"

"No more doubts," she agreed, rising on her tiptoes to kiss him again. "I love you too."

Their guests broke into fresh applause and cheers, but Farah barely noticed. She was too busy thanking whatever twist of fate had led her to hide in Rockwell's trunk that day and journey to Ireland. Sometimes the greatest adventures and the greatest loves came from the most unexpected places.

As Rockwell led her back down the aisle, she caught sight of Wolf standing with Tiffany. He winked at her, and she had to laugh. Perhaps she owed her brother-in-law a thank you for giving Rockwell that final push.

But that could wait. Right now, she had a lifetime of adventures to begin with the man she loved.

"Ready to face the world together, Lady Ware?" Rockwell asked softly.

She squeezed his hand, feeling the perfect fit of their fingers intertwined—like two pieces of a puzzle finally coming together. "As long as we're together, I'm ready for anything."

EPILOGUE

Suffolk—6 years later

FARAH STOOD AT the nursery window, watching the sunrise paint the Suffolk countryside in hues of gold and pink. In her arms, eighteen-month-old Sarah dozed contentedly, her tiny fist curled around a lock of her mother's hair. From the window, she could see the rolling fields dotted with hundreds of white Merino sheep, their wool gleaming in the early morning light.

"There you are…" Rockwell's voice came softly from behind her. "I woke to find your side of the bed cold."

She turned, smiling at her husband as he crossed the nursery to join them. At thirty-six, he was more handsome than ever, his dark hair touched with the slightest hint of silver at the temples. The past five years of country life had added a healthy tan to his complexion and strengthened his already impressive physique.

"Your daughter decided dawn was the perfect time for her breakfast," Farah explained, leaning back against his chest as his arms encircled both her and the baby. "And then I couldn't resist watching the sunrise over our kingdom."

Rockwell pressed a kiss to her temple, then one to Sarah's downy head. "Our kingdom indeed. Though I suspect you're really checking on the new lambs."

She laughed softly. "You know me too well. The twins will be desperate to see them when they wake."

As if on cue, the pounding of little feet echoed down the hallway, followed by excited whispers that weren't nearly as quiet as their owners believed. Moments later, their five-year-old twins, James and Elizabeth, burst into the nursery, already fully dressed in their outdoor clothes.

"Mama! Papa! Can we go see the baby sheep now?" James asked, bouncing on his toes. He was the spitting image of his father, right down to the mischievous glint in his dark eyes.

Elizabeth, fair-haired like her mother but with her father's adventurous spirit, was already heading for the door. "Cook said there were three new ones born last night!"

"Shh," Farah cautioned, nodding toward the now-stirring baby in her arms. "Let me put Sarah in her cradle, then we can all go down to breakfast. After that, if Papa isn't too busy with business today…"

"Actually," Rockwell interrupted, "I think checking on the new lambs is exactly the sort of business I should attend to this morning. Especially with my most trusted advisors." He winked at the twins, who beamed with pride.

As Farah laid Sarah in her cradle, she marveled at how naturally Rockwell had taken to fatherhood. The man who had once feared being tied down by family life now seemed to live for these moments with their children.

The nursery had become one of her favorite rooms in their sprawling country house. The walls were covered in maps and illustrations of far-off places—Rockwell's way of sharing his love of adventure with their children. But unlike the restless explorer he'd once been, he now found his greatest adventures at home.

"Tell you what," he said to the twins. "Go down and ask Cook to pack us a picnic breakfast. We can eat out by the south pasture and check on all the new lambs at the same time."

The children raced off, their excited chatter fading down the hallway. Rockwell pulled Farah into his arms, finally giving her the proper good morning kiss he'd been waiting to deliver.

"I missed you this morning," he murmured against her lips. "Six years of marriage, and I still hate waking up without you beside me."

"Even though you know exactly where to find me?" she teased, running her fingers through his hair.

"Especially then." His expression grew tender as he cupped her face in his hands. "Do you know what today is?"

"Mmm, Thursday?"

He chuckled. "It's exactly six years since we moved here. Six years since we started this crazy venture with the Merino sheep. Six years since you made all my dreams come true—even the ones I didn't know I had."

Farah's heart swelled with love. "I remember how nervous we were, wondering if it would all work out. The sheep, the mill investments, starting a family…"

"And look at us now." Rockwell's voice was thick with pride. "The breeding program is more successful than we ever imagined. Armley Mills has tripled in size. People consider our wool the finest in England. But more importantly, we have three beautiful children, a home filled with love, and I fall more in love with you every day."

"Flatterer," she whispered, though her eyes shone with happy tears. "Though I must say, your latest letter to the Royal Agricultural Society was particularly eloquent. I especially enjoyed your passionate defense of our crossbreeding program."

"Ah, so you're the one who's been editing my correspondence again!" He grinned. "I thought those sentences seemed more polished than usual."

"Well, someone has to make sure England's premier sheep breeder sounds appropriately dignified," she teased. "Besides, I enjoy being part of every aspect of our life here. Remember how you once thought I was just a timid mouse?"

"Never." He shook his head firmly. "I always saw the fire in you, even if I was too blind to realize how much I needed that fire in my life." His hands slid down to rest on her still-flat stomach. "Speaking of which, when shall we tell the children about their new sibling?"

Farah's eyes widened. "How did you know? I only just realized myself!"

"My love, you forget I know every inch of you." His voice dropped to a husky whisper. "I noticed the changes in your body, the way you've been glowing lately. Plus, you turned down Cook's excellent kidney pie at dinner last night, and you never turn down kidney pie."

She laughed, leaning into his embrace. "I was planning to tell you today, actually. Happy anniversary, darling."

The twins calling from downstairs interrupted their tender moment. "Mama! Papa! Cook has the picnic ready!"

"We should go," Farah said reluctantly. "Before they decide to head to the pasture without us."

"Heaven forbid," Rockwell agreed. "Though I must say, James already has quite the eye for picking out the best breeding stock. Did you see him with that new ram last week?"

"Like father, like son." Farah smiled, reaching for her shawl. "Though Elizabeth is the one who's been studying your maps and asking about your travels."

"Perhaps we could take them all to London for the Season this year," Rockwell suggested as they headed downstairs. "Show them a bit of the world beyond Suffolk. Though I must say, I don't miss those endless balls and social obligations."

"Liar," Farah teased. "You miss watching me cause scandals and hide in your trunks."

He caught her around the waist, pulling her close for one more kiss. "The only thing I miss is having you all to myself. Though I wouldn't trade our life now for anything."

They found the twins in the kitchen, supervising as Cook packed the last of the breakfast items into a basket. The children's governess, Miss Wilson, was attempting to convince Elizabeth that she needed a warmer coat for the morning chill.

"I'll carry the basket!" James announced, though the large hamper was nearly as big as he was.

"Perhaps we should share the burden," Rockwell suggested

diplomatically, taking one handle while his son grabbed the other. "That's what partners do, after all."

As they made their way across the dew-covered lawn toward the pastures, Farah's heart felt full to bursting. The morning sun illuminated the scene like something from a painting—her handsome husband and son carrying the picnic basket, Elizabeth skipping ahead to point out interesting clouds, the magnificent house rising behind them, and beyond that, the vast flocks that represented their shared dream.

They settled on a blanket near the south pasture, where several ewes were tending their new lambs. While the twins exclaimed over the wobbly-legged newcomers, Rockwell pulled out fresh bread, hard-boiled eggs, and slices of cold ham.

"Look Papa!" Elizabeth called out. "That one has spots like the ram from Spain!"

"Good eye, sweetheart," Rockwell praised. "That's one of our experimental crosses. We're hoping to combine the fine wool of the Merinos with the hardiness of some of our local breeds."

"Will it make the mills happy?" James asked around a mouthful of bread.

Farah smiled at her son's precociousness. "The mills are already happy, darling. Thanks to your papa's breeding program, Armley Mills now supplies wool to half of Yorkshire's textile trade which is shipped around the world."

"And thanks to your mama's careful management of our accounts and clever investments, we've been able to expand faster than anyone thought possible," Rockwell added, squeezing her hand.

"Tell us again how you met," Elizabeth begged, settling into her mother's lap with a piece of honeycomb.

"Well," Rockwell began, his eyes twinkling, "it all started when your mama decided to hide in my trunk..."

"That's not the beginning!" James protested. "First you have to tell about the boot!"

Farah laughed. "Your father's Hessian boot, yes. Though

perhaps we should save that story for when you're older."

"Much older," Rockwell agreed with a wink that made her blush.

They spent a blissful hour watching the sun climb higher in the sky while the twins alternated between eating breakfast and checking on the lambs. Farah leaned against her husband's shoulder, his arm warm around her waist, and thought about how different her life might have turned out if she hadn't found the courage to defy convention all those years ago.

"What are you thinking about?" Rockwell asked softly.

"How grateful I am that you taught me to be brave," she replied. "To take risks for what I wanted."

He turned to face her, his expression serious. "You were always brave, my love. I just helped you see it." His hand drifted to her stomach. "Though I must say, I'm rather grateful you took the risk of hiding in my trunk that day."

"As am I." She covered his hand with hers. "Though I think this little one might be our biggest adventure yet."

"Every day with you is an adventure," he murmured, bending to kiss her.

"Papa!" James called out. "Come quick! I think another lamb is being born!"

Rockwell jumped to his feet, helping Farah up as well. "Coming, son! This is a very important part of being a sheep breeder, you know."

As they hurried over to where the twins were watching the miracle of new life unfold, Farah's heart swelled with love for her family and the life they'd built together. She might have started out as a timid mouse, but with Rockwell's love and support, she'd found her true self—and her true happiness.

The bleating of lambs, the excited chatter of children, and the warm laughter of two people who had found their greatest adventure in loving each other filled the Suffolk morning air.

THE END

ABOUT THE AUTHOR

USA Today bestselling author, Bronwen Evans grew up loving books. She writes both historical sexy romances for the modern woman who likes intelligent, spirited heroines, and compassionate alpha heroes. Evans is a three-time winner of the RomCon Readers' Crown and has been nominated for an *RT* Reviewers' Choice Award. She lives in Hawkes Bay, New Zealand with her dogs Brandy and Duke.

You can keep up with Bronwen's news by visiting her website
www.bronwenevans.com
and get a FREE book by signing up to her newsletter
https://bit.ly/3eqYJx0
Or Amazon: amazon.com/stores/Bronwen-
Evans/author/B004LKXYLC
Or Facebook: bronwenevansauthor
Or Goodreads: bronwenevans
Or Bookbub: bookbub.com/authors/bronwen-evans